Convergence at Two Harbors

CONVERGENCE AT TWO HARBORS

Dennis Herschbach

NORTH STAR PRESS OF ST. CLOUD, INC.

Saint Cloud, Minnesota

Copyright © 2012 Dennis Herschbach

Cover photo by Diane Hilden

ISBN 978-0-87839-590-3

First Edition, June 2012

Printed in the United States of America

Published by
North Star Press of St. Cloud, Inc.
P.O. Box 451
St. Cloud, Minnesota 56302

www.northstarpress.com

Dedication

This book is dedicated to the members of the St. Croix Writers group who not only encouraged my writing, but also supported me when I needed support the most.

Preface

Although we are not slaves to our past, I'm sure we would all agree that we are deeply affected by the joys and the traumas that occur along our life's journey. In the three principle characters of *Convergence at Two Harbors* I see this tenet in action.

Even as an author, I was influenced by past experiences. During my tenure as a high school teacher, I encountered many students who faced difficult times, much as did Deidre, the student who in the book becomes the first woman sheriff of her county.

I had the privilege of visiting Honduras on mission trips, and it was there that I first learned of the Palestinian immigrants to that country. I met several Americans who were concerned with immigration issues and illegal workers.

In the early 2000s I took a class at a Lutheran seminary taught by a professor who had lived with Palestinian Lutherans for a year, and there I first heard of checkpoints that are randomly set up, so called flying checkpoints, and the delays that can result.

Further research revealed that, according to the World Health Organization, sixty-nine women were forced to give birth at checkpoints from 2000 to 2006. Of these, thirty-five of the newborns died and five mothers perished while they were detained. There are no records of how many surviving mothers developed septicemia because of the unsanitary conditions surrounding their deliveries. There are no records of the aftermath of these traumas experienced by the Palestinians.

Convergence at Two Harbors is a purely fictional account. Names were made up from a list of names of Palestinian prisoners held by the Israelis, selecting a first name at random and pairing it with a randomly chosen last name from someone else on the list. Names of the Americans were put together by the author, and have no connection in the least with actual people.

Dunnigan's is a pub in Two Harbors and is a delightful place to visit, to have a sandwich, and to even order a beer if you'd like. From there, it is a short walk to where *Crusader* sits high and dry on her blocks.

Brimson is a real community in the north woods. Its residents are independent-minded people who are good neighbors but who do not interfere in each others lives. Today, several of the old homesteads have been sold or abandoned, and many have been converted to hunting camps.

If you are so inclined, you can probably use the places described in this book to follow the fictionalized events. A visit to the North Shore of Lake Superior will be its own reward.

CHAPTER
ONE

FROM INSIDE A RUNDOWN HUNTING SHACK, four men spotted a black SUV slowly winding its way up the quarter-mile-long dirt driveway. They had their hands on their guns until they saw a tall, athletic man get out of the vehicle. They rushed out to meet him.

"Ah, Zaim. It's good to see you again, my friend," Jibril greeted him. They hugged, brushed cheeks, first on one side, then the other. They took turns until the greeting had been repeated by all. Only then did the five enter the shack.

Inside, it took a minute for Zaim's eyes to adjust to the dimly lit room, but as they did, he could see that his orders had been carried out. Well away from the propane-fueled cookstove, a dozen backpacks were piled against the wall. In the other room, which served both as a living room and as a bunk room, he noted with approval six fully automatic assault rifles lined up between the two rows of stacked bunk beds, and on the floor, three dozen loaded clips of ammunition.

"I see you have been busy," Zaim praised the four men. "Soon, we will begin to strike fear in these smug northern dogs."

Then he turned to his companions and laughed. "You looked nervous when you came out of the shack to greet me, Imad. You still had your hand on your pistol."

"We can't be too cautious out here, Zaim. What if you had been one of the sheriff's deputies come to check on this place?" Imad said, trying to excuse his obvious fear.

Zaim laughed a snort of contempt. "These backwoods oafs, they wouldn't know a threat if it was a rat running under their noses." He spit in contempt. "Soon they'll pay for their ignorance."

1

Not too convincingly, Imad smiled a broken smile, and Zaim put his arm around his shoulders.

"Don't worry my friend. By the time they know we have been here, we'll be gone," he said reassuringly to his jumpy companion. "Come, let's eat. I'm starving."

The five men sat down to a meal of taboon bread, rice, and chicken. From a pan, they each spooned a healthy serving of *shakshoukeh*, and they talked while they stuffed their mouths with food.

"This is why we picked you, Murad." Zaim said with a grin. "You think it is because you can shoot straight, but really, it's for your cooking." Murad slapped him on the back and ladled another spoonful of the cooked tomatoes and peppers onto Zaim's plate.

"I can do both," Murad answered. "You should have seen the stares I got yesterday when I bought groceries in Two Harbors. They looked at me like I was going to bring down the store." Murad laughed until he almost doubled over. "I asked for lamb and the butcher looked at me like I had asked for yak. There's nothing good about this country, not even their food."

Zaim got up from the table and fumbled through his pack. He came back with a bottle.

"I've got a treat for you boys," he said with a look on his face that belied his joy. "Afu, bring some glasses and a pitcher of water. Jibril, get some ice from the freezer."

Afu and Jibril jumped at the command, and in seconds Zaim poured from the bottle he had secreted into the shack. He half filled each of the five glasses and then added water. Immediately the mixture turned a milky white. Then he added ice and invited each man to take one.

"Arak, lion's milk," and Zaim took a sip of the potent alcoholic drink. "Lion's milk for warriors," and he downed the rest in three gulps.

After their evening meal, the five men needed to stretch their legs and escape the confines of the tiny shack that would have been crowded if only one person were staying in it. They walked around

2

to the back of the building and wandered up a dirt trail that had once been a logging road. Soon they were slapping at mosquitoes.

"How can anybody live up here," Jibril grumbled. "Bugs and trees, that's all they have. The only ones who will live here are those fair skinned Finns," he continued his rant. "They are so sour, even the bugs don't bite them. I saw two of them picking berries yesterday, and they weren't even swatting the bugs away. I think they cannot feel the bite." Then he went on, "I wonder if it will sour the lake when their blood runs off the docks?" and he laughed at his own joke.

When the five of them returned to their shelter, they relaxed in chairs in the screened porch, and the talk turned to their mission.

"By this time next month we'll be on our way home," Zaim reminded them. "By then they will know we have been here, including the sheriff and her slow-witted deputies. But first we have a matter to eliminate in Two Harbors." The others nodded knowingly.

AFTER HIS FOUR COMPANIONS RETIRED TO THE SHACK, Zaim sat alone in the screen porch. The stillness of the night was stifling. Only the buzzing of some unidentifiable insect and the occasional hoot of an owl in the distance broke the silence to which he was unaccustomed.

The shack was all that was left of a hundred-year-old homestead in northeastern Minnesota. During a previous visit, Zaim had chosen this location because of its remoteness. With help from a group in the twin cities of Minneapolis-St. Paul who were sympathetic to their cause and through the complicity of a phantom buyer, he had acquired access to it. Located in the middle of a very rural community, Brimson, it was over twenty miles north of Two Harbors. Zaim thought it an ideal place to hide.

By ten thirty he decided he'd better try to get some sleep and ground out the glow of his cigarette before going inside. He climbed onto his bunk and lay in the dark. He ran his fingers over the painful lump on his left forearm. Zaim was wide awake, too tense to doze off, and his thoughts returned to the day he got off the plane at the Gaza International Airport in Gaza City, Palestine.

That was a hundred years ago, or so it seemed. It was January of 2000, eleven years ago. Then, he was only three days short of his twenty-third birthday, and it was a few months after he had started to make plans to visit Palestine.

Zaim's ancestral family had immigrated to Honduras during the time of the fall of the Ottoman Empire. He was a third generation of Palestinian descent, born and raised in Honduras. He had no real political view on what had happened in Palestine during the collapse, or even what was happening in 2000 for that matter. He had come to Gaza as a tourist seeking some of the pieces to complete the puzzle of his heritage.

When Zaim and his young wife, Dania, had begun to plan their trip, they poured over maps and travel brochures of the Palestinian region. With the help of Zaim's mother, they made contact with a couple of distant relatives still residing in Gaza, and Dania had started to prepare a list of what they would need to take on their adventure. Everything was falling into place like well thought out squares of an intricate quilt.

However, one day Dania made a startling request.

"Zaim, do you think there is room for three of us to make the trip?"

Zaim rolled his eyes toward the ceiling. "Have you been talking to Mama? I thought this was going to be a special trip for the two of us, time to be together and enjoy an adventure."

Dania laughed. "No. I mean the *three* of us."

Zaim still didn't grasp the implication. Finally, Dania had to spell it out. "I'm pregnant. You're going to be a father." She threw her arms around her husband.

They laughed and hugged, held each other and talked far into the night. Then reality hit Zaim. "What about our trip? Do we cancel our plans? What do we do now?"

Again, Dania laughed. "Don't be silly," she pretended to scold. "I'll be six-and-a-half months along when we leave and only into my seventh month when we return. I'll be fine."

They continued to plan, only this time with the knowledge that their child, a son, would be traveling with them as stowaway baggage. The days sped by faster than either of them anticipated, and almost before they were prepared, they were on an intercontinental flight to Palestine.

ZAIM AND DANIA WERE MET AT THE AIRPORT BY AN OLDER MAN, Tareq, who lived with his wife in the Muslim Quarter of Jerusalem. Zaim's mother had made arrangement for the older couple to provide a place for her children to stay while they were in Palestine and had asked them to help the young people avoid the pitfalls of visiting a sometimes hostile territory.

That night, as they had shared a meal together, Tareq inquired of Zaim, "So, my son, why is it that you have developed this interest in finding your roots?"

His mouth full of *musakhan*, Zaim had to take time to swallow before answering. "Ever since I was a young boy, people tell me stories about our family living in Palestine. I don't remember Great-grandfather Hamza. He died years before I was born, but Grandfather Ahmed told me stories about him and of how he came to Honduras." Zaim paused to take another bite. "Momma has kept those stories alive in my mind ever since. I suppose I need some images to fill in the blank spots of my family's storybook."

"I can tell you some about Hamza but only what was told to me by my parents," Tareq said, looking up from his meal. "Your great-grandfather lived in the town of Al-Zahra. He owned rich farmland and grew olives and dates to sell to the merchants in the marketplace. They were close friends, and they visited together every day, even worshipped together on the holy days.

"In those days, when the Ottoman emperor was on his throne, it seemed like everyone could get along." Then he added with a shrug, "Christians, Jews, Moslems: all shared the land in those days."

"In 1910 or twelve, Jews began to flood to the area, many of them sponsored by wealthy Zionists from America. They pretty much moved into the marketplaces and took the jobs of your great-grandfather's friends. The Moslems became nervous because of the imbalance, and at the same time, the empire began to exert its control. Eventually, the Empire cracked, and in response, the Palestinian Christians became the scapegoats. That is when your great-grandfather Hamza and his friends decided to leave their homes and go to Honduras."

Tareq looked Zaim square in the eyes. "You know, my son, you may not like the picture you are going to find. There is so much trouble in the land today, not unlike the trouble that forced your great-grandfather from his land. Be careful."

Over the next three weeks Zaim and Dania expanded the bounds of their explorations, each day venturing a little further from Tareq's home. They would return home in the evening with pictures and full of stories of the life they imagined Great-grandfather Hamza having lived.

One late afternoon, after a particularly long day of walking, Dania excused herself to the bathroom. Zaim heard her cry out, "Zaim, come quickly."

He bolted from his chair. Dania was crumpled on the floor, her arms clutching her abdomen.

"Zaim, something is wrong. Get me to a hospital."

Zaim panicked when he saw a flow of blood creeping down the legs of Dania's cream-colored slacks.

"Tareq!" he screamed. "Call an ambulance! Something is wrong with Dania!"

In only minutes, an ambulance bearing the sign of the Red Crescent was outside. Paramedics rushed in, and with a cursory evaluation of the situation, placed Dania on a gurney and wheeled her to the open doors of the vehicle. Zaim jumped in beside his wife, and the look in his eyes stopped any objection to his riding along. With sirens blaring, the ambulance sped through the streets.

After traveling six blocks, the driver pulled to a sudden stop. Zaim screamed, "Why are we stopped? What's going on?"

From the look on the medics' faces Zaim knew something was wrong.

"It is an Israeli flying checkpoint," one of them said as he stared at the floor in anger.

Zaim tried to search their eyes, but they were averted. "Surely they will let us pass. This is an emergency," he said, still trying to read their faces.

The back doors of the ambulance were thrown open, and heavily armed Israeli soldiers stood outside looking in.

"You three, out!" they ordered Zaim and the two medics. The three hurried out onto the street. Then the soldiers began a methodical search. At the same time, two other soldiers entered the back of the ambulance where Dania lay on the gurney.

"Identification papers," one of the soldiers demanded of the three men. The two medics produced theirs, but in the confusion and haste Zaim had left his at Tareq's.

"I haven't my papers on me," he began to explain, but before he could get the words out, two soldiers had grabbed his arms.

"Wait," he pleaded. "There is a mistake. Dania and I, we are Honduran—only here for a visit. We are not Palestinian."

The soldiers laughed and mocked him. Zaim begged. "Please let us pass. My wife is not well and needs help. She is bleeding badly. Please, I beseech you, let us pass."

One of the soldiers looked at Zaim and asked again, "Where are your papers?" Zaim answered again, more forcefully. The soldier thrust his finger at Zaim's chest. "Don't use that tone of voice with us. We will not tolerate insubordination from your kind."

Zaim could see the interior of the medical van where Nadia lay writhing on the gurney. The blanket that had been covering her had fallen in a heap on the floor, and it was obvious to Zaim that she was in agony. Her moans and occasional shrieks fell heavily on his ears. Meanwhile, the soldiers seemed to be delaying every action, repeatedly calling headquarters for clarification of names and dates.

Zaim was distraught beyond reason, begging the officers to allow him to go to his wife's side, but they pushed him aside. Finally, in an act of desperation, he rushed past the men detaining him only to have one soldier hit him across the back of the neck with a riot stick. Zaim fell to the street, blood gushing from his nose.

"What is wrong with you people?" he screamed at them. "Can't you see she is in trouble. What are you, animals?"

With two men holding him down, Zaim was helpless to move. A third man stepped on Zaim's outstretched forearm. He could feel the heavy heel of the soldier's boot grind into his flesh as the man slowly shifted his full weight onto the arm, and Zaim heard his bones break. The pain was excruciating. Zaim vomited. He was handcuffed and pulled so he leaned against the wall of a building.

As he regained his senses, he could hear the cries of Nadia grow weaker, but the search of the vehicle continued at an exasperatingly slow pace. Eventually, no more sounds came from inside the ambulance. A half hour later the driver was told he could pass, but now there was no need for urgency.

"Well, that's one less we'll have to contend with," Zaim heard one of the guards say, his face contorted with a sneer as the ambulance drove off with Dania's body. Then the soldiers turned to him.

They jerked Zaim to his feet, oblivious to the pain caused by the movement of his broken arm.

"It's Friday," one of the three announced. "We better take care of this one before Sabbath begins," and they shoved Zaim into a van.

CHAPTER
TWO

ZAIM JOSTLED FROM SIDE TO SIDE AS THE DRIVER sped through the narrow, winding streets. There were no windows in the back, and there was no way Zaim could tell where he was being taken.

The van lurched to a stop. Zaim was dragged out and shoved across the walk into a rundown brick building. He was hauled up a flight of stairs and shoved into a dingy bathroom with a shower stall. There, the soldiers looped his handcuffs around the shower head, forcing Zaim to stand, hands stretched above his head.

"This ought to cool you off," one of the men said as he turned on a trickle of cold water from the shower head. He laughed at his own joke. "Come, we'll be late for Sabbath," and they left Zaim hanging.

Zaim stood in the shower for as long as his legs would hold, but by midnight he was numb with cold, and his shivering depleted even more of his energy. Eventually, his legs could support him no longer, and his knees buckled. The handcuffs looped over the shower head kept him from crumpling in a heap on the floor. The metal of the cuffs cut into his wrists, and soon his hands were numb.

As his body's temperature dropped, Zaim began hallucinating. For a while, he was a fourteen-year-old sitting at Mama's table, and he felt the warmth of her small clay cooking oven radiating from the corner of the kitchen.

Zaim's thoughts switched to both his Mama and Papa, and for an instant he was back home, hearing stories of Grandpa and Great-grandpa and of their homeland. He saw himself sitting on his parents' porch, enjoying the cooling evening breezes cascading down from the mountains.

9

Abruptly, his comfort was disrupted when, in his dream state, an ambulance pulled up, sirens blaring. Zaim saw himself get up from his chair and peer into the back. He saw his Dania, covered in blood and holding a just born baby. Before he could act, the ambulance screamed away, and in his nightmare he panicked, not knowing where she would be taken.

Zaim regained consciousness long enough for him to realize his plight, but again he slipped off into that other world of horror. Repeatedly, over the next twenty-four hours, he would lose his grasp on reality and would see Dania. Sometimes she was being accosted by soldiers with no faces, sometimes she would be lovely and well, almost always she held a healthy, happy baby in her arms.

Then he would come to his senses and realize he was not in Honduras. Dania was not with him. She did not and would never have his baby.

After nearly a full night and day, Zaim completely lost consciousness for a time, how long was impossible for him to know. When he partially regained consciousness and was yet in a dazed state, he saw Dania leaning on the fence around her father's small plot of land that was filled with three banana trees, a mango tree, and other flowering plants. Squash vines climbed a trellis, and chickens scratched in the dirt. Dania had a gardenia in her hair, and she was gorgeous.

Zaim saw himself walk over to her, saw her flash her beautiful smile, teeth white against her light-brown skin and highlighted by her black hair. Zaim was in love. In his stupor, he saw himself take her hands and slip a wedding ring on her finger. He held her, and gently kissed her lips. They were warm and soft.

He regained total consciousness for a few minutes but drifted back into the gray mist where he was haunted by more hallucinations.

In his troubled dreams, Zaim held Dania in his arms, tried to protect her from danger, but no matter how he tried to shield her, a part of her was constantly exposed, and he frantically tried to cover her with his own body. Finally, too exhausted to be able to respond, Zaim was not able to prevent some unseen force from prying her from his arms, and she was dragged away into the encroaching darkness that closed around him like a camera shutter that never opened.

CHAPTER
THREE

On Sunday, two Israelis walked into the room where Zaim was still shackled to the running shower head. "You're still with us. Good. We need to talk."

When they unshackled Zaim, his knees buckled, and he fell to the floor, his damaged arm beneath him. He moaned in pain, but they grabbed his arms and led him down the hall to a bare room with a table and three chairs. Then the interrogation began.

The questioners worked in teams until Zaim was too exhausted to respond. Then they would let him sleep for what seemed only minutes, and the ordeal would begin again.

"What is the name of your father, your mother?"

"Why were you at the checkpoint?"

"Where are your papers?"

"You say you are Honduran. Why are you here?"

"Where are your papers?"

The same questions were repeated over and over until Zaim didn't know the answer to even the simplest. Finally, after days of torture and as Zaim slumped over the table too spent to raise his head, an Israeli officer entered the interrogation room. With no explanation, no apology, he said to Zaim, "You are free to go," and he and the others turned on their heels and left the room.

"Free to go?" Zaim thought. "I don't even know where I am in this hellish place."

He managed to grope his way to the hallway and from there he located a stairwell. With his right hand on the banister and his shoulder pressed against the wall, Zaim dragged and stumbled his way down to the first landing. Through his blurred vision he detected light and assumed it must be the doorway. When he opened it, fresh air rushed passed him, and he inhaled as best he could.

Most people on the street wouldn't talk with him. They only stared at the disheveled specimen of a man and moved away. Finally, one bearded person stopped and offered to help.

"My son," the man addressed him with a gentle voice. "You look like you could use someone to lean on."

Zaim's left eye was completely swollen shut, and his right eye was so puffed that he had to tilt his head back to see who spoke. His Samaritan had a short-cut, graying beard, and wore a bisht, a short sleeved traditional jacket. Zaim could see through his partial vision that the man wore a white laffeh, a kind of turban usually worn by older Palestinian men.

"Come with me," the older man offered, and took Zaim by the arm.

"I am Asem," the man introduced himself. "I won't ask you to explain your appearance. I have a good idea of what happened to you."

Zaim began to respond, but before he could form the words through his swollen lips, Asem shushed him. "No need to talk now. We'll have plenty of time as you heal. I'm taking you to a safe place where we can find help."

Asem led Zaim down a narrow street and through an even narrower alley. They stopped outside a solid wooden door that looked almost like a barricade, and Asem knocked loudly with his fist. Zaim heard someone slide back a dead bolt, and he heard, more than saw, the door swing inward. Asem led him inside and helped him into the cradle of a lounger. Zaim settled back with a sigh. He would have closed his eyes had they not already been swollen shut.

He heard another person moving nearby, but Zaim could see nothing, could not make out the dimensions of the room or see that there was a large table with many chairs around it in the center of the room. Where he was smelled of good things: some kind of fresh fruit, a mixture of spices, and freshly baked bread. For the first time in many days he felt as though his life was not in danger, and he struggled to make sense of his surroundings.

"Ibrahim, get some cold compresses for his face while I seek help. Keep our friend calm while I am gone. He's hardly in any condition to cause trouble, but help him rest."

With those words, Asem left through another door that opened to an alley on the opposite side of the building. He returned in a few minutes with a man who was carrying a leather bag.

"My friend," Asem said to Zaim, "this man is a doctor. He'll treat you, and soon you'll be back on your feet."

Turning to the other man in the room Asem asked, "Did he say anything while I was gone?"

"Nothing I could recognize. He seemed to be mumbling something about Dania. At least that's what I think he tried to say."

Zaim felt the doctor probe at his ribs, and he winced when the man's fingers touched the places where he had been struck with clubs. When the doctor palpated Zaim's abdomen, a sharp pain made him draw up his legs into the fetal position, but when the doctor moved his arm, Zaim couldn't control himself, and he cried out in pain.

He heard the doctor say to Asem, "I don't think there are any serious internal injuries, only very deep bruises, but his arm is badly broken. It has already begun to heal crooked, and I'm afraid we'll have to re-break it if we are to set it anywhere near what it should be."

Zaim felt the jab of a needle in his upper arm, and an all too familiar veil of darkness engulfed his mind.

THREE WEEKS LATER ZAIM HAD BEGUN TO REGAIN SOME OF HIS strength. His arm had been re-broken while he was anesthetized, and it was encased in a heavy cast. The doctor had told him that it would heal but not exactly right, and he would always feel a lump and some discomfort.

"Good morning, Zaim," Asem announced before breakfast. "A wonderful day. What do you think?"

Zaim could only look at him through eyes clouded with pain. Not physical pain. That was pretty much gone. The pain he felt was far worse. It was the pain of loss, the kind of pain that never goes away.

Asem didn't seem to be daunted by Zaim's silence. "You say you are Honduran and that your great-grandfather emigrated from Palestine years ago. We haven't pushed for more information, but don't you think we should know where you were staying before this incident? Surely someone must be missing you—your mother, father, a friend? Think of them. They would want to know you are safe. Come, my son. Say something."

There was a long silence, and Zaim stared at the food on the table. Finally, in a voice that even he didn't recognize, he said, "Tareq. Tareq Al 'Abd. Moslem Quarter." Then he was silent.

Asem pressed for more. "A wife? I see you have the marking on your finger where a ring was placed." Zaim's eyes flared, and he shook his head.

Asem continued as if Zaim were interacting with him. "Today, a friend of mine is going to pay a visit. I have told him we have a guest in my house. He would like to meet you."

Zaim only sat and stared straight ahead.

Later that day, just as Asem had foretold, someone knocked at the same door through which he had escorted Zaim two weeks ago. Asem checked through a peephole and opened the door part way. A well-dressed man in traditional Palestinian garb slipped in, and the door was quickly shut and bolted behind him.

He pulled up a chair alongside Zaim.

"Asem has told me about you and what happened to you, although I'm sure we don't know the whole truth. That will come in time, but for now, Zaim is it? I would like to talk and have you listen. Is that all right?"

Zaim didn't move, just stared at the opposite wall as if nothing was registering.

"My name is Aymen Yunus Baroud. I am Palestinian, and I want to be your friend, if you will allow it. Let me tell you about Palestine. We are being strangled by the Israelis. They claim we are terrorists, murderers, and worse. But we are not stealing their land. We are not preventing their men from traveling to work. We do not cut off their electricity but for two hours a day. We do not deprive their people of water."

Aymen paused to let his words sink into Zaim's thoughts.

"We do not stop ambulances and allow pregnant women to die during childbirth."

At those words, a scream erupted from Zaim's throat, and he jumped to his feet. The nearest object to him was a glass bowl filled with fruit. He grabbed it and threw it against the wall. Then he hoisted the straight-backed chair in which he had been sitting and smashed it over the table. The effort jarred his injured arm, and he sank to the floor, holding it against his chest and rocking back and forth in pain that wasn't totally physical.

Aymen slowly rose to his feet and said quietly, "We'll talk again tomorrow, my son," and he let himself out the door and disappeared into the alley.

CHAPTER
FOUR

THE NEXT DAY, WHEN AYMEN CAME TO ASEM'S HOME, he didn't go directly to Zaim as he had the day before. He huddled with Asem in another room.

"Asem, were you able to locate this man, Tareq?" Aymen asked.

Asem nodded, and then added, "He is a distant cousin of Zaim. They have been worried about him, and his wife. As we suspected, she was the one who died at the checkpoint a little over three weeks ago. Tareq was very cooperative when we told him of Zaim's condition. He turned over his papers to us so Zaim will have identification. But wouldn't it be better for Zaim to have Palestinian papers. We could easily arrange that."

Aymen shook his head. "Zaim will be of great value to us once his hatred has been allowed to fester. Then documentation of his Honduran citizenship will be of far more value than being just another Palestinian."

Aymen walked into the adjoining room where Zaim sat silently at the table. This time there was no glass bowl with fruit.

"You look well, Zaim," Aymen greeted him. "Will you listen to me today?" Zaim didn't blink, didn't register any kind of emotion.

"I am sorry for what I said yesterday. Evidently my words opened a bitter wound in your soul. I am sorry."

He sat for a moment, waiting for a response. This time Zaim turned his head to look at Aymen, and for the first time, Aymen saw a profound sadness in his eyes.

"What you have suffered has been suffered by countless Palestinians, and we continue to suffer. With no warning everything we have can be taken from us: our homes, our land, our families, even

17

our very lives. And no one is ever called to pay the price for our losses."

Once again, Aymen paused long enough for his words to register. Then he continued.

"The whole world ignores our plight. Some pay lip service to our suffering, condemning the fact that even humanitarian aid does not reach us. The worst is the United States of America. They send seventeen million dollars a day to Israel in the form of guns and planes and bombs, and they deny us even the use of our slings. They condemn our right to defend ourselves. Some of their politicians even declare that we do not exist, that we are not a people."

Aymen paused. "We'll talk again tomorrow. I will be your friend, if you will allow me."

The one-way conversation went on day after day, with Aymen quietly, relentlessly, telling stories of suffering and pain, always placing blame where he saw fit. One week, two weeks, three weeks passed, and then one day Zaim spoke before Aymen had hardly sat down.

"Why did they do this to me?" he asked, his eyes dark with hate and pain.

"Because you looked Palestinian and had no papers on you."

"But why? Why did they allow my Dania to die—and my son?"

Aymen sat quietly, sensing a turn in the situation.

"For no reason, Zaim. For no reason."

From that day on, Aymen worked at fueling the hatred behind Zaim's eyes. Increasingly, he grew the idea in Zaim's mind that although the Israelis had committed the murder of his wife and child, it was really the fault of the United States, and it was they who should pay.

CHAPTER FIVE

DURING THE WEEKS AFTER DANIA'S DEATH, Aymen stopped by each day.

"So, my son. It looks like Asem's food agrees with you. You've gained weight."

Zaim only shrugged and looked at Aymen.

Unfazed, Aymen continued. "I heard that the Israelis set up a road block only a few blocks from here yesterday. Word is another pregnant woman was forced to give birth in an ambulance. She lived, but no one knows if she will become infected."

Aymen paused and studied Zaim's face, waiting for a reaction, but all he observed were eyes so dark they were almost black, staring straight ahead. Zaim hardly blinked.

"They tell me that in the past year over thirty women have faced the same fate. Some lived, some died."

After another pause Aymen stood up from the table and announced he would return tomorrow, and he did. This same ritual was played out with only occasional reaction from Zaim. Finally, one day Aymen stood to leave, and Zaim reached out and grabbed his arm.

"Is there nothing we can do to stop this from happening? Is there no one who will stand up to those dogs?"

Aymen slowly sat down. "There is, and there are. All over Palestine, all over the world, we have brothers who will do anything to avenge what is happening. Not only do they seek revenge on the Israelis, but also on their puppeteer, the United States.

"Yes, there are those who are taking a stand, and, yes, we are avenging the crimes committed against us.

19

"We need more men, though. Our army is relatively small in the eyes of the world, and we need brave men to fight, men like you, Zaim. Will you join us? Don't answer now. I will be back tomorrow, and we can talk then."

That night Zaim was more restless than ever. By morning his hatred for what the Western World represented to him was boiling like melted lead in a caldron, and he had made his decision. All he wanted was to make those responsible pay for what he had lost, and he clearly knew who they were: Israel and the Evil Empire that supported them, the United State of America. He vowed they would pay.

When Aymen arrived at Asem's home the next morning, Zaim was the first to speak. "I am ready. What do I do?"

A smile broadened Aymen's face. "Come with me. I have someone I'd like you to meet."

Before following Aymen, Zaim turned to Asem. "What can I ever do to repay you for the kindness you have shown me?"

"Learn well, my son. Learn well."

With that the two men embraced each other, brushing first one cheek and then the other, and Zaim left for a new life.

"I am taking you to meet our spiritual leader," Aymen announced as the two men walked through a crowded marketplace.

It was the first time in months that Zaim had been out in public. Time had smoothed the sharp edges created by the extreme trauma of Dania's. Left in place was a distrust of people, an emptiness of being alone even in this crowd, and a hate that would never die. Several blocks later, Aymen led him into a brick building, and they were met by two others who were dressed in traditional Palestinian garb similar to what Asem had been wearing the first day the men met on the street.

"Wait here," Aymen demanded, and he left the room to return in a few moments accompanied by someone who was a total stranger to Zaim.

He thought he was beyond being cowed, but this person carried himself in such a way that Zaim knew who was in charge before any words were spoken. Dressed in a black robe and with his head wrapped in a black turban, the man looked at Zaim through scowling eyes overshadowed by dense, bushy black eyebrows.

"You are Zaim," the man announced with not so much a question as a statement.

Zaim could only nod.

"Come! We must talk," the black-robed cleric ordered, and he led Zaim away to an inner room.

Zaim spent the next few days in this hidden residence. The cleric interrogated him daily, sometimes lecturing him on the evils of western society, sometimes probing to ascertain his commitment to avenging his loss.

One day Aymen retuned, bringing with him a person Zaim had never met. He was introduced only as Haitham, the leader of a group calling themselves freedom fighters, what the United States called terrorists.

CHAPTER
SIX

HAITHAM WASTED NO TIME WITH IDLE CHATTER. "Aymen tells me that you have experienced what so many of us have endured for years, perhaps more so. I am sorry for your loss. The question is, do you want to take action or are you content living with your memories?" He allowed time for his words to sink in.

"What do you mean, 'take action'?" Zaim wanted to know. He didn't immediately pick up on what Haitham was getting at.

Bluntly, Haitham said, "Do you want to avenge your wife's and son's deaths, or do you want them to remain only a memory you carry? If you believe someone should pay, I can help. If not, then forget I came today." Again he waited out the silence.

Through pursed lips Zaim spit out the words, "They must pay for the pain and the loss they have caused me. Tell me how."

"First, I have connections with warriors who seek revenge for the degradation with which we Arabs are burdened. They will welcome you into their group with open arms. In various places, we have training sites where fighters are taught how to strike back at our enemies. It is at such places that plans are made to plant fear in the minds of those who would step on us and to cause as much damage as can be done.

"Second, after your training you will be assigned a project designed to avenge the wrong done to you. Aymen tells me that you are sure that the real power behind Israel is the United States and its people. You are right, and we believe you are an ideal person to carry our war to their shores. Are you willing to sacrifice yourself for this cause?"

Zaim stared at Haitham. "When do I begin, and where do I go?"

LESS THAN A WEEK LATER, HAITHAM ESCORTED ZAIM to the airport. He handed the younger man his ticket.

"Do you have your passport?"

Zaim checked his breast pocket another time. "Yes, it is right here, and I have the papers verifying why I wish to enter Afghanistan. Will it not seem strange that I am entering the country at a time of such turmoil?"

"Everything has been taken care of as far as that is concerned. The Russians have all but left the country, although you might still experience their presence at the airport. The marketplaces in the cities are still able to function. Yours is not a difficult story to tell. You are a merchandiser of handmade rugs who wishes to establish contacts with several of the home businesses where the valuable rugs are woven. You are an importer who in turn sells to outlets in the United States.

"Once through customs, you will be met by one of ours who will take you to the training camp. Don't worry about being stopped by security. That matter has already been arranged for with a few dollars changing hands. As for having to verify your profession, it is only a cover to be used for nosy fellow passengers or airline workers.

"We'll meet again, I'm sure. Have a pleasant trip."

IT WAS AS HAITHAM HAD PREDICTED AT THE AIRPORT in Afghanistan. The customs officer smiled and ushered Zaim through with barely a cursory look at his passport and a quick stamp of the papers. Once inside the terminal, Zaim looked around, hoping to be able to identify the person who was supposed to meet him. A man about his own age was leaning against a pillar. He held a hand-lettered sign: ZAIM.

Together, they proceeded to the baggage claim area where they found the two bags holding all of Zaim's possessions, and they left the airport without exchanging more than a few dozen words. Zaim was instructed by the man who had not even introduced himself to toss his bags in the back of a battered Toyota pickup truck. They drove from the city in silence, the driver constantly checking his side mirrors and glancing from side to side whenever they approached an intersection or alley.

Once out of the city, Zaim could sense the driver begin to relax, and for the first time a slight smile formed on his lips.

"I am Fadi. You I know, Zaim. We have approximately five hundred kilometers to travel before we reach our destination in the mountains. It is a well-hidden camp. In the meantime, I would guess you are hungry and thirsty. If you look in the cooler behind the seat, I brought some fruit and roasted lamb from the city, and there are a few bottles of cold water, too. Feel free to help yourself. Do you have any questions of me?"

Zaim shook his head and reached for the food. It had been a long day, and he was hungry and tired. He ate in silence.

Long after dark, Fadi braked the pickup to a stop. Zaim had fallen asleep, his chin bouncing off his chest as the road had become narrower and rougher until it was nothing more that a goat trail into the mountains. His eyes opened wide when the vehicle stopped moving, and in the head lights he could see a few dilapidated buildings. There was a lamp burning inside one of them, and the flame produced a flickering effect when viewed from outside.

"Come with me," Fadi urged. "I want you to meet our leader and instructor before you go to bed." Zaim followed, slightly intimidated by being in a situation so totally foreign to him.

It took his eyes a second to adjust to the dim light in the building, but when they did, Zaim was struck by the starkness of the room. Two rows of tables with benches were arranged across its length. At one end was a kitchen with several large pots and pans hanging from nails driven in the wall. At one of the tables sat a rough-looking character whose weathered face and ragged beard presented an image of one who had spent most of his time in the wilderness.

"Our new recruit has arrived." Fadi said matter-of-factly. "Samer, this is Zaim. Zaim, meet our leader. Samer is one of our patriots who helped drive the Russians from Afghanistan. He is your teacher and trainer. Listen to him, and follow his orders."

Samer looked up from his cup of hot tea. He placed his right hand over his heart and nodded slightly. "Zaim, how are you after your long trip? Well, I hope."

Zaim, taken aback by this custom of always asking about a visitor's health and more than a little awed by Samer's intense eyes, was a little flummoxed.

"I am fine," he managed to get out.

"That is good. We begin early tomorrow with your training, and I am glad you are in good condition to start.

"Tell me, Zaim, are you afraid?"

Zaim was not quite sure how to answer that question. Finally, he gathered his thoughts and said, "Not so much afraid as uncertain. I don't know what to expect, and that is a little frightening. Should I be afraid?" he asked of Samer.

"To a degree, yes. You probably know that last summer President Clinton of the United States ordered a cruise missile attack on one of our training camps. It killed several of our lieutenants and narrowly missed killing one of our leaders, Osama.

"I will say that we are quite confident in our safety here. Few of us are notable targets, and we are well protected not only by the terrain and but also by the tribal chiefs who rule this area.

"Fadi, take our new friend to his quarters and get him settled. Zaim, be ready for a very difficult day tomorrow."

As the sun was rising above the mountain peaks the next morning, Fadi opened the door to the barracks and called out to the men. Zaim opened his eyes and looked around. He was surprised to see twelve other beds in the room. Last night he had been ushered to one near the door, had slipped into bed, and had fallen asleep without seeing much of the room. Bodies began to rise from beneath the covers, and Zaim found himself to be one of thirteen recruits who would begin their training that day.

There were no amenities. A latrine was located behind the building, there were no places to wash up, and the place was as cold as the air outside. Zaim wondered about his choice.

Breakfast was served with little fanfare, and the men were told they had roughly fifteen minutes to finish their meal. Samer sat down with the men.

"We are not here to break you. We are here to help you become warriors against the sins of the Western World. For the next weeks you are going to be toughened both physically and mentally. It will be difficult, for sure, but in the end you will thank us."

The men ate in silence after that, until Samer stood and in a quiet voice said, "It is time."

They were pushed through physical drills day after day: running, climbing banks of loose sand, pushups, pull ups, all sorts of strenuous exercises. Whenever someone faltered, Samer was there to talk to him, to remind him of what hurt had been suffered. When Zaim wanted to quit, Samer was there to remind him of Dania, of his son, of his suffering. At night he needed no reminder. His damaged arm throbbed and renewed his hate.

Day after day, the men were told stories of atrocities against the Arabs, some true but most grossly exaggerated or fabricated. Day after day the men were led to hate more deeply than they had the day before. A group mentality took over, reinforcing their beliefs. Eventually, between the physical hardship and the constant talk of reprisal, the men came to hold an irrational hate for all things Western.

Training became less physical. The thirteen were taught how to shoot assault rifles, how to assemble and disassemble their firearms, how to safely handle explosives, how to use hand-to-hand combat tactics, and most interesting to Zaim, how to build bombs and detonate charges. He excelled beyond what he thought possible, and soon it became apparent that he had emerged as the leader of the thirteen. They looked to him for inspiration and for guidance. This did not go unnoticed by Samer.

CHAPTER
SEVEN

THERE WAS NO FORMAL GRADUATION FROM THE CAMP, no diplomas handed out, only an acknowledgement by Samar that their training was drawing to an end. One day Zaim noticed that two of the men he had bunked with were not at breakfast in the morning. The next day, one more was missing, and the day after, two more.

That day Samer sat next to Zaim at his table.

"I have noticed how well you have performed, my son." Samer had never called him that endearing term before. "We have decided that it would be a waste of time to place you on the lines or even in minor covert duties. Instead, we have an important project for you to do.

"You will take charge of training a six-man team. When the training is complete, you will be given your directions. This will involve patience on your part. It will not take place immediately. Word is that a monumental attack on U.S. soil that has been years in the planning is scheduled for the near future. Your attack will be of a different nature and will occur after the Americans have once again become complacent."

Zaim continued to shadow Samer, until one day five new recruits were brought to camp: Imad Diqqa, Murad Judal, Jibril Al-Nams, Afu Jaber, and Yusuf El' Elyam. Samer and Zaim put the men through the same routine he had endured. Little by little Samer stepped out of the picture, until the recruits knew who was their superior. Zaim was their leader, and what he said was their law.

ZAIM WAS SURE THAT HIS TEAM WAS READY. Although he was a demanding leader, and although none of the recruits fully measured up up to his exacting standards, he reluctantly admitted to himself they were good.

He had been in this camp for months now and had been allowed to sit in on many of the strategy sessions attended by Samer and various other individuals who came and went. One day Samer summoned Zaim to his makeshift office where he was instructed to have a seat. Another freedom fighter Zaim did not recognize was already there, sipping from a cup of strong spiced tea.

"Today, I have received a plan intended for you and your group," Samer began. "The others will be assigned to return to their homes until everything is ready for their action. In the meantime, you will return to Honduras for only a few days. Then you will travel to the U.S. under the pretext of seeking buyers for Afghan rugs.

"Here is a map of the U.S." Samer unrolled a large page that looked like it had been torn from an atlas. He pointed at a spot midway across the North American continent and close to the nation's northern border. "This is Minneapolis, Minnesota. We have a group of people who have lived in this city for many years. Some members have actually been born there. Most are respected business men who are above being suspect in any subversive activities.

"Now here, even further north," and Samer moved his finger almost to the line representing the Canadian border, "is the town of Two Harbors. It is small, about thirty-five hundred residents. Most importantly, it is a village on Lake Superior where one of only two sets of ore docks is located. Much of the iron ore that feeds the steel mills on the eastern end of the Great Lakes is shipped from there." Then he pointed a little more north.

"Here is a place called Brimson. It is in the middle of a northern wilderness, remote and sparsely populated. That is where you will set up your base of operation. For now, I want you to make contact with those in Minneapolis. They will help you purchase a secluded place up there.

"Here are two phone numbers for you to use when you arrive in Minneapolis. Do you have any questions?"

By the time their meeting ended, Zaim had a good idea of what he was to do. The most difficult part of the assignment was the part about being patient. Before he was dismissed, he was assured he would not be left to carry out this mission alone. He would have assistance along the way.

Two days later, after instructing those he had trained and setting up means for them to be in communication, Zaim was back at the airport, ready to board a plane that would eventually return him to Honduras. He was not the same person who had left over a year before.

CHAPTER
EIGHT

STILL IN BED, DAVID CRAINE STRETCHED LUXURIOUSLY. The glow of pale-green light flickered through the thin shade covering the window of his single room, and a neon sign shaped like a shamrock above Dunnigan's Pub blinked on and off. The pub was a watering hole for the locals in this small Minnesota burg, Two Harbors. It was also a regular stop for the surge of tourists who spilled from the excursion train that pulled into town every other day in the summer. David lived above that tavern in a rented pillbox of a room, and the dim light from a street lamp below was enough for him to see the extent of his worldly possessions—except for his lake cruiser moored at the Silver Bay Marina.

From his bed in the corner, David took in the sights: a lounger facing an ancient television set, a Minnesota Twins baseball cap hanging on the doorknob, the short counter with a toaster and microwave parked on it, a one-tub kitchen sink, and a small round oak table with a cup and saucer waiting to be bused.

This room was the place where he slept in the summer when he was not on Lake Superior in his boat. It was the place where he spent his winter months, hibernating until spring. At the first glimmer of open water, the boys at the marina placed slings under his pride and joy, *Crusader, Too*, and cradled her into the ice-cold water of the harbor slip.

From then until freeze-up, he virtually lived on his boat, returning to the room above Dunnigan's only when he needed a place to rest and while he restocked the boat with necessities and took on a load of fuel. She was a wonderful craft—thirty-four feet long with twin screws powered by two 454 Chev engines.

31

The cruiser was big enough to handle Lake Superior's waters quite well. She had ample room for guests to sleep over, and he was thankful for all the adventures she had brought into his life.

He remembered the parties they had on her, remembered the times when as many as seven people spent days on her without leaving. It was cramped, but no one cared as long as the steaks, wine, and beer held out.

"Well," he said to himself, "time to get up and face the music," and he rolled out of bed, stretched to his full six feet and looked out the window. It was dark, and under a lone streetlight two blocks away, *Crusader I* sat high and dry on timbers. She was a museum piece by that time, a reminder of those who decades ago fished bluefin herring on Lake Superior. No one would mistake *Crusader, Too* for her namesake. David's version had a streamlined fiberglass hull that could cut through the waves—far different than the lumbering hulk of a workboat propped up by the marine museum, a crippled and useless vessel.

David dressed and gawked in the mirror. He looked all of his sixty-seven years, and he combed his hair by running his fingers through the few gray strands protruding from his nearly bald pate. He put the coffee pot on and realized he wasn't hungry, then checked his watch. Four-fifteen in the morning.

He poured a cup of steaming black stuff, placed the cup on the table.

David wandered around his tiny upstairs apartment, and his mind drifted to the time he had driven up the Old Scenic Highway to Two Harbors for the first time. That was in the spring of 1978, and he was going there to be interviewed for a teaching job in the Lake Superior School System. He was single then, a relatively young man with few worries.

He was hired by a curmudgeonly superintendent, and he remembered starting teaching there that fall. David had planned to stay only two years but had ended up teaching history and political science for the next twenty-one. He remembered why he stayed.

The fall of 1980 brought changes to the school system: some teachers left amid farewells, but new faces were hired to fill their slots. Among them was Alicia, an attractive redhead hired to teach sophomore English.

He remembered how her appearance stopped him in his tracks the first time they had met in the hallway. She was tall and slim, fair skinned with a faint sprinkling of freckles. David was instantly mesmerized by her sparkling green eyes and her ready smile. And when she said hello, well, her voice had a certain seductive quality that had to be natural. No one could conjure up that quality.

After learning she was his age, thirty-seven, and a divorcee, he made a point of stopping by her room to inquire if she needed help with anything. He convinced himself he was only trying to be helpful.

But as the school year progressed David found himself taking the long way to his room past hers, and to his delight he noticed Alicia spending more time near his room. The day came when he finally screwed up enough courage to approach her.

"Hi, Alicia," David had said trying to sound nonchalant. "I have two tickets to the playhouse in Duluth on Friday night. The performance is *The Seductive Life* . . . I mean *The Secret Life of John Doe*. He turned three shades of red and thought to himself, *Oh, God. Where did that come from?*

Alicia burst out laughing, and asked. "Well, which is it, David?" Then she added, "Either way, I'd love to see it, if that's what you were talking about."

That day began a love affair that lasted for the rest of their lives.

They taught in the same school for the next nineteen years, and retired on the same day in 1999. They were fifty-six, young and in good health, and over the years they had accumulated a comfortable retirement account. David thought of their plans: travel to places they had never been, evenings in a villa in Greece, perhaps a visit to Italy, or even to the Swiss Alps.

A month later, Alicia had driven to the nearby city of Duluth, and David had stayed home to finish packing for their first post-retirement adventure. The doorbell rang, and when he answered it, David was surprised to see a state trooper at his door.

"Are you David Craine?" the trooper asked. David nodded, his stomach beginning to knot. "May I come in Mr. Craine?"

Again David nodded.

Once inside, the trooper cleared his throat. "Do you mind if I have a seat? Perhaps you would sit down as well." David slowly sat down without saying a word.

"Mr. Craine," the trooper began. "There was an accident on the expressway this morning. A person in a pickup truck ran a stop sign and broadsided your wife's car. I'm so sorry to have to tell you that your wife was killed in the crash." David slumped out of his chair onto his knees and lowered his head onto the carpet. His body shook as he repeated over and over, "No, no, NO . . ."

The trooper placed his hand on David's heaving shoulders and asked, "Can I call someone for you, a relative, a friend, perhaps a pastor?"

David looked up, his eyes already swollen red. "We have no children, no close relatives either. We only have, had, each other. Will you call the pastor at Bethlehem Lutheran? Tell him I need him."

The next three days were a blur for David, but somehow he survived. After Alicia's funeral, after she was laid in the ground, he was lost. For days, he sat and looked at his living room wall. After a week, he realized he had to get moving—or perish.

As with most widowed people, he made it through the first year of living alone, and only then could he think about putting his life together.

For as long as he could remember, David had wanted to own a boat, a big boat, and he wanted to travel on Lake Superior. Now he had a plan. He would sell the house, take the proceeds from that and his savings if necessary and buy his dream. He would put together a new David Craine.

FROM HIS APARTMENT WINDOW above Dunnigan's, David looked out past *Crusader I* sitting high and dry on her blocks, looked over the harbor's ore docks, and he remembered the day he visited the Silver Bay Marina. It was that day he fell in love for a second time. She was a beauty, all thirty-four feet of her. And he christened her *Crusader, Too.*

After all the required courses, after hours of practice and trial runs, David eventually received his captain's license. Finally, he could travel the Great Lake, sometimes with friends, sometime alone. He lived on the boat as much as he could, and life got better.

The winters, though, were a drag. During the long, dark hours from December to April, David found himself sitting in his tiny apartment, staring at the walls too much like he had done after Alicia died. After church service one Sunday, his pastor took him aside.

"David," his pastor began, "Our synod is organizing a mission trip to Honduras. Your name has been brought up as a possible participant. Do you have any interest in such an adventure? I think it would be a perfect fit for you. Would you give it some thought?"

After a few seconds to let the pastor's words sink in, David asked, "Just what would I be doing on this trip?"

"I'm not totally sure, but I know part of the time you could be working with children at the orphanage in the town of Valle de Los Angeles. The mission group will be divided into four teams of approximately six people. One group will be researching the need for outreach to Hondurans who have relatives in the U.S., legally or illegally. With your political science interest, that might be right up your alley."

David mulled over his pastor's proposition for a couple of days before deciding to sign on for the February trip. Over the next eight years, David made a dozen trips to Honduras, each time becoming more appalled at the conditions in the country which forced workers to leave everything and to risk their lives to come to the States. They grasped any opportunity to earn money and send it home so their families could survive.

With each trip to that Central American country, David developed a real love for the people. They had so little, yet were willing to share what they had. Most suffered physical problems from rotted teeth to chronic infection without complaining. His attitude concerning immigration laws soon changed because of what he saw and experienced in Honduras.

In 2007 in Willmar, Minnesota, the INS made a raid on the town. Because of the practice of some employers hiring illegals to work in their plants, many Hispanics without documentation lived in that community. The INS used what some considered unnecessarily heavy-handed tactics during the arrests that had been made.

David traveled there to make sure workers rights weren't trampled by overzealous officers. He joined with a naturalized U.S. citizen, Marietta. Acting as an interpreter, she and David objected when the workers were treated in ways less than what he expected from his country.

It was because of his actions that he appeared on the radar screen of two groups: the FBI and a loosely organized group of Latinos concerned for the welfare of their people.

David snapped out of his daydream and checked his watch. To his surprise, only a few minutes had passed since he last looked. He sat down at his table.

"DAVID CRAINE, YOU IDIOT. HOW DID YOU GET yourself into this mess?" he said to the floor, but it didn't answer, didn't have to. David knew how he had dug himself into this hole without being reminded by any impartial floor.

I wonder what I'd be doing today if I hadn't answered the phone? he thought. "No use asking the floor," he mused out loud. "It doesn't know any more than I do."

He took a sip of the coffee. In his memory he could actually hear the ring tone of the phone. Given the chance, he'd probably answer it again. As he sat at his table, he thought back to the call, and he could almost hear the voice on the other end of the line.

"Hello. Is this David Craine?" the heavily Spanish-accented voice asked.

"Yes it is. What do you want?" David snapped back, expecting to hear a telemarketer stammer out some prewritten plea for money.

"Mr. Craine, my name is Herminio Valesquez. May I speak to you for a moment about a matter of some urgency?"

David could not force the memory of the phone conversation with Herminio from his mind. It was as fresh as the day it had occurred a year ago.

"Mr. Craine, you have come to my attention because of your many mission trips to Honduras and especially because of your work with the immigrant laborers during the Willmar problem."

Before David could say a word, Herminio continued. "I am a representative of a group, the Americans for Immigrant Justice, AIJ, and we commend you for your stand on behalf of our people."

David remembered responding, "Well, I didn't do much, only advised people of their rights. In the end, they were all deported."

"We know that," Herminio affirmed, "but you stood up for human dignity, and that's what counts."

By this time David was wondering where the conversation was heading. "David, I would like to meet with you so we can converse more. Would you meet with me?"

David's mind immediately told him to hang up, but something inside of him answered, "I guess I could." Then the thought occurred to him that he should be the one to select the time and the place.

"How about tomorrow at 2:00 in the afternoon?" David said, thinking that would be a quiet time in any of the restaurants in town. "I'll meet you at the Vanilla Bean Cafe on Main Street."

David penciled in the date of the meeting on his calendar, April 22, 2011, and so the stage was set for the greatest act of David Craine's life.

He made sure to arrive early at the small cafe and was already seated facing the door when a man with definite Latino features entered. David stood and extended his hand. "Herminio? I'm David Craine. Please be seated."

The lone waitress came to their booth and handed each of them a menu while the two men paused, each sizing up the other. When she left, Herminio spoke first.

"Thank you for meeting with me, David. I know this is unusual, and you must be wondering what I want from you. And you are right, David, I do want something."

With that, David sat more upright in his seat. Herminio continued, "I told you over the phone that you have come to the attention of the AIJ because of your work in the Willmar situation. Also, we know you have a large boat capable of carrying several passengers on Lake Superior."

David nodded.

"Here is our predicament, David. We have six men, three Hondurans and three Mexicans who have been in your country working without documentation. They are eager to leave here and return home, but it is difficult for them to make connections so far from the Mexican border. We would like to hire you to smuggle them out of the country before they are apprehended. If they can make it past the Canadian border, we have a network set up that will allow them to secure passage to the port in Thunder Bay, Ontario. A transport there is scheduled to be loaded with wheat in early June at the port. If we can get them on that ship, the captain has agreed to let them stow away for the trip to Panama. From there, they can jump ship and find their way safely home."

"Stop right there," David interrupted. "There's no way I'm going to break the law, so don't waste your time or mine." He started to stand.

"Please wait and hear me out," Herminio quickly said, placing his hand on David's. "We certainly do not want you to break the law or to go against what your conscience tells you. But consider this. Is it wrong to help these men get out? Your government doesn't want them here. Many of your people don't want them here, and these men don't want to be here. If they are caught, after months of waiting in jail and taking up your resources of space and time, they will be sent home. Is it wrong to spare everyone the trouble and trauma they will experience if caught? We thought that with your humanitarian attitude you might be willing to help. We can't pay much, but I can offer you fifteen hundred dollars to ferry them to a spot on the lake's shore just past the border."

David sat back down to think. He remembered the way the immigrants had been treated in Willmar, and what Herminio said did make some sense. Herminio could see David's pause and took the opportunity to continue his argument.

"It is how far from here to the border, a hundred-fifty miles at the most, probably less? Why, in eight hours or so you could make your delivery and be on your way home. You'd have your money. Your country would have six fewer illegal workers to worry about, and they would be on their way home."

With those words, Herminio motioned for the waitress. "Order what you'd like, David. This is on me. Come let's eat. Take your time. I don't need an answer today. I just ask that you think about this opportunity to correct a wrong."

They placed their orders, and when the food was served, Herminio did not bring up the subject again. Instead, he spoke of the conditions that David had witnessed in Honduras. The two men discussed the need for social justice in the world and the role individual people filled to help.

After the meal, Herminio shook David's hand and said, "I'll call you in two days. Whatever answer you give me, I'll take as final." With that, the two men went their separate ways.

Two days later, David gave Hermino his answer. "Yes, I'll do it."

CHAPTER
NINE

AFTER HE MET WITH HERMINIO, PLANS WERE MADE to smuggle the six aliens out of the country. David tried to convince himself that what he was doing was not illegal, but the thought haunted him.

The idea was for him to have his boat fueled at the Silver Bay Marina. Herminio and the six men were to arrive just after nightfall, which in May would be around 8:30 p.m. Chances were, no one would be at the marina at that hour.

The Silver Bay Marina was small, having only fifty-six berths. Harbor traffic was always slow during the week, and even on holidays there was little rush. Best of all for Herminio's purpose, it was hidden from traffic passing on Highway 61.

All went as planned, and on the night when the men were to board David's boat, the moon was in its waning phase. David had the cabin lights dimmed in his boat, and *Crusader, Too* rocked gently in the swells. He was greeted with several, "*Holas,*" as the Latinos came aboard, and David shook the hand of each. As he did, he noticed that each man had his own distinctive look. One was of definite native descent, Aztec in appearance, another had very Spanish features, and the others resembled so many of the indigenous people he had met on his trips to Honduras. Two of the six were a little different, though. David had met several of the descendants of Palestinian immigrants in Honduras, and these men reminded him of those with whom he had contact. Nothing seemed out of the ordinary with the group other than he was beginning to feel like a criminal.

With an, "*Adios,*" to Herminio, the mooring lines connecting *Crusader, Too* to the dock were hauled in, and David started the trip to the Canadian border. It was smooth boating, and the lake was un-

40

usually calm. The forecast was for the weather to hold for at least another twenty-four hours. Within eight hours he had reached the drop-off point, a private dock in one of the few sheltered bays along the shore.

The men jumped to the dock with repeated, *"Muchas gracious."* In his hurry to get back into American waters before he was discovered, David did not stay long enough to see them climb into a dark-colored van.

It didn't take long for him to make it back to Grand Marais on the U.S. side of the border, and the sun was beginning to rise in the east, a red fireball edging up over the horizon. He pulled into the Grand Marais Marina, grabbed a cold bottle of juice and a bag of cashews while his boat was being re-fueled, and immediately set out for his berth in Silver Bay.

DAVID WAS A METICULOUS MAN, AND BEFORE he left *Crusader, Too* at her mooring, he swept the floor and picked up even the smallest pieces of debris left by his passengers the night before. He noticed what looked like a piece of black plastic wedged into the crease between two seat cushions, but when he pulled it out, he discovered it was a flash drive for a computer, left behind by one of the men.

David assumed it had fallen out of one of their pockets and had gotten pushed down without the man realizing he had lost it. He put it in his pocket, assuming it had records of time spent in the U.S., perhaps a record of earnings, or even e-mails from home. His computer was at home in his apartment, and he thought that after he rested it might make interesting reading. With that, he jumped into his car parked at the marina and drove to Two Harbors.

By the time David arrived there it was evening again, and he was exhausted. He had been without sleep for almost twenty-four hours, and with a great deal of effort, he climbed the stairs to his second story apartment. When he unlocked the door at the top, all he could do was fall into bed. He tossed and turned in a restless sleep, dreaming that everyone, the county sheriff, Latinos, and the towns-people, were trying to capture him. When he awoke, it was seven in the morning. David had a headache, and his muscles were stiff as though his pursuers had caught up with him and given him a gang-land going over.

As he splashed cold water on his face, he wished he had never agreed to smuggle the men into Canada. He knew he had broken the law. He spotted the flash drive that had been found on his boat. It was lying on the table where he had tossed it before going to bed.

More for something to take his mind off what he had done than anything else, David turned on his laptop and plugged the flash drive into the UB port. For a second the computer made its working sounds, and then a notice popped up on its screen asking him if he wanted to open the files. Another click on the control pad and the screen was filled with file numbers.

David clicked on the first file, and it opened. To his amazement it was a high resolution picture of the ore docks rising six stories above the harbor's water behind his apartment.

He opened the next file to find another picture of the docks, this one taken from a different angle. Each file was one of a series of pictures from the same site. Some showed the road in Two Harbors leading to the yards behind the docks, some were of the docks taken from the breakwater across the bay, and it was obvious that several were taken from the water just below the massive steel beams that supported the huge ore hoppers of the docks. Still another had ob-viously been taken from the top of Pork City Hill, an area off limits to all but the dock and railroad workers.

David thought, *This is odd. Those men didn't appear to be tourists, and if they were, why didn't they just get a passport and enter the country legally?* He opened the next file.

To his complete amazement, the file was a daily log of activities: the time a train pushed its load of cars onto the top of the dock, how long it took the train to empty the gondolas into the ore hoppers. It detailed the time a ship arrived, where it docked, how long it took to load. The journal documented how many workers could be seen on the dock, what they were doing, and if they were vigilant of what was occurring on the ground.

Most troubling, though, was the record of security personnel, where they moved, and when they took their stations. The hair on the back of David's neck began to bristle, and a wave of heat flushed over his body. He opened the next file.

This time, there was no mistaking what the files were about. On this file were estimates of the type of explosives and the quantities that would be needed to completely take down the docks. There was little doubt that the files were plans to blow up the ore docks in Two Harbors.

Opening the last file, David found six names:

1. Imad Diqqa
2. Murad Judal
3. Jibril Al-Nams
4. Afu Jaber
5. Yusuf El 'Elyan
6. Zaim Hassan Zayed

Sweat poured from his forehead as David realized he had bumbled his way into a situation far more serious than helping some illegal workers leave the country. As he sat holding the flash drive in his shaking fingers, his telephone rang.

"Hello," David said, his voice shaking with trepidation.

"David, this is Herminio," the man on the other end blurted out. "I'm not sure how they know, but I received a call from an FBI agent named Erickson a few minutes ago. He said he wanted to ask me some questions about my organization, the AIJ. He said it was nothing serious but to be at his office in forty minutes or he would send two of his assistants to pick me up."

David felt his insides knot. Then he heard Herminio say in a hushed voice, "Hold on a minute, David. Someone is knocking on my door. I guess he didn't want to wait for me to come in on my own."

David waited, fiddling with the flash drive in his hand. After five minutes, he was getting agitated because Herminio did not return to the phone, and after a full ten minutes, he hung up the phone and paced the floor, trying to make sense of all that had happened in the last twenty-four hours.

CHAPTER
TEN

SHERIFF DEIDRE JOHNSON WALKED INTO HER OFFICE and quietly closed the door behind her. She sat at her desk, cradled her head in her hands, and closed her eyes, and she wondered how David Craine could have gotten himself in so deep. It seemed like yesterday that she sat in his political science class when she was a high school junior. She remembered his caring manner.

"Deidre," she remembered him asking, "Will you stay after school today? There are some things we should talk about."

Mr. Craine looked up from his desk when Deidre knocked on his office door.

"Come in Deidre. I'm so glad you could stay for a few minutes today," he said with his characteristic politeness. That was one thing about Mr. Craine—he treated every student as though they mattered.

"No, leave the door open please," he said. "It gets stuffy in this little room if the door's closed." Deidre knew better, and she respected him for his propriety.

"Deidre," Mr. Craine had started, "I'm not sure what is going on, but your grades have begun to plummet. At the beginning of the year all your assignments were turned in on time, and you were almost straight A. Now you're so far behind it'll be a miracle if you can pull out a passing grade for the semester."

Deidre remembered how her face reddened, and tears welled up in her eyes. All she could do was look at the floor and swallow hard.

Mr. Craine continued. "I've taught long enough to know that something destructive is going on in your life. If I didn't know better, I'd think you are using drugs, but your eyes are too clear and you

45

don't show any other symptoms of that sort of thing. Is there anything I can do to help?"

Deidre could do nothing but shake her head no and continue to look at the floor. It was becoming more difficult for her to hold back her tears.

"Deidre, if you're in trouble, I can help, but only if you'll let me."

With that Deidre crumbled. "How can you help?" she sobbed unintelligibly. "Do you know what it's like? He came home drunk last weekend and lined us up against the wall while he pointed a shotgun at us, all the while screaming he was going to kill us!"

Deidre buried her head in her hands, and said nothing for a few minutes. Mr. Craine was quiet while he waited for her. Finally she could speak again. "My step-dad always drank a lot—too much I suppose—but he was never like this. This past fall he lost his job, and now he drinks all the time. My little brother's a nervous wreck. His hands shake so badly he can hardly tie his shoes, and Dad's so cruel to Mom. He throws things at her, and lately has been slapping her around when she doesn't do what he expects." With that Deidre slumped in the chair and wept into her hands.

Mr. Crain handed her a wad of tissue but never said to buck up or to stop crying. Instead he said, "I don't know how you kids can take what some of you go through. Deidre, I'm required by law to report this to the authorities. Please don't think I'm betraying your confidence, but it's something I must do. Do you understand?"

Deidre remembered nodding and blankly staring ahead. Snot ran from her nose in stringy threads, and she tried wiping them away only to smear everything around.

Then Mr. Craine got out of his chair and put his arms around her, and said, "You'll be safe now."

He returned to his desk and picked up the phone. "I'm calling a friend at Social Services. She's a wonderful lady."

Deidre saw him dial and wait for a pickup on the other end of the call. "Hi, Jan? Say, I've got a real problem here. Do you suppose you could stop by my office right away? I'd like you to come as soon as you can." There was a pause, and then he said, "Yes, I think we could say this is an emergency." Another short pause and, "Great, we'll see you in five minutes."

With that Deidre's Mr. Craine turned to her. "The Social Service Office is only a block down the street. Jan's dropping everything and coming right now." Deidre remembered how calming his voice was to her. "It's easy for me to tell you not to worry, but believe me, she'll help you and your family."

Jan burst into Mr. Crain's office like a whirlwind. Deidre hadn't known what to expect and was a little taken aback by this dynamo. Jan plunked her five-foot-eleven-inch frame onto the one remaining chair in the office, and it groaned under her ample weight. Her gray hair looked like it had been combed by a windstorm. Deidre looked into her eyes and was immediately taken by their kindness.

"So," Jan began the conversation. "David tells me things are a little tough for you right now."

Deidre nodded.

Jan looked right at her, and said, "I want you to know how proud I am of you for seeking help before something really bad happens. I want to be the one to help, if you'll let me. Is that what you want?"

Again Deidre nodded.

Jan asked Deidre to repeat her story, and this time the words came easier, more matter-of-factly. After hearing the details, Jan said, "We have to get you and your mom, your brother and sister out of this situation. It doesn't seem that any of you are safe at home right now. Will your mother talk with me?"

Deidre only shrugged.

After that, events began to move so quickly they hardly registered for Deidre. That very afternoon Jan met with her mother, and by early evening, while Deidre's step-dad was out drinking, Jan helped Deidre, her mother, and her siblings pack a few pieces of clothing in an old suitcase. She escorted them to the women's shelter in downtown Two Harbors. By bedtime the three of them settled in an upstairs apartment in the safe house.

Deidre didn't know much of the details after that. A restraining order was taken out against her step-dad, and he was scheduled for a hearing before Judge Anderson, but before that happened he skipped town. Rumor was he had run to California where he became lost in the crowd. At any rate, he never contacted them again.

By this time Deidre was so far behind in school there was little chance that she could enter her senior year with any chance of graduating on time. That was when Mr. Craine had come to her rescue again.

Deidre remembered how he offered to tutor her during the summer, how Mrs. Craine had helped her take care of the incomplete her English teacher had given her, and how much time the two of them had devoted to her.

Even during her last year of high school, after she was back on track to graduate with the rest of her class, the two of them had continued to support her. They invited her family to share Thanksgiving dinner with them, and Mr. and Mrs. Craine made sure they had a Christmas. Mrs. Craine took her shopping for a dress for graduation. She remembered Mr. Crain encouraging her to begin college, and she remembered the day he had told her to call him David from then on.

CHAPTER
ELEVEN

THERE WERE SOME PROFESSIONS TRADITIONALLY OUT OF BOUNDS for women, and Deidre had set her mind on becoming a law enforcement officer. For those trying to break the barriers, their efforts were often met with male resistance.

At first, the biases were subtle. When she had enrolled in college at Great Lakes University, she met with a counselor. He opened her file, and they began to discuss her future.

"Well, Ms. Johnson," he said as he scanned her records. "You seem to have been an exemplary student, with the exception of two quarters of your junior year. Do you have an explanation for the significant drop in your grades for that time?"

"I do, but I don't care to discuss them with you. They are of a very personal nature," she replied.

That stopped the counselor for a second. "I see," he remarked and made a note in her file.

"Do you have a goal you're trying to reach, or will you be taking courses to explore where you want to focus your studies?"

Deidre looked at him, and resolutely said, "I want to major in criminal justice. After graduation, I would like to be a law enforcement officer."

Her counselor offered a patronizing smile. "Ms. Johnson, have you thought this decision through? I mean look at you. How tall are you? Five-two?"

"Five-one," Deidre interjected. It only made the counselor continue with his line of distorted reasoning.

"And you probably only weigh one-ten at the most. Have you thought about how you could possibly pass the physical requirements

49

at a police academy? Have you thought about what it would be like to have your nose mashed across your pretty face? Why don't you be realistic? Did you ever consider a more traditional woman's profession, like nursing? You'd certainly bring comfort to any patient, especially the men."

Deidre's eyes narrowed, and she blurted out, "You might have been able to counsel this way ten years ago, but not today, and not with me. How does sexual harassment sound to you? Do you like the sound of those words?"

She stopped to compose herself, and with a forced calm to her voice said, "Can we get on with what courses are required for my degree and the sequence in which they should be taken?"

Almost in disbelief, the counselor looked at Deidre and responded by first clearing his throat and then saying, "Of course. It's your life, I suppose." He matter-of-factly went through the list of required and selective courses and helped Deidre draw up a tentative schedule for her first year.

School had always been easy for Deidre, and college classes were no exception. She was totally engrossed in what she was learning and in four years walked across the stage to accept her diploma. But that was only the beginning.

In order to become a police officer candidate, Deidre had to complete a program at an accredited academy. Centralia, Minnesota, was the closest and most affordable she could find. She applied, but before being accepted, she had to pass the required physical tests.

The medical exam presented no problem. Deidre had always been healthy, but the requirement of being able to carry a two-hundred-pound weight over her shoulder was another consideration. During her last year of college she had spent hours in the gym lifting free weights and working out with a couple of friends who were on the football team. The contrast between them was comical. They were six-four and roughly two hundred seventy-five pounds, and she was five one—if she had her shoes on—and weighed in at one-o-five and a half. But Deidre earned their respect with her dedication.

During the academy's test, she had no trouble with pushups or pull ups. In fact her lower body weight worked to her advantage, but the lift and carry was another matter.

A sack about the size of a large man's torso was filled with two hundred pounds of some sort of grainy material. Deidre would have to lift it to an upright position, place her shoulder under it, and stand up. Then she had to carry it ten yards before setting it down.

She muscled it up, but her knees almost buckled. One staggering step after another, she made her way across the floor before dropping the bag. The rules didn't say the bag had to be set down gently. She passed, and no one could deny her claim to admission.

CHAPTER
TWELVE

THE FIRST DAY OF HER FIRST CLASS AT CENTRALIA, Deidre was introduced to Female Bias 101 when the instructor took attendance.

"Johnson," and there was a palpable pause, "Deidre."

"Present," Deidre responded.

The instructor looked up from his computer printout. "Oh, excuse me," he said. "I didn't know they let high school cheerleaders take this course."

Everyone in the room burst into laughter, except Deidre. She knew it would be hopeless to respond in this setting, and she looked at the top of her desk.

After that, the day went a little smoother. When she had completed her last class of the afternoon, an introductory class on law enforcement ethics, her instructor, Pete Hovland, took her aside, and encouraged her. "I know this is going to be tough on you, but hang in there. Not all of police work involves brawn, and, anyway, you'll find ways to cope. Brain usually wins out over brawn."

Pete was one of the older instructors, probably ready for retirement, and he smiled at her. "Hang in there."

As it turned out, one of her male classmates from high school in Two Harbors was following the same path she was taking. Ben VanGotten had been a jock in high school. At six-two and two-hundred pounds, he had starred in both football and hockey. Even then he was noted for his crudeness, especially the things he said to his female classmates. Now, of all the police cadets, he was the one who treated Deidre with the least respect.

In their self-defense class, which was not supposed to involve actual force, students were paired up by approximate size, all except Deidre. More often than not, her partner was Ben.

52

During the first class exercise, Ben was to be a belligerent drunk, and Deidre was supposed to control him with a handhold designed to inflict debilitating pain. It was supposed to be a walk-through exercise, and when Ben flung his free arm around and knocked Deidre to the mat with her lip bleeding, she was taken completely by surprise.

The instructor smirked. "You have to always be prepared, because you never know what's going to happen."

Day after day Deidre experienced the same abuse. It was especially bad when Ben was paired with her. Whether she was playing the part of the officer or the part of the suspect, she always ended up absorbing punishment. By the end of the second week, she was a mass of black-and-blue marks.

Deidre had reached her breaking point. On Monday of the third week, she was once again paired with Ben. This time, she was to be a fleeing suspect, and Ben the arresting officer. Ben grabbed her from behind, his hands conveniently finding her breasts. Deidre had enough.

With one quick stomp of her foot on Ben's instep, she felt the snap of one of his metatarsals. Ben let go in surprise, and Deidre spun around, delivering a forceful kick to Ben's groin. He fell to the mat like a felled tree, writhing in pain, not knowing which part of his anatomy he should hold.

Deidre looked down at Ben, and said, "You always have to be prepared, because you never know what's going to happen." Then she stalked out of the room, wondering if she had just kicked her way out of the academy.

That evening, as she straightened her dorm room for what she thought might be the last time, someone knocked at her door. She opened it, expecting the worst, but it was Pete, the one instructor who had encouraged her.

"Hi, Deidre. May I come in?" Pete asked.

Deidre motioned with her hand to enter. *So,* she thought, *this is who they send to tell me I'm through.*

"Deidre, I heard about what happened in class today."

Deidre sat silently.

"I want you to know that I'm proud of you. I knew at some point you were going to have to put an end to this harassment, but I didn't know how you were going to do it." Pete laughed. "Well, you did it."

Deidre looked at him. "Mr. Hovland, am I finished here?" she asked with a quaking voice.

"No. No, not at all," Pete responded. "There was meeting of the faculty with the dean to discuss your status. A couple of the instructors wanted you dismissed. You probably know who they are?"

Deidre nodded.

Pete went on. "I told the group that times are changing, and they had better get used to it. I also told them that if they terminated your education here, I would consult you about filling a civil sexual-harassment suit, and also a Title Nine federal suit. That opened a few eyes, I can tell you."

By this time, all Deidre could do was mumble her thanks.

"Ben has a broken foot, and I suspect some swelling elsewhere. His foot's in a cast. I don't know about the other part," and Pete chuckled.

"His education will be delayed for a while, but he'll be allowed to come back next term to finish. You hang in there, Deidre." With that, Mr. Pete Hovland excused himself from Deidre's room.

AUGUST 16, 1998, WAS A CLOUDLESS DAY, and as Deidre stood on the graduation platform at the Centralia Police Academy, she felt taller, stronger, and ready to take on the world. She had made it through four years of college and received a degree in criminology. Now she had completed the six-week training course at Centralia's police academy.

After those first two weeks of harassment she had endured, and after she had taken care of Ben, her life had been much more bearable. At least no one had tried anything funny during the mock arrests they had to make from then on.

But on that beautiful Thursday in August, Deidre put the past out of her thoughts. This was a day she would enjoy and remember.

Deidre had applied for an opening with the Lake County Sheriff's squad in her home town. They were interviewing for one position now, but another would open up the following November. She figured if she put her application on file now, she might stand a better chance for the second opening. That was why she was somewhat shocked when she received a call from the sheriff a few days before graduation.

"Hello," Deidre answered the phone in her room.

"Is this Ms. Deidre Johnson," the caller wanted to know.

Deidre didn't recognize the voice, and almost hung up. "Yes, this is Deidre," she said after a slight pause.

"This is Sheriff Thorton of the Lake Country Sheriff Department. After reviewing your application and resume, we would like you to come in for an interview. I know your graduation is set for this Thursday, but could you come to the law enforcement center next Monday morning?"

Deidre could hardly believe what she was hearing, and her first thought was that someone was playing a prank on her.

During the pause that ensued, the sheriff spoke again. "We particularly were impressed with your reasons for choosing the law enforcement profession, and we were especially moved by your familiarity with domestic violence."

That was when Deidre realized the call was for real. Few people, none at the academy, knew about that night during her junior year of high school when her father was going to kill her and her family.

Finally, Deidre stammered, "Yes, yes, I can be there. What time did you say?"

"I didn't, but is ten o'clock okay with you?"

Once again Deidre stammered, "Yes, yes, that'll be fine."

Sheriff Thorton said goodnight, and hung up. Deidre slowly sat down on her bed and placed the phone on its cradle. Then she let out a "YES!" at the top of her lungs.

GRADUATION HAD BEEN EVEN MORE EXCITING than she had believed it would be, and as she received her diploma, her eyes met those of her instructor, Pete. He gave her a thumb up and a broad smile.

As she drove the two hundred fifty miles up from Centralia in southern Minnesota to Two Harbors, Deidre sang along to the tunes on the car radio until she was hoarse and couldn't sing any more.

At 9:50 on Monday, Deidre entered the law enforcement center. She climbed the flight of stairs to the second floor and opened the door. On her right was an area closed in with darkened glass. She stepped up to the speaker mounted on her side of the window, and even then could barely see into the dispatcher's office. This was also the room from which the inmates were observed around the clock.

"Can I help you," the person behind the glass asked. Deidre couldn't help but notice the jailer was a woman and was wearing a black uniform of some sort.

"Yes, I have an appointment for an interview with Sheriff Thorton at ten o'clock," Deidre managed to get out of her desert-dry mouth.

"Place your keys and any other metallic objects in the well under the window. You can pick them up after your interview. Good luck."

She heard a buzz and then the click of the lock in the door to her left.

Deidre thought she could see the woman smile behind the cover of the tinted glass. She opened the door and walked into Sheriff Thorton's world behind the glass. When the door closed behind her, she heard the lock click shut.

"You must be Deidre," the sheriff's secretary said, and she pushed a button on the intercom.

"Yes, Joyce, what is it?" Deidre heard a now familiar voice come out of the machine.

"Deidre Johnson is here for her interview. Would you like her to come to your office now?"

Deidre heard the sheriff answer, "Yes, send her in please."

Deidre entered his office, and she was almost stunned by the size of the man. For an instant he stood and looked at her, trying to come to grips with a five-foot-one-inch blond who wanted to be on his force. Finally, he stuck out his huge hand. "Bill Thorton," he said.

Deidre placed her hand in his meaty paw. She tried to present herself with a firm handshake, but the sheriff's oversized hand totally engulfed hers.

"Please, sit down," the sheriff offered. His voice was quite gentle for such a large man.

"Your interview will be attended by five people: two county board members, the director of the Lake County Human Services, the community liaison representative, and me. Just be yourself. Answer each question honestly, and don't rush your answers," he advised. "I see the others are already in the conference room. Let's join them, and good luck," Sheriff Thorton smiled at Deidre.

The two of them entered the room together. Four people rose to shake her hand, but the community liaison representative , a grossly overweight, balding man, stayed seated and didn't offer her his hand, only scrutinized her from top to bottom with what she called the "elevator look," giving her the once over. Deidre privately gave him a name, "*Oinker.*"

Everyone sat, and the interview began with Sheriff Thorton referring to a list of prearranged questions. "I will be reading the questions as they appear on this sheet. Each interviewee will be asked the same set of questions so there can be no sense of bias. At the end of the session you'll have an opportunity to ask whatever you would like of us. Do you agree to this format?"

Deidre nodded and quietly said, "Yes."

The questions started out easy enough. "Deidre, will you tell us something about yourself?" That she could handle. From there the questions became more about theoretical situations and what actions she would take.

The interview went better than for what Deidre could have hoped. Part way in, she was able to relax and be herself. When the interview was about to end, Sheriff Thorton stood from his chair and once again held out his hand, but before Deidre could rise, Oinker interrupted.

"Just a minute," he leered. "I look at your, ah, size and I wonder how you would react if a man say my size, came after you. How could you ever handle him," and he smiled a strained smile.

Deidre felt her face flush, and she almost blurted out something that wouldn't have been appropriate.

Sheriff Thorton stepped in. "It was agreed before this interview started that only the questions on this sheet would be asked, and Ms. Johnson accepted those terms. Ms. Johnson, you do not have to answer that question." He glared at Oinker.

"That's all right, Sheriff. I'll answer the question." Then she looked at Oinker and calmly said, "If you'd care to step outside, because this hypothetical man is your size, I'd be happy to demonstrate."

Now it was Oinker's face that flushed, and his jaw clamped shut. He shook his head. The others shook Deidre's hand and expressed their thanks for her coming to the interview. Oinker looked out the window.

"We have one last interview to conduct this afternoon," Sheriff Thorton informed her. "Then we'll make our decision during a late afternoon meeting. One way or the other, you'll receive a call tomorrow at 8:00 tomorrow morning. Have a pleasant afternoon."

Deidre left the center with mixed emotions: hopeful but cautious, elated but exhausted. The next morning she sat with her cell phone in one hand, a cup of coffee in the other, and a knot in her belly.

At eight o'clock, her phone rang. It was the sheriff's secretary, and Deidre's heart sank. Surly if she had been the chosen candidate, the sheriff would have called her personally to tell her the good news.

"Good morning, Deidre," the receptionist said. "Sheriff Thorton was called out early this morning to the scene of a rather tragic accident on one of our county roads. He left a message asking me to tell you that you have been chosen to be on the force. Your orientation will begin next Monday morning at seven sharp." The secretary added, "Congratulations, Deputy Johnson."

CHAPTER
THIRTEEN

DEPUTY DEIDRE JOHNSON FELL INTO A ROUTINE. The other deputies, all male, treated her with more aloofness than animosity, and she guessed they talked behind her back. As long as they let her do her job, she was okay with that.

In the community, she was building a reputation for being fair and thorough. Among women dealing with domestic violence, Deidre was close to reaching sainthood. She also gained a reputation for being able to defuse tense situations without the use of physical force.

Her most rigorous test had been one night when she was working the 9:00 p.m. to 7:00 a.m. shift.

"Deputy Johnson, report in with your current location," her police radio had crackled.

"I'm traveling north on Highway Three, almost to the Silver Bend Cemetery."

"There is a report of a domestic about another three miles up Number Three, fire number 2129A. Respond immediately. The caller indicated an armed male was making threats against his family. Backup is on its way, but the nearest squad has about twenty minutes ETA."

"I read you," Deidre responded. Her heart sank at what the dispatcher had said. She was being called to a situation that was all too familiar.

She turned on her warning lights but chose to not go in with a siren screaming. Her vehicle raced through the darkness, and she prayed that a deer wouldn't leap onto the road from the brush-lined ditches. It took less than three minutes for her to reach the driveway, douse her warning lights, and park behind a red F-150. Deidre's SUV had hardly stopped rolling when she leaped from the driver's seat and drew her pistol.

60

When she reached the door she could hear familiar sounds that twisted her insides. A woman's voice was pleading, "Please, please, don't do this. They're your children."

Deidre heard a male voice yell, "Shut up, you damn woman. Don't ever tell me what I can or can't do. You're the cause of all this. If you'd keep your trap shut, I'd be okay."

In the background, Deidre could hear children wailing. Her instinct was to barge in and shoot the abuser, but she took a second to calm herself. Then, her pistol still drawn, she quietly turned the door knob. The door was unlocked, and she let herself in.

The entryway led to a small living room. A table lamp lay broken on the floor, and a picture had fallen or been knocked off the wall. There was a slight blood smear on the doorway. The screaming and wailing was coming from the next room.

Deidre stepped around the corner into the kitchen, and the scene burned its way into her memory. Lying on the floor was a young woman. One sleeve of her dress was ripped and hanging from her shoulder. A trickle of blood ran from her nose, and the skin on her cheek had been scraped as if her face had been rubbed along the stucco wall.

In the corner, three children huddled together, seeking shelter behind each other's body. Their crying didn't cease, and they looked at Deidre like three trapped animals.

In the center of the room stood a man, their father Deidre assumed. In his right hand he held a butcher knife, and he swayed back and forth in a way that made Deidre believe he was extremely drunk.

"Who the hell are you?" he slurred, spotting Deidre.

Deidre held her handgun hidden behind her back. He had a knife. She had a gun, and she didn't want the situation to escalate.

"My name's Deidre. What's yours?" she responded with a calm voice.

"Why're you here?" the man demanded, ignoring her question.

"I was told that times have been tough for you. Thought I'd stop by and see how you were doing."

"What do you know about me? What business is it of yours what I do?" he challenged, but at the same time looked at her quizzically.

"Well, I know you've got three kids here who look like they could use a break."

Deidre caught the reflection of headlights as another car pulled up behind hers. She assumed it was another squad responding, and she gave a silent prayer of thanks that they had made such good time.

"I've got a friend outside. What do you say we let the kids go out and sit in his car until we get things settled in here?" She hoped he would at least spare the children the memory of what might happen.

"Why? You think I can't take care of my own kids," he argued.

"Oh, that's not it at all. Sometimes it's good for adults to make their decisions without a bunch of crying kids around. Know what I mean? They just get on our nerves sometimes . . . I forget, what did you say your name is? Charlie?"

The man with the knife pointed it at Deidre. "Just like a woman, can't remember anything. My name is Kurt. I told you that, but you weren't listening, were you?"

"Oh, right. I'm sorry Kurt. I guess with all the excitement here I forgot. Say, Kurt, how about letting the kids leave? They can't help us here, anyway. What d'ya say?"

Kurt looked at the terrified little ones. "Go on. Get out before I give you what you got comin', you worthless brats. Git!"

Deidre motioned for the children to move toward the doorway. When they were close to her, she quietly said to the oldest, "There's a nice man outside. Tell him Deidre said everything is good in here, and she wants you to stay in his car. Can you do that?"

Through his tears, the child nodded and helped guide the younger ones from the room. Now it was just the three adults.

"Okay, Kurt, what's the problem? Your wife looks like she can use some help. She must have fallen down, right?"

"Uh, yeah. Yeah. She fell down and hit her face," Kurt explained, using the excuse Deidre had given him.

"How about we let her go into the living room and lie down on the couch? It looks like she could use some rest, don't you think, Kurt?" Deidre was hoping to have Kurt's wife out of the line of fire before she took more forceful action.

"Ah, she's okay," he responded. "She falls down a lot."

Deidre motioned for the woman to move. "But if she's resting in the other room, then you and I can talk. Come on, Kurt. She'll just be in the other room."

The lady began to crawl toward Deidre. Kurt stood looking at her through his alcoholic fog, the butcher knife still in his hand, but he made no move to stop her. Finally she disappeared into the darkened living room.

As soon as they were alone, Deidre brought her arm from behind her back, and for the first time, Kurt saw that she had a gun.

"Kurt, this is no time to be foolish. A gun beats a knife every day of the week. I'd like you to drop the knife right now."

Kurt looked straight into the barrel of Deidre's service revolver. The bore looked as big as a canon. The knife rattled onto the floor.

"That was a smart move, Kurt," Deidre said with an even tone. "Now kick it away from yourself."

Suddenly all of the fight had gone out of Kurt. He slumped.

"Kneel on the floor." Kurt knelt. "Place your hands behind your back." He did without objection.

Deidre circled behind him and placed a handcuff around one wrist and then the other.

"Okay, Kurt. I'll help you to stand. Then we'll walk outside. Do you understand?" Kurt nodded.

As the two of them, Kurt in front and Deidre behind with her weapon still drawn, moved down the steps of the porch, Deputy Anderson stepped forward and led Kurt away. Deidre heard the deputy reading him the Miranda act.

Deidre was still shaking when she went to her vehicle and opened its door.

"Come on, kids. Your mom's waiting inside for you. It's safe now."

They followed her into the house, and Deidre turned on a dim light in the living room. She went over to the couch.

"Can you tell me your name?"

"Mary."

"Mary, I'm not so sure it's good for you and the kids to stay alone tonight. Not that your husband will be back. He'll be in jail. But I think you could use someone who'll help you get cleaned up and who'll help get the kids settled. Please let me take you to the women's shelter in town. They can help. They'll help you decide what to do from here."

Mary could only mumble, "That would be nice."

It was a silent ride into Two Harbors that night. Deidre phoned ahead to make sure someone would be waiting at the shelter.

Over the next days, Mary was well taken care of, and she told anyone who would listen about how Deidre had rescued her family. Deidre's reputation grew.

SIX MONTHS AFTER BEING HIRED, DEIDRE and another deputy arrived at the scene of a fender-bender at the intersection of Seventh Avenue and Waterfront Drive. It was a minor mishap, no injuries, only bruised egos. One of the cars had its front fender caved in, and it was pressed against the tire so it couldn't be driven away. The situation was handled with no problem, and while they waited for a wrecker to come tow the disabled car to a garage down the street, Deidre and the other deputy, Jeff, had time for some small talk.

"Our department sure has a thing for homegrown talent," Jeff stated with a little displeasure in his voice.

Deidre bristled for an instant. Then she asked, "What do you mean by that?"

"Well, first it was you," but he paused when he saw the fire building in Deidre's eyes. "I mean they hired you, and . . ." Jeff knew he was digging the hole deeper. Finally he said, "Oh, hell. I didn't mean that the way it sounded. You've done a great job in a tough situation. I mean, now that they've hired another hometown boy, along with the other two on the force before you were hired, we seem to be a little lopsided with Lake County people."

Deidre looked surprised. "I didn't know they had hired someone. I thought they'd take a little more time. The posting closed only yesterday."

"That's what I mean," Jeff shrugged. "It seems they rushed their decision through awfully fast."

"Do you know who they hired?" Deidre asked, eager to catch up on the department gossip.

"Ben something-or-other. VanBotton, VanGotter. I don't remember exactly, but it's something like that."

Deidre looked at Jeff with disbelief. "VanGotten," she said, hoping it wasn't him.

"Yea, that's it. Do you know him?"

Deidre pulled her hair back with both hands. "A little," was all she said, but inside she knew Ben hadn't forgotten her and why it had taken him three months longer to graduate from the academy than it had the rest of the class.

The wrecker arrived, and Jeff and Deidre were too busy directing traffic to chat any longer, but Deidre was mulling over what the hiring of Ben would mean for her. By the time the wrecker lumbered away with the car and her shift was over, Deidre had conjured up all kinds of scenarios of what life would be like on the force with Ben Van Gotten around. Maybe she could request shifts opposite his. In the end, she decided to ride out any storm and let the situation work itself out.

The following Monday, the deputies met at seven o'clock in the morning. The night shift was ending, and the day shift was just coming on. Deidre had gotten used to the schedule: coffee and a sweet roll, staff meeting, reports filed, then either go home and get some sleep or go out on patrol.

This morning was different. The new deputy was joining the group. Deidre stood back, not wanting to be in a situation where she would be forced to speak to Ben. Once she caught him looking at her, and his eyes narrowed reflexively.

Sheriff Thorton entered the meeting room, the same one where Deidre had been interviewed. "Good morning, everyone. Please, take a seat."

Deidre pulled up a chair at the end of the table away from Ben.

"I'd like to introduce the newest member of our force, Ben Van-Gotten. Ben and Deidre were classmates in college and also at the academy. Ben had an unfortunate accident, broke his foot during a training exercise, or they would have graduated together. Welcome aboard, Ben."

Everyone gave Ben a round of applause. Deidre's hands hardly made contact with each other, and she was the first one to lower them to her lap. Ben's face was crimson by now. The others thought it was out of shyness, but Deidre knew better. She knew Ben had not forgiven or forgotten. Neither had she.

After that introductory meeting, Deidre avoided Ben as best she could. He wanted nothing to do with her either. They worked together, each behaving the way professionals should, but the air was definitely icy when the two of them were in the same room.

One day Jeff, the officer who had sprung the news about Ben that day of the traffic accident, and Deidre were alone in the meeting room, looking over the next month's schedule.

"Deidre, is it just me, or do you and Ben have something going on between the two of you?"

Deidre flared. "What do you mean by that? Are you trying to start some sort of office gossip about the two of us? We're hardly able to stomach each other, let alone have something going on between us."

"Whoa. Wait a minute, Deidre. What I meant was, is there some kind of bad blood between the two of you? I sense it, and so do the others. I'm just curious."

Deidre looked at Jeff for a few seconds before answering. "You know how it is, Jeff. Oil and water will never mix."

CHAPTER
FOURTEEN

ONE MONDAY MORNING AT THEIR WEEKLY MEETING, Sheriff Thorton came in late. His deputies were getting a little restless, anxious to be off on their beats or to go home. When he entered the room, he looked tired.

"It seems like I have been at this job an awfully long time." He paused to swallow hard before continuing. "I've decided not to run for re-election again." He cleared his throat. "It has been a privilege to work with each of you. Every one of you has strong talents that, when blended, have made this force effective. I know we haven't had any extremely difficult cases in our time together, but I have complete confidence that we could have handled just about anything."

Sheriff Thorton paused again to settle his voice. "I know some of you will make a run for this position, and I wholeheartedly want you to do that. In fact, I encourage you to. I will say, I'm not going to endorse one of you over another, because I have utmost respect for each of you." He cleared his throat again before continuing. "Now, let's get on with our reports."

The deputies had a difficult time keeping their minds on business. Ben had made his decision the moment he grasped what the sheriff was saying. Two others were thinking about the possibility, and the remaining deputies were wondering what it would be like to work under another person other than Thorton. Deidre put those thoughts out of her mind and concentrated on the business at hand.

After the meeting was adjourned, the deputies stood around in small groups mulling over what had transpired. Ben sounded like he was already politicking. Deidre started to leave the room, and Jeff hurried to catch up with her in the hall.

"Your going to make a try for it, aren't you?" he asked. Deidre looked at him in disbelief, but Jeff's eyes told her he wasn't joking.

She paused, and for the first time allowed her mind to go there. "No, I don't think I want the job. I like what I do, and, frankly, I'm not sure I could herd this bunch of cats," and she laughed, but she meant what she said. "What about you, Jeff? I think you'd be a good fit, don't you?"

Jeff answered without hesitation. "Holly and I have already talked about this possibility. We knew Thorton would be done one day, just didn't know when that would be. You know we have two little girls who need their daddy home, and I know Holly would rather not get involved in campaigning and all the animosity that can stir up in a community as small as ours. No, I decided months ago that if this situation arose I wouldn't run."

The two walked down the stairs together, and when they were about to climb into the separate vehicles, Jeff turned to Deidre once more.

"I do wish you'd give running for sheriff some thought. You'd make a good one." With that he got in the SUV, waved to Deidre, and drove away.

For the remainder of her ten-hour shift, Deidre kept trying to put the idea out of her mind, but it had a way of crawling back in. By the end of her shift she couldn't shut off her thoughts, and a plan began to emerge.

That evening she turned on her TV to a SIRIUS show tune channel, heated her meal of leftovers in the microwave, and sat at the kitchen counter, eating and thinking. By bedtime, Deidre had made her decision—not to run. She slept peacefully that night.

She was comfortable with her decision and had all but put the matter out of her mind. When word leaked out that Sheriff Thorton was retiring, that changed. Near strangers stopped her on the street.

"Deidre, are you going to make a run for office?"

"Deidre, have you given any thought of running for sheriff?"

"Deidre, remember me? I was the kid you picked up for shoplifting eight years ago, and I'm the one you helped get straight. Any chance you'll be wanting to fill the vacancy left by Thorton?"

One day the director of the battered women's shelter stopped her. "Deidre, a number of women were talking last night, and your name came up so frequently that we'd like you to drop by this evening, if you have time. We'd like to chat with you."

Deidre thought it a little odd, but she figured they wanted advice concerning restraining orders or protection for those who felt endangered. That evening when she entered the lobby of the shelter, she was greeted with more than a surprise.

Propped up against the walls of the room were numerous placards that read, "JOHNSON FOR SHERIFF." Deidre was dumbfounded.

Amid the staccato applause from the ladies, Deidre was finally able to blurt out, "What is this all about?"

One woman, her eye still blackened and her arm in a sling, spoke first. "Deidre, we invited you here to offer you our whole support if you'll put your hat in the ring for sheriff. We believe our concerns and needs will be better met by you than by any of the other candidates who have filed."

The air went out of Deidre's lungs, and she groped for a chair behind her.

"We can't make the decision for you," Judy went on, "but we want you to know we will work for you in any way we can."

One by one the other dozen ladies provided their input, until Deidre felt overwhelmed.

"You know I understand your situations, but I had decided not to run. Now you've started me thinking again. Tomorrow's the last day for filing for the primary. Let me have tonight to make my decision."

That night Deidre did not sleep well.

THE CLERK'S OFFICE IN THE COUNTY COURTHOUSE was located on the main floor. Deidre climbed the fourteen limestone steps to the front door. She wondered how many trips up and down had been made by the folks of Lake County to wear such deep depressions into the treads. Inside, she walked up to the clerk's window and rang the call bell.

Andrea Wasburn, the elected clerk, came to the window.

"Well, hello, Deidre. Anything special I can help you with this morning?" She grinned at Deidre.

Deidre turned a little red, a characteristic she had always disliked in herself. Blushing gave the impression she wasn't sure of herself.

"I'm here to file for the primary election. For sheriff," she added and then mentally kicked herself for sounding so dumb.

Andrea handed her a form. "Fill this out, and I'll notarize your signature. Pay the $100 filing fee, and you're in."

Deidre swallowed hard, picked up the pen, did as she was instructed, and handed the signed paper back to Andrea. She wrote out a check for the fee, noticing that its deduction brought her account dangerously close to zero.

"That makes four of you. I'd be surprised if anyone else shows up before closing time," Andrea predicted. As Deidre turned to walk away, she heard Andrea say, "Oh, and good luck. We're behind you."

The next weeks were filled with activity. Not only did Deidre pull four ten-hour shifts a week, now she also had to use every spare moment calling on homes to distribute her literature. True to their word, those who said they would support her placed campaign signs wherever they were allowed. They passed out literature, made calls. For a rather cobbled-together campaign, they were effective at what they did.

Financing all of this was another worry. Deidre had some savings, but not nearly enough to run a full campaign. The staff at the women's shelter used their expertise in this area, and soon had raised enough for Deidre to do a decent job of presenting herself.

Ben was the only other candidate who seemed to be able to out-spend her, and she couldn't help but notice his signs popping up in yards all over town. A talented high school jock, Ben was able to capitalize on his notoriety in his home town.

A debate was scheduled between the four candidates for sheriff. It was in the high school auditorium and was intended to allow the public to see the candidates, to ask impromptu questions, and to allow a moderator to ask pre-distributed questions.

Deidre had noticed that whenever there was any sort of gathering, Ben always moved closer to her. He was always friendly, but it seemed he sought her out, where before he had ignored her.

This time she found that her name plate was next to his on the table behind which they were seated. The four candidates walked out on stage with Deidre leading the way. When they got to their chairs, Ben pulled hers out for her and motioned for her to sit. Then he slid the chair under her as if he were seating a date at a dinner table.

It suddenly dawned on Deidre what was going on. Ben was a good foot taller than she and outweighed her by a hundred pounds. He was using this opportunity, as he had been all along, to contrast the difference between their physical sizes.

The questions and answers went well. There didn't seem to be any animosity on display, and the redness receded from Deidre's face.

The moderator of the panel asked questions related to finance, the jail occupancy, what was the central problem each candidate saw looming in the future, questions of that sort. Near the end of the time limit, the moderator opened the floor to questions from the audience.

Immediately, the man sitting in the front row, one she recognized as being a high school pal of Ben's, raised his hand. The moderator called on him.

"I would like to direct my question to Deidre," he said, not doing a very good job of disguising the sneer on his face. "I can't help but notice there's quite a difference between you and the other candidates relative to your size. Do you think you're able to defend yourself against a much larger man, say someone Ben's size?"

The words had hardly left his mouth when Deidre shot back, "I don't know about that. Perhaps Ben could answer the question for you."

Now it was Ben's turn to blush. Enough people in the audience knew the meaning behind her words, and an audible wave of snickers could be heard traveling through the auditorium.

There were no other questions for Deidre that night.

THE NIGHT OF THE PRIMARY ELECTION, any interested person could enter the courthouse to watch as the precinct numbers were posted. Shortly before midnight, it became obvious the election for sheriff was a two-person race. After that, nothing surprising happened, and the final tally was posted at four in the morning: Ben VanGotten, 2,329; Deidre Johnson, 1,942; John Persons, 358; and Mike Craig, 221.

It didn't take much math to figure out that if Deidre was going to win, she would need the support of virtually all of the losing candidates' supporters.

There were only weeks left before the general election, and both sides ramped up their efforts. After the high school auditorium incident, Ben abandoned his efforts to contrast their gender differences. Instead, he and his cronies spread as much mud over Lake County as they could. Deidre continued to pound away at what she would do to improve the way the department responded to calls. She especially brought up the need for more effective domestic dispute enforcement and for more effective ways to deal with the children involved in those cases.

Another question-and-answer session was held at the high school, this time between only Ben and Deidre. No one questioned her size.

Finally, Tuesday, November 4th arrived. Deidre's polling place was at the high school, and she was there when the doors opened. She took the usual friendly jabs about who she was going to vote for and laughed them off. After voting she had her ten-hour shift to work. By the end of the day, she felt like she needed more than a glass of warm milk to settle her nerves.

Deidre went home when her shift was done, showered and dressed in her civvies. She ate a frozen dinner heated in her microwave, and then tried to watch TV. Before the ten o'clock news she climbed into her car and drove to the courthouse to stand vigil another time.

All night long the count wavered between her and Ben. Deidre would go up by a hundred votes, and when the next precinct was posted, he would move ahead by fifty. The lead changed hands almost every time a new posting was added.

Finally, with only one precinct yet to report, Deidre led Ben by a mere two hundred ninety votes. When the final count was put up on the bulletin board, Deidre sat down. Then she got up and read the totals again. Deidre Johnson, 2,798; Ben VanGotten, 2,490.

Deidre was jolted out of her thoughts of the past by the demanding ring of the phone on her desk. She picked up the receiver.

"Hello, Sheriff Johnson speaking."

CHAPTER
FIFTEEN

DEIDRE STOOD BY THE CONFERENCE TABLE in the Lake County Law Enforcement Center. She looked from the face of one deputy to another, and jammed a pencil through her tightly pulled back blond hair. She was aware of how far her relationship with the men had come.

It had been two years since she was elected sheriff. There had been some tough sledding at times. Not long after her taking office, Ben had filed an unfair labor practice suit against her and the county.

Only a few weeks after the election, he had walked into Deidre's office with no invitation and announced, "I've drawn the night shift two weeks in a row, and I'm tired of this harassment. One more stint like this and I'll have to report you to the county board."

Deidre looked at him with little emotion. "Ben, you know that we all cover for each other during vacations. We always have, and you never complained before. Who is harassing whom?"

"All I know is now that you have the authority, I'm not going to allow you to push me around. The other guys recognize that you would like me to leave."

Once again Deidre kept her cool. "Ben, do what you have to do, but I doubt if the other guys, as you say, have any gripes. As for scheduling, we'll all draw night shifts equally. That's documented, and you're free to look for any pattern of discrimination."

Ben's complaints didn't stop there. He claimed he was always given the oldest squad vehicle to drive. He complained about the assigned routes to patrol, and he continued to complain whenever his number was called for two weeks of nightshift. He objected the most strenuously when he drew the assignment of patrolling the entrances to the dock area. He said it was impossible to stay awake just sitting there in the shadows. Anyway, why were they wasting taxpayers' dollars over that pile of rusting steel? Who would ever be able to do anything to them?

Ben made the claim that he was being bypassed when overtime assignments were made, and he contended that it was in retribution for his having run a close race with Deidre.

Eventually, Ben took his grievances to the union. They were obligated to take them to the full County Board of Commissioners who wanted to throw out all allegations but who, themselves, were fearful of a law suit. A state arbiter was appointed, and he promptly threw out all charges, claiming there was no evidence to support Ben's case. Since then, she and Ben had been living under a fragile, unspoken truce, and the other deputies had come to respect her fairness and her willingness to stand up for them during times of public and county board scrutiny.

After looking each of the men squarely in the eye, Deidre said, "I have been contacted by the FBI from their Duluth office. Something is going on in the Brimson area, and believe it or not, they'd like our help. They didn't really ask for it, more like ordered it."

This made the deputies sit up straighter in their chairs. Deidre continued. "West of the old Brimson school is a homestead at the end of a quarter-mile-long driveway. It's changed hands several times in the last fifteen years and most recently has been used as a hunting shack by people from the Cities. Most of the buildings have caved in, and the fields are pretty much grown up in brush, but you can still see what had been the farm house from the county road."

One of the deputies spoke up. "I know that place. It used to be the Erholti place back in the nineteen-teens and twenties. Then the Havamakis bought it and farmed it up until the nineteen-fifties or so. I think it stood empty until about twenty years ago when some hunters from the Twin Cities bought it. Waino Jarvinen told me about it one day when we went trout fishing together in the river on the back of the property."

"That's the place all right," Deidre confirmed her deputy's information. "I received a call from an FBI Special Agent John Erickson yesterday afternoon. He requested that we set up a routine surveillance of the homestead. He wants us to keep track of anyone using the place, any increased traffic in or out of the driveway, anything out of the ordinary. Needless to say, we're not to let on what we're doing. We'll up our coverage of the area, but only randomly drive by so as not to arouse any suspicion."

Standing, she reminded the men, "This isn't the way the FBI and Homeland Security usually work. They actually said they need our help." Deidre paused to let those words sink in. "Because this is a small community, strangers stand out like glow-in-the-dark markers, and the agency is afraid their people will be spotted as outsiders. That's why we are doing the surveillance on what's going on in Brimson."

Before she adjourned the meeting, Deidre cleared her throat, having to make one more announcement. "We've also been asked to keep David Craine under surveillance. Agent Erickson made it clear we're not to allow anything to happen to him until they are ready to make a move."

Ben looked up from the doodles he'd been making on his note pad, a startled look in his eyes. "What has he done to deserve this attention? We all know him. He couldn't be a person of interest in any crime."

"I know that as well as any of you, but those are our orders. Erickson couldn't or wouldn't go any further with his information."

She dismissed the group to their duties.

Following the usual routine, the staff meeting was held every morning with each deputy going off duty informing those coming on of what was happening in the county. After several weeks of recording the comings and goings at the hunting shack, nothing much had been noted. At their Tuesday meeting, Deidre informed the deputies that the FBI had been in close contact with her.

"That Agent Erickson is getting to be a real pain in my butt," she told the group. "He's on the phone every day, wondering if anything different's going on up there. All I can tell him is, 'the same old, same old,' and that seems to make him all the more edgy."

She continued, "You've done a good job of not giving any notice that we're aware of the group in Brimson. Be careful to keep it that way."

"John," Deidre asked of the under-sheriff, "When you drove past the place last evening, did you notice anything different?"

"You know the driveway's a long one, and I couldn't stop to glass the area," John answered with a shrug. "I could tell that there was a different vehicle parked next to the shack, though. The others have been spotted here in town driving a silver Land Rover, but this one was black, a Ford Explorer, I think. That's about all I could make out."

At this point, Deidre began to bring the deputies up to date. "Like I said, Special Agent Erickson's called me from the FBI offices in Duluth every day wanting the latest information. They're certain there have been four men living in that hunting shack in Brimson, and from what I gather they're involved in some sort of crime. The agency isn't sharing with me what. But they think the four are only underlings, and the agency doesn't believe they'll act alone," she said, looking over her shoulder out of habit to be sure no one was behind her. "The one we've been waiting for arrived last night. The under-cover agents who've been doing surveillance at the Duluth airport spotted him yesterday afternoon. He rented a black Ford Explorer and was followed into Two Harbors where he turned up the State Road, heading for Brimson. You were right on with what you reported, John," and Deidre gave her deputy a nod of approval.

"The FBI surveillants in Duluth identified its driver as Zaim Hassan Zayed. He's the missing leader," Deidre said, upping the ante. "Now that he's arrived, we think things will begin happening and soon. You and I just don't know what."

One of the other deputies interrupted. "How does this change our mission? Will we get a crack at this bunch, or are we going to sit back until they do something?"

Deidre stared at him for a moment and then said, "The most important thing we must do is not to let on that we're in the know in the least. We continue acting like small-town hicks with nothing more to do that cruise the dirt back roads. If they suspect for a minute that we're on to them, they'll evaporate, and no one will have a thing for all the effort and man hours that have gone into this operation—so be careful."

She reminded her deputies, "If you meet them on the road, just give a nod and a smile. Show them we are not into profiling. Show them how accepting we are. Do not, and I repeat—do not—do anything to put them on guard."

Deidre dismissed the crew. "Meet here tomorrow, same time. Oh, by the way, Bill and Cass, keep your eyes out for David Craine. His boat was spotted heading into the Knife River Marina. I'm sure he'll go to his apartment above Dunnigan's so watch for him."

Bill questioned, "What do you want us to do if we spot him? Anything?"

Deidre answered, "Just don't call attention to the fact we know he's back. Okay guys, you know what we have to do. Have a good shift."

CHAPTER
SIXTEEN

VIC AIALA SAT IN HIS CHAIR ON HIS DECK, READING A BOOK. It was a few minutes past midnight, and he could hear the rhythmic pulse of a siren coming from the ore docks two miles down the hill from where he lived. He could see the rows of lights delineating the railroad tracks that ran along the top of the massive hoppers into which iron ore was dumped from strings of gondola cars. From his vantage point, he could see lights illuminating the hundreds of yards of conveyor belts that moved ore from the mountainous stockpiles heaped near the base of the docks. All those steel chutes and bins and belts were essential for loading the thousand-foot-long ore carriers that carried their cargo from Two Harbors on the Great Lakes to steel mills out East.

Vic was the supervisor for the entire facility and operation. To him the sirens that sounded every time the conveyor was moved, the train whistles that signaled an outbound string of empties being returned to the mine, and the boat horns that communicated with the ore dock workers were sounds of comfort. The night sounds told him all was well.

He thought it ironic that he could fall asleep peacefully when the harbor symphony was playing in the middle of the night, but when all went silent he would wake with a jolt as if from a nightmare.

The peace that night was a far cry from the turmoil that had erupted on September 11, 2001. That morning he had received an urgent call from Sheriff Thorton commanding him to shut down all operations. No trains were to be allowed onto the docks, and the conveyors were to be shut down. Any lake traffic was prohibited from entering the small, single use harbor, and no one was to enter or leave the road entrances until several deputies arrived to help sort things out. At the time, Vic knew nothing of the tragedy taking place in New York, and he was more than irritated until the sheriff told him to turn on a TV. After that, no explanation was needed.

Within minutes three deputies had pulled up outside his office, their SUVs immediately enveloped in the cloud of dust trailing them. One deputy was posted at each plant-site entrance, and the third, a petite blond whose name tag read Deputy Johnson entered his office.

"This isn't a good morning, Mr. Aiala," she said with a catch in her throat. "Sheriff Thorton will be here in just a few minutes.

"You have a full shift of workers on right now, and he wants you to call them to your office right away. I know you have security on duty all the time. Have them continue to monitor the docks. Especially, have them watch for any small boats motoring around the dock abutments. That shouldn't be a problem, because the Lake County Search and Rescue is already patrolling the harbor entrance, but just in case, have them be alert for any movement."

Vic was impressed with Deidre's take charge attitude, and he made no objection to her commands.

As she had predicted, in only a few minutes Sheriff Thorton pulled up in his SUV marked LAKE COUNTY SHERIFF.

"Well, Vic," he said. "I'm thinking things have changed forever, and not for the better I'm afraid. Is this your entire force?"

Vic looked over the group of men now assembled outside his office. He counted the number listed on the work schedule and then counted the confused faces before him.

"This is all," he affirmed, "Except for security, and they're doing what Deputy Johnson asked."

Sheriff Thorton cleared his throat. "If you haven't heard, the Trade Center towers in New York were attacked only an hour ago by terrorists. It's turning into a real disaster, and all sorts of alerts have been put out. All air traffic has been grounded. All possible strategic targets have been placed on alert, and all unnecessary travel is being discouraged.

We have been issued an alert for the ore docks, and while it doesn't rank up there with the Prairie Island nuclear power plant, the docks are of national security importance because of the need to move ore to the steel plants at the other end of the lakes."

Then, Sheriff Thorton began to divide the workers by crew assignment. "How many of you work at the water's edge, helping to moor the lines from the carriers?" Three men raised their hands.

The sheriff pointed at two others. "You go with these three who are familiar with the bases of the docks. Search each steel support one by one. Look for anything that in your opinion seems out of the ordinary. Especially, look for any backpacks strapped to the uprights or any wires running along the I-beams. If you find anything at all that looks out of place to you, do not touch it but call me immediately."

He spoke to the remaining workers. "I'll let Vic divide you up into respective search groups. I'm not sure what goes on around these docks, and he can assign you areas that are most familiar to you. Be thorough in your search, and don't try moving anything you find."

Before turning the group over to Vic, Sheriff Thorton turned to him. "Meet me in your office when you're done. I need your opinion about what we can do to make this area more secure."

It took the rest of the shift and another three hours of overtime for the workers to inspect every angle of iron that formed the lattice supporting the tracks above. In the end, nothing was found that was of any significance.

When the group gathered again in the business office, a comprehensive list of findings was drawn up. Sheriff Thorton stood up from where he had been sitting. "Thank goodness everything here is stable. Unless anyone has something to report, I think we can continue our stepped up patrol, and you can go home."

Ben cleared his throat. "You had me stationed at the southwest entrance, and things were so quiet there, I was scanning Pork City

Hill for any sign of deer. I saw something that I suppose I should mention."

Sheriff Thorton's head snapped around. "Well, what did you see?"

Ben's face started to flush, and he regretted having said anything. "Somebody was on the hill glassing the docks. He was only there a second and then ducked behind a boulder. After that, I didn't see anything more."

Sheriff Thorton's face contorted, and he blurted out. "And you didn't call that in right away? What in the hell were you thinking? You're hired to act like a law enforcement officer. Do your deer hunting on your own time."

He glared at Ben as he said to Deidre, "You and Jeff go up there and see what you can find. Ben, if I didn't need every warm body here, I'd send you back to the office. Take your blasted binoculars and go to the breakwater. Take a good look at Pork City Hill as Deidre and Jeff come up the backside. By a stroke of luck they might flush something out."

Ben packed up his humiliation and left.

The night of 9/11, Vic Aiala had sat up well past midnight looking at the strings of lights on the docks and listening to the steady pulse of sounds coming from the harbor. That night he slept restlessly, waking every time the warning siren on the conveyor stopped sounding.

Now, ten years later things were different. Deidre Johnson was the sheriff. Although her department still kept tabs on the docks, there was usually only one deputy on watch during a shift. Time caused even traumatic memories to fade, and tonight, hearing the sounds of activity from the docks and knowing that increased security was on duty during the dark hours, Vic slept well.

CHAPTER
SEVENTEEN

SHERIFF DEIDRE JOHNSON TRIED TO FORCE HERSELF to stop thinking of the past. As she was about to dive into a stack of backed-up paper work, her desk phone rang. She answered.

"This is John Erickson," Deidre heard from the other end of the line.

"Hi, John. What's up with you this morning?"

"Not much on this end. How about there? Anything to report on those fellows up north?" John wanted to know.

"We might have something developing. That black Ford Explorer you told me about yesterday might have been spotted by one of my deputies. Last evening, it was parked outside the old farmhouse in Brimson.

"John, is it possible for you and me to meet this morning. I really feel we're being kept too much in the dark here. You know that old saying about feeling like a mushroom, 'kept in the dark and being fed too much BS.'"

Surprisingly, he seemed eager to talk. "There is a great little place on the scenic highway between here and Two Harbors. They serve wonderful gourmet food, and the place is quite private. Can you meet me there at noon? Better wear civilian clothes though. No need to attract attention to ourselves."

Deidre was pleased with his response. "I know the place you're talking about. See you there at noon."

When she pulled into the parking lot of the small restaurant, Deidre knew she was ten minutes late, and when she entered the eating area, she noted that John was already seated at a table in the far corner of the room. Deidre had never allowed herself to get involved with any man. She had not dated, had not sent out any vibes to anyone, but when she looked across the room to where John sat, she couldn't help but notice that he was quite good looking, for a man.

The place was almost empty, and John had picked a table well away from other customers. To the other diners, the two of them were just a man and a woman meeting for lunch. Neither of them carried a notebook or computer. The only tools they brought with were concealed in holsters beneath their clothes.

John stood and shook Deidre's hand. "Sheriff Johnson, it's good to see you again. We want you to know that we appreciate the job you and your deputies are doing. So far, everything is falling our way."

Deidre nodded her approval to his words. A waiter appeared and with much fanfare described the day's specials. He recommended the halibut on toast with asparagus spears. Deidre decided to have the grilled egg and asparagus sandwich instead. Agent Erickson took the waiter's recommendation. Each ordered a glass of white wine. It was against regulation, but they decided it would be a good way to look like an ordinary couple. Anyway both of them liked a glass of wine with their meals.

The waiter immediately brought their drinks, and to make things appear even more normal, they toasted the day and took a sip of the wine.

"So," Deidre began, "We're doing a good job. I wish I knew a little more about what we are doing." She paused a moment before asking the question that was troubling her the most.

"We have been told to keep and eye on David Craine but to not let on that we are. I would like to know just how deeply he is involved in this whole mess, whatever it is. What can you tell me?"

John Erickson took another sip of wine and stared into his glass, then swirled the wine a few times, stalling for time. "There are some things I can't tell you yet. My higher-ups have not given me clearance to share much more than I have." He took another sip of his wine before continuing.

"Your job is to continue surveillance on him. Don't let him out of the sight of your deputies, and if it appears he is in any danger, apprehend him. He is too valuable to allow anything to happen to him. We need him alive at any cost."

Deidre realized it wasn't going to do much good to press the point, yet, she needed to know. "But what has he done? If it's been so serious, why don't you arrest him now?" she pressured, her face becoming red from frustration.

John looked her square in her eyes and shook his head. "All I can say is keep him alive."

The waiter hurried to their table carrying two very warm plates with his bare hands. After placing their meals in front of them, he asked almost sincerely, "Can I get anything else for you?" Both Deidre and John shook their heads, and he left.

Deidre cut her sandwich into smaller pieces. "Look, John. I have a personal interest in this David Craine. He's a good man, and if he's into something way over his head, I'd like to know. Can't you give me something?"

He picked at his fish dinner, took a forkful of the meal, and gestured with his thumb and forefinger that it was good. He chewed and swallowed.

Finally he said, "I suppose I can share with you that David is in serious trouble. In a twist of events he probably could never have envisioned, your Mr. Craine has become involved in a plot with considerable consequences. You must have guessed that there's a connection between him and the group under surveillance in Brimson. Please don't press me about the details."

He picked at his fish some more, and then added, "I know the special relationship you have with him and how he is almost like a father to you, but you have to keep focused on your job and your priorities."

Deidre gathered the subject was closed. The two finished their meals, talking mostly chit-chat, but when they had paid their tabs and placed the waiter's tip on the table, John turned to Deidre.

"I wish I could have said more to relieve your worry, but for some reason or other, my superiors will not allow me to say more. They might have a legitimate reason, or they might be afraid if you know too much, you'll steal their thunder. I *am* sorry."

As they left the cafe, Deidre thought to herself that things hadn't really changed at all.

CHAPTER
EIGHTEEN

THE NEXT MONDAY MORNING, SHERIFF JOHNSON was finishing reading the reports from the nightshift dispatcher. Just as she was thinking she could slip out for a cup of coffee and a treat, her phone rang. She glanced at the caller ID and saw it was Deputy VanGotten on the line. She finished putting away the file in her hand before picking up.

"Deidre," the deputy said, the strain in his voice immediately evident to her, "Deidre, you better get up to the Old Drummond Pit right away. We have what appears to be a homicide here."

Those words made Deidre sit bolt upright in her chair, and immediately David Craine's name popped into her mind. "Do you recognize the body," she asked a bit too hurriedly.

"No," Ben replied. "I haven't moved the corpse at all, haven't even touched it. It's obvious that he's been dead for a while, at least long enough for blowflies to have laid their eggs and had them hatch."

"I know that pit. Make sure both entrances are blocked off and that no one comes into the pit. And don't you move around until we get there with the coroner and our equipment." Then she added, "It should take me only about eight to ten minutes to get out there," and she hung up.

As she rushed past the dayshift dispatcher, Deidre barked orders at her. "Get two squads out to the Old Drummond Pit as fast as you can. Find the two closest, and tell them not to spare the horses getting there."

By this time she was at the top of the stairs leading down to the parking lot, and she reached the ground in four bounding steps.

87

When Deidre arrived at the pit, a place where the county had mined gravel for years, she was met at the first entry road by her deputy.

"Good to see you in the field, Deidre," Ben said with a smirk. "This is your first homicide, isn't it?"

The sheriff ignored the not so subtle barb thrown at her. The animosity from the election hadn't completely evaporated, she thought.

"What do you think, Ben? Did you see any tracks leading into the pit?" she asked.

Her deputy shook his head no. "Like I said, the body's been here at least since yesterday, and you know how hard it rained last night. I bet we got an inch. That soaker wiped out any marks in this fine sand."

Deidre looked down at the two bare ruts in the road. In between them, grass had grown, evidence that not many people passed this way. She saw two sets of footprints in the still moist sand of the road ruts. "What about these?" she asked, pointing at the imprints that led into the pit and then back out again.

"Those were left by the couple who found the body this morning. They're waiting in Joe's squad car over at the other entrance. Their shoes match these tracks, and I don't think we have to worry about them having anything to do with this. Anyway, they're waiting for you so they can make a statement and then get out of here. They're pretty shook up."

Deidre left Ben at the entrance and walked the thirty yards into the pit where a third deputy stood, waiting for her.

"You've done a good job here Jeff. Thanks." And then quickly she added, "Well, let's go take a look at what we have."

Off to the side and under a huge white pine tree, sat a blue Toyota Corolla. Its paint was peeling in several places, one headlamp was smashed out, and the driver's side front fender was caved in. Deidre noticed the windows were rolled down and thought that strange. The trunk lid was propped open as wide as it could be.

Even before she moved around to the back of the vehicle, Deidre could smell the stench, but she was hardly ready for what she saw. Curled up in the trunk was the body of a man. Blood caked his matted hair, and Deidre could see that the front of his forehead was missing. Blowfly eggs had hatched, and tiny maggots wormed their way in the wound. Deidre gagged but forced the acrid tasting stuff back down.

"Jeff, I've seen some gross stuff, but this is about the worst." she said, wiping tears from her eyes. "There isn't much doubt this is a homicide, is there? Who climbs into the trunk of his car, closes the lid, and then shoots himself? Secondly, I don't think he put those plastic ties on his wrists afterward, do you?"

Jeff looked at her and smiled a crooked smile at her attempt at black humor. "Why don't you go talk to the couple who found the car so they can leave? I'll stay here until the coroner and the others get here."

Deidre walked to the other entry road and met the couple who had found the mess.

"Sheriff Johnson, these are Cal and Judy Bender," the deputy, Joe, informed her. "I just saw the coroner pull in, along with the search and rescue squad. If it's okay with you, I'll go see if I can help out at the scene."

Cal fidgeted with his car keys, and Judy kept covering her mouth as though she wanted to prevent a scream from escaping.

Deidre broke the uneasy silence. "Thank you for being patient. I understand you're the people who discovered this," and she motioned with her head in the direction of the pit.

The two nodded.

"Can you tell me how you happened upon this gravel pit? How about you, Cal?" Deidre needed to shake them out of their stupor and get them talking.

"Well, Judy and I decided we would take a walk today, and I remember reading about this experimental forest with hiking trails. We drove out here early this morning. Our car's parked about a half mile back from here."

Deidre nodded her approval, encouraging him to keep talking. Judy stood with her hand over her mouth, saying nothing.

Cal continued. "We took the trail through that white pine stand and came out where the snowmobile trail crosses the road to the other pit. Then we started to walk back to our car on this road."

Deidre looked at Judy. "Is this what you remember, Judy?" she asked.

Judy nodded. Then it was as though a dam had finally burst, and Judy's words came gushing out. "We got to this entrance to the pit, and we decided to take a detour up this entrance and out the other. It joins up with the road back to our car you know, and when we were in the pit we noticed an old junker of a car under that big white pine tree, and—"

"I think you should try to slow down a little," Deidre said, interrupting her. "I have to write this down, and I can't keep up with you." She smiled a reassuring smile at Judy.

"Of course," Judy stammered. "I'm sorry. It's just that this has really hit me hard. I can't get that awful picture out of my mind."

Again, Deidre nodded her understanding. "So when you saw the car, what did you do?"

Judy began again, this time slower and more controlled. "We thought it strange that a car would be parked out here, so we walked over to it. Both of us commented on the foul smell coming from it. Cal thought maybe someone had poached a deer and stuffed its remains inside of an abandoned car." With that Judy covered her mouth again. "You tell her, Cal. I can't do it."

Cal looked at Sheriff Johnson, and his lips trembled. "I saw what looked like a bloody rag hanging from the trunk. It was balled up and thick enough that it didn't allow the lid to latch. When I lifted the trunk lid, there he was. That's all I know. We immediately left the pit and raced back to our car. We used our cell phone to call 911 and asked the dispatcher to send a deputy here, and we waited in our car until he arrived." Judy looked away, her hand still covering her mouth.

"Did you touch anything else, touch anything inside the car or walk around the car?" Deidre wanted to know.

Cal answered again. "No. As soon as we saw the body, we left. Was that all right?" he asked as though fearful he and his wife had made a serious mistake.

Deidre assured him they had done exactly what they should have. Then she said to the couple, "Why don't you go home and try to settle yourselves. Do you have a clergyperson you can talk to? If you don't, I can have someone at the Human Development Center meet with you right away, if you think you need support at this time. I know this must be terribly upsetting for you, so please take advantage of my offer if you want."

Cal thanked her and said they'd speak with their minister. Deidre called one of the deputies on her two-way and had him come to drive the Benders back to their car. As they prepared to get into his vehicle, Deidre had one more thing to say. "I'm going to have to ask you to not talk with anyone about this, except your pastor, until the details have been released in the news. It's important that you agree to this. Do you understand?"

Cal answered for both of them. "I certainly do. We'll do anything to help you that we can."

They left with the deputy, and Deidre trotted back to the pit.

By that time the coroner had made a preliminary scan of the area and was ready to roll the body over just as Deidre came upon the scene. Looking for some form of identification, he took the victim's wallet from his pants pocket.

"He wasn't a robbery victim," the coroner stated with flat affect. "There are five one-hundred dollar bills in here. And they left his driver's license, too. Our man in the trunk is known as Herminio Valesques."

CHAPTER
NINETEEN

AFTER RETURNING TO HER OFFICE, DEIDRE WAS JUST beginning to draw up a flow chart of what her plan of action would be when her phone rang.

"Sheriff Johnson," she spoke into the receiver.

"Hi, Deidre. This is John Erickson," the voice on the other end responded.

Deidre's hackles immediately went up. "Hello, John. What can I do for you this morning?" she asked, making no attempt to disguise her abruptness. Of all mornings, she didn't need the FBI cluttering up her time with questions about what's going on in a shack up in Brimson.

"Deidre," John said, using her first name as though they were close friends. "Deidre, I've heard that a body was found in an abandoned car up in your neck of the woods."

Before he could get another word out, Deidre's voice became even more curt. "How did you get that information so fast? The body's hardly cold, and already you've got your feelers into this case. We're doing everything we can to follow your other request, and that uses up a lot of man hours. If we weren't sitting on our behinds up in Brimson watching a bunch of wannabe Jack Pine Savages, we might have time to take care of law enforcement where it would do some good."

"Now, Deidre, cool down a second and let's talk. First of all, I don't think there's anything your people could have done to prevent this homicide. This case runs a lot deeper than you think. This Herminio Valesquez . . ."

Before he could finish his sentence, Deidre almost screamed into the phone. "Herminio Valesquez! Herminio Valesquez! We

92

didn't have an ID more than an hour ago, and you already know the victim's name. In fact, we aren't even sure it is him. Just because he had a wallet on him with that name doesn't mean it's him. Most of his face was blown away, so his picture ID didn't help much. The coroner still has a lot of work before we can come up with a positive."

"Oh, don't worry, Deidre. The body is who his wallet's credentials say he is. It's Herminio all right. His finger prints matched those in our data base."

Deidre exploded again. "What's going on here? I'm the sheriff of Lake County, and you know more about what's happening than I do. You must have a snitch in this department to have gotten the information so fast. It's VanGotten isn't it. Ben has been trying to undermine this department ever since I beat him out in the election. If it wasn't illegal, I'd have fired his butt the day after the votes were counted."

John Erickson didn't seem too surprised or excited by Deidre's outburst. "Deidre, don't get your shorts in a bundle."

He knew the instant the words left his mouth that it was the wrong thing to say.

"You listen here, John Erickson, or special agent, or first-class jerk, which ever fits. You might not respect me, but you will respect my office. Either you treat it with the respect it deserves or I'll have you up on charges. I don't care if they are sexual harassment, harassment, meddling or . . ." and Deidre couldn't think of anything else to add to the list. All she could do was sputter.

"Listen Deidre, I apologize for what I said. It was way out of line. I'm sorry, and you're right. You deserve more respect than that."

That took the wind out of Deidre's sails, and she was left speechless. "Well, okay, but don't ever talk to me that way again."

John continued. "Deidre, Ben isn't in cahoots with us. We've never talked to him, but we have been in touch with the county coroner. And don't get all fired up about him," he added as fast as he could. "Several months ago, he was informed by Homeland Security that all suspected homicides in the Two Harbors area must be immediately reported to us. He had no other option."

By this time, Deidre was ready to throw in the towel. A person could only stay as angry as she was for a short time, and then all of the steam would be gone.

"Okay John, you win. I suppose you're going to come in here and take over the whole investigation, take all the credit, and then paint us as though we are a bunch of incompetent hicks." She felt another head of steam building, and John sensed another eruption coming.

"Deidre, we need to talk. I mean really talk this time. The agency can't sweep in and start mopping up, at least not yet. There's too much you don't know. Give me a couple of hours to get some clearances, which shouldn't be too difficult with what happened to Herminio. There's a park in Duluth, Chester Bowl. Meet me . . . *will* you meet me there at one o'clock. I'll bring along a couple of box lunches."

AGAIN, DEIDRE WAS A FEW MINUTES LATE FOR THEIR MEETING. By the time she arrived at Chester Bowl, John had already selected a picnic table down near the creek. He had a disposable table cloth spread and on it an assortment of deli salads and a platter of deli fried chicken.

"Hi, Deidre," John greeted her. "As you can see, I slaved all morning cooking a special lunch for us," and he laughed. Deidre couldn't help but notice his curly blond hair and piercing blue eyes.

"Please, sit down and eat," he offered. "We can talk business afterward."

For the next half hour the two visited over the picnic meal. The sound of the stream trickling through time-worn rocks was soothing, but eventually Deidre's patience ran thin.

"John, we have to get down to business. I have a murder to investigate, and you promised to fill me in on what's happening up in my neck of the woods. Now what's up?" she demanded.

John cleared his throat and looked at the table top as he fidgeted with the salad left on his plate. "I thought I could get clearance to tell you everything, but it appears that isn't the case." He paused once more, and Deidre got an uneasy feeling in her stomach.

"Here's what they said I can share. You're to continue to shadow David Craine. You're not to allow him to know he's being followed. I can tell you that he's involved in a case we're investigating that puts his life in jeopardy, and it's your department's job to make sure nothing happens to him until we're ready to move."

Deidre sat up straight with those words. "But can't you tell me what he's done that's put him on the radar of your agency?"

John looked at her through his clear blue eyes. "I'm really sorry. Really. But I haven't been given clearance to tell you anything more. My boss told me to tell you that you're doing everything we've asked, and to tell you to continue to keep an eye on the group up north in that hunting shack. You're to report any of their observed activities to us."

"But, John," Deidre pleaded. "What about the murder in the Drummond pit? What am I supposed to make of the fact that you undercut my department by having an inside track with the coroner? We deserve more for what we're doing than what we're getting."

Again he pushed his salad around on his plate.

"I know you do, but what can I say? I'll be in trouble if I get caught telling too much. And I have to ask that you don't pursue the murder case too vigorously. Make it look like you're working on it, but make it take some time. Eventually, things will work their way out, and you'll know the reasons for everything."

Deidre didn't say anything to that request, but she thought, *Yeah, right. I'm going to let a murder happen in my county and not investigate it. In a pig's eye.*

"John, I've got to get back to work. Thank you for the picnic lunch."

She was surprised when John took both of her hands and said, "I wish I could share more, but orders are orders. Maybe when this is over we can meet here again for a picnic and talk about all that happened."

With that he gave Deidre's hands a gentle squeeze and said, "Keep up the good work. I appreciate what you're up against."

Deidre got into her SUV and drove away, unsure of her emotions. She should have been seething, but she realized she was more confused than anything.

CHAPTER
TWENTY

ZAIM LAY IN HIS BED, LISTENING TO THE WHEEZES and snorts of the others as they slept soundly. Unlike them, the place was strange to him. They had lived here for the past several months and were used to the complete silence of the wilderness night, but to Zaim it was unnerving, like the feeling one gets during the calm that precedes a storm. He quietly rolled out of bed so as not to disturb the others and made his way to the porch where he found a comfortable chair. Zaim took out a cigarette and lit it. The cigarette's glow was a burning ember in the blackness of the night.

Periodically, the horizon would dimly light up because of some distant electrical storm, and he thought there must be a storm approaching.

As he sat in the dark, Zaim ran his fingers over the easily palpable lump on his forearm, massaging it as he did so often when he was deep in thought. Sometimes it ached so that he had to take pain pills to numb the discomfort, but he was thankful for its presence. Like a bur under a horse's saddle, it was a constant reminder to him of the day his arm had been so viciously broken. It was a constant reminder of his lack of medical attention and the days of abuse he endured for no other reason than he had protested over Dania's treatment. He was thankful he would never be allowed to forget.

Zaim contemplated how quickly plans could be altered. Every part of his plan had been meticulously arranged. The cell had been successfully set up in this wilderness area, and no one seemed to be suspicious. He thought it fortunate that these north woods people kept to themselves and didn't meddle in other people's affairs. In fact, not one person had ever stopped in to see who was living in the old shack that had been all but abandoned for years.

97

But now, one careless act by someone who should have known better had perhaps compromised the entire operation. Yusuf was to have brought with him a flash drive containing information about the docks, but when he boarded the freighter in Thunder Bay and Zaim had met him, there was no flash drive. After searching every possible place it could have been on his person, he had to admit it was gone.

Zaim was furious and had forced Yusuf to backtrack in his mind and relive the time leading up to the discovery of the loss. The careless one insisted he had it in his pocket when the men boarded David's boat at Silver Bay, but now it was missing.

After more prodding, he finally admitted to Zaim that he discovered its loss after getting in the SUV at the dock in Canada. The only logical conclusion was that it had fallen out of his pocket on David Craine's boat, and somewhere on *Crusader, Too* incriminating evidence lay hidden.

For weeks Zaim had waited for some sort of fallout because of the lost flash drive, but as the days passed and law enforcement seemed oblivious to the men living in the hunting shack north of Two Harbors, he came to believe that nothing was going to come of it and the only ramification would be that much of the plan would have to be constructed from memory.

Eventually, Zaim settled on several explanations of why the docks weren't swarming with security guards. One, if David Craine had found it, he had realized that by alerting the authorities about the information contained on the flash drive, he would have incriminated himself and would, himself, face prosecution.

Or, second, the flash drive had been lost by Yusuf as he either boarded or left the boat. If it had fallen into the water, no one would find it. It may have even been lost on land and might be lying in the weeds and tall grass near their Canadian landing site. In which case, at the worst, someone other than David might have picked it up. But with no point of reference, a stranger probably wouldn't make much of it. For all they would know, it might have been notes for a book an author was writing.

Zaim sat inside the screened porch of the rundown shack. Its wooden floor tilted downward away from the building, suggesting that the foundation timbers had rotted away, and the screens had a few small tears in them that persistent mosquitoes found. The night was calm and peaceful, the kind of peace that would nurture an inner quiet in most people. For Zaim, however, silence only allowed the hatred stemming from his memories to fester and become more inflamed. More than ever, he wanted to punish someone for his Dania. Someone had to pay, and it would be those who propped up and offered unwavering, unthinking support for the Israelis who destroyed everything he had in life. They would pay.

CHAPTER
TWENTY-ONE

AFTER THE CORONER HAD FINISHED HIS INVESTIGATION of the crime scene at the Drummond Pit, Deidre had ordered the abandoned car to be towed to Denny's Automotive in Two Harbors. She had it stored in a locked stall in his shop. On the way back from her meeting with John Erickson, she stopped at the garage. She knew that the first step in solving Herminio's murder would be to trace the ownership history of the Corolla.

"Hi, Denny," she shouted in greeting.

Amid the din of hammers pounding out dents and grinders smoothing steel, Denny called back, "Hey, Deidre. How's it going? Haven't talked with you for a long time."

The whole while he talked, Denny strode to where Deidre had entered the building.

"What's up?" he wanted to know?

"I need your help for a few minutes, if you can spare the time."

Denny had been involved in other cases when Deidre needed help with automotive incidents. "Sure, any time. What can I do?"

"I need to find the VIN of that car." She pointed at the blue Corolla sitting crooked on its flat tires inside the shop. "Usually it's found on the dash where the windshield meets, but the glass was broken out and the number had been scraped off. I checked the inside of the door frame, and the number had been obliterated there as well. Any suggestions?"

"Shouldn't be a problem," Denny said confidently. But then he added, "Unless, of course, whoever owned this car knew about the third location."

He lifted the hood of the wreck and took out his flashlight. Denny aimed the beam of light at the fire wall, and said, "It should be back there, behind the engine. Not all cars have it at this location, but this year Toyota does." He scraped away the dirt and oil grime from an aluminum tag. "Here it is . . . 4TZQAJ8TN067084. I hope this is what you need."

Deidre walked the half block back to the law enforcement center and climbed the flight of stairs to her office. Logged into her computer, she began a search for a Corolla with the matching VIN.

That's strange, she thought, *this car was last registered to a couple who live in Duluth.* She found their telephone number listed in the directory and dialed it up.

After several rings, the party at the other end answered.

"I'm calling for Alf Larson," Deidre said.

"This is he. May I ask who's calling," a man with a reedy voice responded.

"This is Sheriff Deidre Johnson of the Lake County Sheriff's Office. Do you have a minute to talk to me?"

After a moment's silence the man blurted out. "This is about my son, James, isn't it? He hasn't lived here for quite some time. Do you know where he is? What has he done now? Is he injured?"

It was Deidre's turn to be a little flummoxed. "No, Mr. Larson. This is probably not about your son, and I'm sorry, I don't know where he is. This is about a 1997 blue Toyota Corolla. Do you own such a vehicle?"

Again there was a long pause on the other end of the line. "I, we did. Actually it was James's car, but it was registered to me. He was pretty hard on it. Had a couple of accidents, fender benders that pushed up the insurance costs. By the time he left home last winter, it was pretty much junk, so I had it towed to a recycling place for scrap. I got sixty dollars for it."

"Do you remember when the car was towed?" Deidre wanted to know.

"Just a second. I've got it marked on my calendar." Deidre heard pages being turned. "Yes, here it is. He came for it on May 9th. Like I said, he paid me sixty dollars for it. I was careful to have him write out a receipt that I have here."

"Mr. Larson," Deidre pressed. "Do you remember the name of the junkyard?"

"Not exactly. It was the one up on Dice Bay Road, out of Duluth, Standard's or something like that."

Deidre was pretty sure she knew the spot, but asked, "Stanford's?"

"Yes. That's it, Stanford's Auto Salvage. Here it is. He signed his name Stanford Williams."

Deidre was about to thank him for his time and cooperation, when the old man asked, "You will tell me if you hear anything about my son, James, won't you?"

Deidre assured him she would, thanked him, and hung up the phone. *Alf Larson certainly didn't murder Herminio*, she thought.

On the way out of the office, she told her secretary to route all calls to her cell phone, because she would be on her way to Duluth.

The Stanford's Auto Salvage yard was anything but usual. A row of flowers—hollyhocks, delphinium, and phlox—lined the ditch by the driveway. The lawn was mowed and trimmed around the edges. There were no car parts lying around. Everything was spotless. Even the three shops looked to have been freshly painted, and the fence, behind which rows of junkers were hidden, was perfectly a lined.

Stanford Williams, the owner and operator of the yard came out of his office to meet her, and Deidre almost laughed, because she couldn't help but think this was an English gentleman coming to invite her in for tea. His clean khaki pants had a sharp crease, and he was wearing a plaid, long sleeved shirt with the cuffs rolled up two turns, and on his head he sported a short-billed flat hat. He was a small man with delicate fingers and a neatly trimmed, gray moustache.

"Can I get you something?" he asked, his friendly smile exposing whitened teeth.

Deidre showed her badge. "Deidre Johnson, Lake County Sheriff." The man stiffened ever so slightly.

"I'm here to check on the whereabouts of a vehicle. It was reportedly picked up by someone from this yard, although it was supposed to have been junked. I'd like to talk to you about that."

"There must be some mistake," Stanford said, still smiling. "This is St. Louis County, and you are from Lake County. That means this is out of your jurisdiction."

"You're right as far as my having no jurisdiction here relative to an automobile registration, but this visit is regarding a junked car that has been involved in a homicide in Lake County. Whoever took that car in as a junker and then allowed it back on the street could possibly be considered an accessory to murder," Deidre bluffed.

Those words had an effect on Stanford's attitude. Suddenly, he wasn't quite so smiling. He became serious.

"I don't know what I can do to help you, Sheriff. I know I didn't have anything to do with any murder or whatever you're talking about. But if there's anything I do know, I'll tell you."

"A 1997 Toyota Corolla is registered to an older gentleman, Alf Larson, who claims you towed it away for scrap. It had some body damage and had been pretty well beat. Do you remember picking up that vehicle?" Deidre asked.

Stanford toed the crushed rock in the drive before answering with a question of his own. "When was that supposed to have happened?"

He's stalling for time, Deidre thought. "Last month, May 9th. Alf has the day marked on his calendar. He's very meticulous with his record keeping. You might remember that he'd drawn up a bill of sale. Will it help your memory if I told you that you paid him sixty dollars for the beater."

Stanford's memory became much more acute. "Now I remember. An older man who complained about his son not appreciating what he had. Yeah, I remember him—and the car. It ran, barely, but I got it started and drove it up onto the trailer."

"So, if you towed the car here, what happened to it? You didn't file the title with the state, indicating that the car had been junked." Deidre had Stanford and he knew it.

"The title's probably in my office. It's a little messy in there, and it's probably under a pile of paperwork I haven't got to yet."

Deidre looked around at the park-like appearance of the yard and thought, *Yeah, right, and you probably have stacks of dirty dishes in your sink, too.*

"If the car hasn't been registered as junked, and if there is no record of the title being transferred to another party, how did it end up in a gravel pit west of Two Harbors?"

Stanford was getting more agitated by the minute. He continued to look at the ground and dig at it with the toe of his boot.

"If I tell what I remember, am I going to end up in serious trouble?" Stanford wanted to know.

"If you don't tell me what you know, you definitely are going to end up in serious trouble," Deidre threatened. "Right now, the only law you've broken is letting a vehicle off your lot without any record of a sale. You sold or gave away or had stolen a vehicle meant to be junked. Because that happened in St. Louis County, I have no reason to arrest you. However, I will be obligated to turn over that information to the St. Louis County sheriff. What they do after that is up to them. But if you're concealing information about a crime that occurred in Lake County, that's another issue. The Corolla was found abandoned in a gravel pit, and there was a body in the trunk. That's serious business, Stanford, far more serious than not registering a junked vehicle."

"Okay, okay," Stanford said, squaring his shoulders as though he was about to face a firing squad.

"A couple of days after I towed it in here, two men stopped by. They said they were looking for an old beater they could use to drive on some rough roads up north, something that wouldn't matter if it was wrecked. I thought it was a little unusual—they didn't seem like the kind who were used to driving on logging roads, but they said they wanted to drive into some brook trout lakes north of Two Harbors."

"How did they pay you?" Deidre wanted to know.

"Cash, $500. Cash if I'd turn over the title to them without signing it. They said they'd register it when they went through Two Harbors."

"And you let them do that?" Deidre wasn't buying the whole story.

"Listen, five hundred bucks is five hundred bucks, and in this business that's not easy to come by. They said if the car broke down in the woods, they wanted to be able to walk away from it. I figured no one would be the wiser."

Deidre now believed she was getting closer to the truth. "Can you give me a description of the two men?"

Stanford looked at the sky as he thought. "I guess they'd be about five-ten, not big not small, if you know what I mean. They had black hair. And, oh yeah, they had darker skin than most people around here. Not black, mind you, but darker. That's about all I can remember."

Deidre prodded his memory. "What about the way they spoke? Was anything out of the ordinary?"

Once again Stanford looked at an invisible something in the sky. "There was something about the way they spoke that *was* unusual. They didn't really have an accent. Maybe it was the way they put their words together. You know how the old Norwegians around here say, 'Ya' or 'You betcha?' Well, these guys had their own way of speaking, but I can't really tell you what it was. I just can't put my finger on it."

Deidre couldn't let it drop. "Stanford, do you watch the news on TV?"

"Sure, who doesn't?" He looked at her curiously.

"Have you ever paid attention to how people from the Middle East sound?"

At that Stanford's eyes came alive with recognition. "That's it! They didn't have an accent like you hear so often, but the way they spoke reminded me an awful lot of what people from that area say."

"One last thing," Deidre announced to the now visibly flustered junkman. "Do you remember anything about the car the two drove up in?"

"Well, yes, of course I do," Stanford answered almost indignantly as if Deidre should have assumed he would notice. "It was a 2010 black Ford Explorer, Minnesota license plate 765 BGY."

Deidre's eyes opened a little wider with that information. "Stanford, are you sure about the license number? Did you write it down for some reason?"

Stanford smiled an unforced smile. "I don't have to write down license plate numbers. For some reason they stick in my memory, sort of like a file index that I can roll and see the vehicle make and the number. It drives me nuts sometimes, because I can't stop it from happening, but sometimes it's kind of fun to show off, if you know what I mean."

"Stanford, what you've told me is a big help. I'll have to report the car thing to the sheriff here, but I want to thank you for cooperating with me. Thank you."

On the way home, Deidre tried to put together the connection between a body in an abandoned car, five Middle Eastern men in a hunting shack, and possibly David Craine.

CHAPTER
TWENTY-TWO

DEIDRE SLOWLY CLIMBED THE STAIRS TO THE SECOND FLOOR of the Law Enforcement Center. She was weary, and her head ached. Deep in thought, she walked past the front desk, and the receptionist's presence hardly registered. In her cool, dimly lit office, Deidre stood in front of a tripod holding a pad of poster paper, and using a thick-lined marker she began to draw a chart. It had three columns, and above each she placed a heading: HERMINIO VALEZQUES, DAVID CRAINE, and HUNTING SHACK. These are the three topics that consumed her days—and nights.

Herminio was a homicide victim found in a gravel pit in her county. David Craine was under protective surveillance, and the occupants of the hunting shack were under watch for some reason. She didn't know for what, but the FBI was "requesting" her department to report on them.

As an afterthought, Deidre squeezed in a fourth column on the margin of the right side of the paper and labeled it STANFORD. Then she started filling in data under each heading.

> Herminio: Honduran, immigrant advocate, dead, found in junked car.
> David Craine: In danger, possibly wanted by FBI, immigrant advocate,
>   Honduran mission trips, boat
> The Shack: Middle Eastern men, FBI interest
> Stanford Williams: Junked car, Middle Eastern men

Deidre sorted the chart's data, dividing it into subsets of information, and she noticed that the only interaction Stanford Williams had with anyone in the group was the sale of the junked car. His name was linked to nothing else. She took her marker and crossed off his name on her pad, and on the large chart, she deleted the column under his name. It was evident to her that Stanford was only interested in making a fast buck. Nothing in her logic connected him to the others in any way.

Then she considered Herminio and his involvement. Certainly he was connected to the car, his temporary coffin, and that car was possibly connected to two Middle Eastern men.

"There aren't too many men of that description in the Northland," she muttered to herself. She wondered how a naturalized U.S. citizen from Honduras ended up in the trunk of a car purchased by the two men, and why.

That brought her to David Craine. The men in the hunting shack north of Two Harbors were under surveillance by the FBI, and so was David, although for different reasons she had been told. Then too, David and Herminio shared one commonality, their interest in immigration issues.

"Could David have been involved with Herminio?" Deidre asked out loud. "Did they know each other?"

By this time it was late in the day, and the only conclusion Deidre had arrived at was that Stanford Williams was out of the picture as far as she was concerned. Other than that, her mind was spinning like the circles she had drawn around the various groupings. All she knew was that Herminio had been found dead in a car bought illegally by two possibly Middle Eastern men; the FBI was interested in a group of Middle Eastern men hold up in a shack twenty miles north of Two Harbors; the FBI wanted David Craine watched, and she had a headache.

On the way out of the office, she asked the dispatcher which deputy had the night shift watching the docks.

"That would be VanGotten," she answered. The information didn't do much for Deidre's headache.

Deidre couldn't stop herself from trying to form connections between the three groups of people, the men in the shack, Herminio, and David Craine. Even after two vodka tonics and a microwaved frozen dinner, she had difficulty falling asleep, and she dreamed about lists with threads connecting them, forming a spider web maze. When her alarm buzzed its wakeup call, it seemed to her that she had just fallen to sleep, and she got out of bed, hardly rested.

After a quick breakfast of some kind of bran cereal soaked in vanilla yogurt, Deidre returned to the office for the morning report from the nightshift crew and to organize the dayshift's schedule.

"Ben, anything to report?" Deidre sipped a cup of hot coffee, hoping the caffeine would kick in fast.

"Not much. It was a slow night . . . except for one person of interest. I drove down to the breakwater a little before nine o'clock last evening and noticed a man get out of a black SUV. He headed onto the breakwater, and I could see him standing by the restraining cable about halfway to the end. He had binoculars and was watching an ore boat being loaded. I thought he was spending more time than usual at that spot, because it was so close to dark. In fact, the lights were on at the docks, and it was quite a sight with the docks and the boat all lit up. I decided to check him out."

Deidre immediately became more alert and not from the coffee. "You didn't approach him did you?" she asked.

"No. There was a group of young people out at the end of the pier, and they were having a little too much fun for being just boat watchers. I walked out to them and checked their IDs. They were all over twenty-one, so I just reminded them not to litter with their beer cans and chip bags—asked them to be careful. Told them we didn't want to have to go fishing for anyone in the morning. Then I walked back to my truck, and as I passed the guy at the cable, I nodded and smiled. He nodded back, and then went back to studying the loading process at the docks."

"Do you have a description of him," Deidre wanted to know. "Or, was it too dark to see?"

"There was still enough light that I could make out his features quite well. He was of average build, about five-ten, I'd say, skin color olive with black hair. I assume he had dark eyes, but the light was too dim to get a very good look.

"When I got back to the parking lot, I jotted down the license number of his SUV." Ben shuffled through his pockets, trying to find his note pad. He found it in his left breast pocket. "It was a Ford Explorer, Minnesota license 765 BGY."

A jolt like an electric shock surged through Deidre's body, and she hoped the deputies didn't notice.

"Good work, Ben," Deidre said, and Ben actually smiled back at her.

"Not much has changed since our meeting yesterday," Deidre said, trying to sound matter of fact. "Jeff, you take the Brimson area today. Don't drive by the shack too often, but take a couple or three spins by to see if anything changes. Report back immediately if things seem different around there in any way. The rest of you are on your regular areas. Oh, and Ben, get some sleep. You deserve it."

The group filtered out of the office, and Deidre moved into the peace and quiet of her own private space. She closed the door behind her and knew the pieces were beginning to fall . . . into place she wasn't sure.

CHAPTER
TWENTY-THREE

DEIDRE PLOPPED INTO HER SWIVEL CHAIR and turned to her computer. With three clicks of the mouse, she was into the Minnesota auto license data base. She entered 765 BGY and hit search. In less than two seconds, the information she sought was displayed on the monitor's screen.

> License number: 765 BGY
> Make: Ford
> Model: Explorer
> Color: Black
> VIN: 3AWPAF8MN056073
> Registration: Arrowhead Auto Rental

Deidre spun to retrieve her phone, and then turned back to her computer, returning to its home page with one click of the mouse. She typed in Arrowhead Auto Rental, Duluth, Minnesota, and clicked on "search." Arrowhead Auto Rental listed its phone number on its webpage. Deidre could hardly dial the number rapidly enough.

"Good morning. Arrowhead Auto Rental. This is Jo Anne. How may I help you?"

"This is Deidre Johnson, sheriff of Lake County speaking." Deidre heared an audible inhalation of air on the other end of the call, and she smiled to herself at this common reaction.

After a moment's silence, Jo Anne responded. "Yes, how may we help you?"

"I need information concerning a SUV you may have recently rented out. It is a black Ford explorer, license number 765 BGY. Do you need the VIN?"

"No, the license is all I need. Has this vehicle been in an accident, and if so can you provide me with more information?"

Deidre checked herself so as not to give out information she might want to hold back. "No. No, not that at all. The driver of this vehicle was stopped for a minor traffic violation is all. We're just touching base to make sure the driver's papers are in order," Deidre lied.

"Here it is. All of our data can be accessed in our computer base with the touch of a button. What would you like to know?"

"First," Deidre inquired, "What is the name of the person who rented the vehicle?"

"Zaim Hassad Zayad," Jo Anne responded, stumbling a little over the pronunciation.

Now it was Deidre's turn to take pause. "Is this person a U.S. citizen?"

"Let me see. No, he's Honduran. All of his papers were in order. He presented a valid passport and visa. It says here it's a B-1 visa for business travel. He listed his business as AHI, Afghan Home Industries. I remember he said that he specialized in carpet sales. Does this correspond to what you have?" she asked of Deidre.

"Yes. Everything seems to be in order and jives with what we have here," Deidre lied again, but her thoughts were flying. "Thank you for your cooperation, Jo Ann."

Deidre hung up the phone and stared at the chart she made last night. Then she began to scribble on the note pad on her desk.

Zaim Hassad Zayad—Honduran—Abandoned car—Herminio's body

Herminio—Honduran—Immigrant advocate—Found dead in car

David Craine—Honduran missions—Immigrant advocate

She scrawled another series: Zaim—Hunting Shack?—FBI—Herminio—David—FBI.

"Is this why we're watching David?" Deidre whispered out loud.

Her next move was to reach for the phone again and dial a number. "Hello, John? This is Deidre Johnson calling from Lake County."

"Well, Deidre, what a pleasant surprise to hear your voice again. To what do I owe this pleasure?" Special Agent Erickson schmoozed into the phone.

"Okay, John. You can cut the B.S. now. I thought that the picnic we had the other day was so relaxing that we should get together again for lunch. I know a nice quiet spot at the mouth of the Sucker River. If you have time we could meet there. I'll stop in Knife River and pick up a smoked fish and some cheese, and I'm sure the deli in Two Harbors has something to go with it. This lunch is on me. What do you say?"

Deidre recognized a definite pause as if John was wondering what the catch was, but he recovered quickly and without more hesitation answered, "Why, Deidre, that's a great idea. I'll bring some soft drinks, and we'll have a real picnic. I can't be long though. I have a meeting with my supervisor at 1:30 this afternoon. Still, I know the place you're talking about, and it is only ten or twelve minutes out of Duluth. I'll be there at noon."

This time Deidre was the first to arrive, and she had everything set out when John came tripping down the bank.

"You certainly surprised me with your call this morning," John said as he settled himself onto the blanket Deidre had spread on the ground. He took a piece of fish and layered it with a slice of cheese on one of the crackers Deidre had brought. He took a bite.

"I never dreamed we would have a social get together like this," and he took another cracker and more smoked fish.

"What do you know about a man named Zaim Hassad Zayad, John?" Deidre asked, forcing her voice to remain as smooth as warm honey.

John inhaled so abruptly at her words that he choked on a good-sized cracker crumb and tried to get his breath.

"John," Deidre said as sweetly as she could, "are you all right?"

After wheezing a few more times and coughing until his air passage was cleared, John looked at Deidre through tear-filled eyes.

"How do you know that name?" he managed to croak out. "So Zaim is what this picnic is all about."

"Now, John," Deidre continued with mock sweetness. "Evidently you know about this Zaim already, but let me fill you in on what I know. Zaim bought the car in which we found Herminio Valesquez's body. He also was seen spending more than the usual amount of time watching a boat being loaded at the ore docks in Two Harbors. I would assume the black Ford Explorer he drives is the same one spotted up in Brimson at the hunting shack. You know, the one you've had us watching for the past month. Oh, and I know that Zaim, although his name doesn't sound like it, is Honduran, as was Herminio. Bear with me, John, while I connect a couple of other dots. David Craine, remember him? He's the retired teacher you've had us watching. He spent a lot of time in Honduras, and both he and Herminio have been active advocates for Latinos who are in this country illegally."

Deidre fixed herself a cracker with fish and cheese, smiled at him, and said, "Is there anything you'd like to tell me, John? Or do I have to keep finding the pieces to this puzzle by myself, because if I do, the only other person who can help me is Zaim. I have plenty of evidence against him to bring him in on a murder charge. Remember, I know where he lives."

Deidre smiled at John as if she really cared for him and took a bite of her fish-cracker sandwich, and she waited.

John cleared his throat. "Deidre, don't do something you might regret. Zaim's not one to mess with. Besides that, the FBI would not look on his arrest with much joy. In fact, his arrest would be the end of your career."

He looked at Deidre. The sweet look on her face had disappeared.

"Look, Deidre, I really commend you on your professionalism and the way you have started to piece things together. Give me twenty-four hours. I'll take what you've said to my supervisor. I might be able to persuade him to let you in on what is going down with this operation, but he's old school. Still has that us-against-the-world thinking. I'll call you later today, and we'll talk."

John began to get up, but Deidre said to him, "Why don't you sit down, John. We've got another half hour before we have to get back. It would be a shame to let this fish and cheese go to waste."

CHAPTER
TWENTY-FOUR

JOHN ENTERED THE FBI OFFICES IN DULUTH AT EXACTLY 1:30. His supervisor, an ex-marine special forces and now director of his division, was waiting for him, looking like he expected John to have been there a half hour ago. John offered his hand, and his supervisor, Enos Pratt, gave it an extra firm squeeze.

"How are things going up north, John?" he immediately began the conversation.

"Well, Enos, I'll tell you. That Brimson area is one tough place. There are people living up there who want nothing to do with the world, and they don't want strangers in their territory. It's tough sledding."

Enos scowled at John from under heavy, black eyebrows that gave his eyes a hawkish appearance. "What do you mean by that? Have you lost contact with our group?"

John matched the scowl with one of his own. "I didn't say that. I only said it isn't easy. I'm sure you remember we have brought in the Lake County sheriff's squad to do surveillance up there as part of their daily patrols, and that's something I want to talk to you about."

"What's to talk about," Enos snapped back at John. "Can't that bunch of hicks handle a simple surveillance?"

The tone of the conversation was starting to get to John. "Listen, they're doing as good a job as anyone, maybe better than we expected."

"What the hell are you talking about? If you have something to say, say it."

With that invitation, John jumped in with his best argument. "We absolutely have to let the sheriff know what's going on . . ."

Before John could utter another word, Enos jumped to his feet, and his face turned crimson. "Impossible! Don't even suggest that crap. The first thing she'll want to do is take over. Her kind always does. This is our operation, and don't you ever forget it. And don't you ever address me with that tone of voice again."

Now it was John who got to his feet. There was no way that he was going to remain seated and looking up at the standing Enos.

"Deidre is the sheriff of Lake County. It's her job and her duty to investigate any crime in her jurisdiction, and that is what she is doing.

"You saw the Lake County coroner's report on that Honduran guy, Herminio, and so did she. We couldn't withhold that kind of information from her, because she was called to the crime scene even before we knew about it."

"Yeah, well so what? So a guy gets knocked off and stuffed into the trunk of a car? Happens plenty frequently," Enos fumed.

Now it was John's turn to fire back. "Here's what. Deidre . . . Sheriff Johnson has traced that car back to Zaim. She strongly suspects he's one of the five camped out in the hunting shack in Brimson, and she would have every right to go in with some deputies and arrest him for being involved in the murder of Herminio. Now, do you want to listen to what I'd like to say?"

"She wouldn't dare do that. She knows it'd be political suicide for her to make that move. She'd never work in law enforcement again. I'd personally see to that. Probably wouldn't be that bad either, one less woman pushing her weight around."

"She would dare, and she will do it. Enos, we've kept her in the dark long enough, and it is time to let her in on what we've got going on. If she goes up there, not knowing what she would be facing, a lot of her men are going to be taken out, maybe even her. I suppose that won't bother you. Just one more woman we wouldn't have to deal with.

"Think of this, Enos, what is important, preserving the integrity of this operation, or keeping ourselves isolated? No matter what, if she arrests Zaim, the whole operation is blown, kaput. She may get shot. She may lose her job, but two years of work by a lot of good people will go down the drain because of your misogynistic slant on the world."

John wasn't sure if Enos comprehended the word misogynistic, but he knew the tone of his voice probably told the story. Enos glared at John for several seconds, and John didn't flinch. He was tired of taking guff from this pompous, self-righteous clod.

Eventually Enos cleared his throat. "I'll overlook your insubordination this time, John. Don't let it happen again. I suppose that woman has us over a barrel. Let her in on why we have the bunch in Brimson under watch. Let her know the importance of our having them continue with their plan.

"But John, you are not to tell her about David Craine's involvement in this. We both know her attachment to him, and I don't want her running to him for any reason. Do you understand me?"

John walked to the door and over his shoulder, answered, "Yes, *sir*."

Before he left the room, Enos had one more word for John. "I don't like this 'Deidre' crap. She is 'Sheriff Johnson.' Do you understand?"

Again, over his shoulder, John answered, "Yes, *sir*."

John went to his car, and from the parking lot called the Lake County Law Enforcement Center. The phone was answered by the dispatcher.

"This is Special Agent Erickson out of the Duluth FBI office. I'd like to speak with Sheriff Johnson, please?" John always found that the mention of FBI got faster results.

"I'm sorry. Sheriff Johnson isn't in her office. She is on her way to Brimson with a deputy, but she left a message for you. 'John, call me on my cell phone with any news about Zaim.'"

Panicked, John used his phone's speed dial option, and listened as it rang, then heard Deidre's voice. "I'm sorry. I am not available to take your call at this time. Please leave a message at the tone."

As calmly as he could, he left a message. "Deidre, this is John. Please do not go after Zaim until we have a chance to talk. My supervisor wants me to fill you in about those guys up there. Again, I'm asking, please don't go to the hunting shack. I'll call again in a few minutes."

CHAPTER
TWENTY-FIVE

WITHIN MINUTES JOHN'S PHONE RANG. It was Deidre.

"Hey, John, what's up?" Deidre's voice sounded agitated.

"I hope I'm not too late with this call. You haven't been up to the shack have you? Tell me no."

Deidre let out a sigh. "No, John, I'm being a good player, even if I don't know the rules. We had an incident up at Big Jimbo's Tavern. Do you know the one at the intersection of County Road 150 and Rock Lake Road?"

"I think I do," John answered, relief flooding his voice. "What's going on up there?"

"Nothing . . . now. We had a domestic that got way out of hand. Some logger was half in the bag and beating his girlfriend around in the bar. A stranger stepped in to stop him. He threw the logger out on his ear and then got back to the bar to finish his beer.

"The bartender told the stranger to watch out, because the guy he threw out is a mean one when he is drunk. Sure enough, when the stranger stepped out of the tavern a little later, the logger was waiting for him with a double-bit axe. Took a swing with it, too. Luckily the guy ducked enough only to catch a glancing blow off his shoulder. Cut him bad though.

"That was when someone called 911, and our deputy got there in about three minutes. Lucky for the guy who got cut up, Jeff was on route to make a pass by the hunting shack. Jeff had to draw his gun to get the logger to put down the axe. For the three minutes it took Jeff to get there, the stranger danced around, avoiding the axe swings and bleeding like a stuck hog.

"I got there about the same time the ambulance did. Typically, the girlfriend accused the stranger of attacking her boyfriend and said he reacted in self-defense. There were a lot of other witnesses, though, who gave us the real story.

"That's tough country up there, not what you city boys are used to." Deidre smirked—John could sense it even though he couldn't see the look on her face.

"So, John, what's the big news that couldn't wait until I was back at the office?"

"First, I was really worried that you had gone to Brimson to pick up Zaim. In fact, in my mind I was sure that's where you were headed, and I wanted to talk you out of doing something that would not only be foolish, but also dangerous.

"Second, I talked to my supervisor. It wasn't a pleasant conversation, but he finally decided it was better to let you in on what we have going up there than let you stumble into something you aren't prepared to handle."

As the words were leaving his mouth, John knew they weren't the right ones. Even over the miles between Brimson and Duluth, John could feel Deidre's hackles rise.

"Whoa there, John. What do you mean something we're not prepared to handle. You still think we're a bunch of Keystone Cops, don't you? You come up here and face a drunk with an axe sometime and see how well you're prepared to meet a situation."

As had happened before when he and Deidre were talking, John found himself on the defensive. "Wait a minute, Deidre. I didn't mean that the way it sounded. I meant you don't know what you'd be facing, and you wouldn't be prepared for what's up there.

"I want to have another face-to-face talk. Once you know the whole truth, you'll understand what I'm talking about."

"So you're going to give me the entire scoop this time?" Deidre asked, her temper cooling down almost as fast as it had heated up.

"Everything," John said, knowing that wasn't quite the truth.

Deidre looked at her watch. "It's 3:30 now. I'll be back in Two Harbors by 4:00. Can we meet at 5:30? I'll need some time to make out a report on the incident at the tavern.

"Let's see, we've been to the Scenic, to Chester Park, to the Sucker River. How about spreading our presence around? We could meet at the Rocky Point Cafe. They don't get much business, because the food and service isn't the greatest, but we'd have some privacy there"

John responded immediately, too quickly he thought afterward. "Sounds, great. See you at 5:30," and he heard Deidre hang up the phone.

CHAPTER
TWENTY-SIX

AT 5:00, DEIDRE WAS STILL SCRAMBLING TO FINISH HER REPORT. *Why is it that women allow themselves to get into abusive relationships and then alibi for the bums instead of filing charges?* She shook her head, because she had no answers.

Finally she put the file into its proper slot and drove out to Rocky Point. It took her fifteen minutes to get there, and John had a table next to the window overlooking Lake Superior by the time she arrived. He rose to meet her.

"Deidre, or should I say Sheriff Johnson?" he said as he extended his hand. "It's good to see you again."

"What's with this formality, John," Deidre threw back at him. "Suddenly I go from Deidre to Sheriff Johnson. I suppose I should be a little leery of what's coming next." Deidre smiled at him.

"Oh, nothing. I just don't want to be too informal if you want formal. Which do you prefer?"

"Deidre's fine," she responded, wondering why he would be concerned about it now.

"Good," John said. "Anyway, have a seat. Why don't we order and enjoy our meal. It sounded like you could use a few minutes away from the job when we spoke earlier, and we can go down by the lake after dinner. That way we can be sure no one's eavesdropping. Did you get everything done that needed doing?"

Deidre had to agree that a few minutes of small talk over dinner might be nice. "That's okay with me. By the way, if I were you, I'd stay away from their ground beef. They make some real belly bombs here. My advice is to stick with the chicken."

When the disheveled waiter came to their table, his shirt tail hanging out in back, Deidre took her own advice. "I'll have the grilled chicken salad, with a side of honey mustard dressing," she ordered. "And ice tea."

The waiter turned to John. "And you?"

John looked at him and then at Deidre.

"Oh, what the heck. I want a hamburger with an order of onion rings and root beer."

The waiter turned to leave, and John hollered at his departing figure, "And make sure the burger's well done." He looked at Deidre and chuckled.

"You're going to be sorry tomorrow," Deidre laughed back at him.

Throughout the meal, neither of them brought up work, and the conversation centered around the weather, the changing shades of color in the lake, and if the Minnesota Twins were going to fold by the time playoffs rolled around.

Finally their meal was done and they paid the waiter, leaving an obligatory tip.

John was the first to get out of his chair. "We better go see the lake before it gets too late," he said to Deidre, and they walked side by side down to the rocky outcrop that formed the shoreline.

Out of earshot from anyone else, John broke the silence first. "I spoke to Enos Pratt, my supervisor. I think I told you that already. I convinced him that if you're going to continue to help us, you have to know what's going on. If you don't, it could be extremely dangerous for your people. It took some convincing, but he finally came around."

Deidre looked at him in surprise. "I thought these were just some minor drug dealers in Brimson. You mean they might be connected to the mob?"

"It's a lot more than that, Deidre. They might not look it, but that group is considered to be as dangerous as anything to ever hit Lake County. We suspect they are heavily armed with more firepower than anything your deputies have."

Deidre's eyes opened wider. "So what's the deal? What are we up against here?" Suddenly, realization hit her. Zaim Hassad Zayad was not your usual northern Minnesota name.

"Are you telling me these are terrorists? That can't be. There's nothing in this county they'd . . ." Her words trailed off. "The docks!"

John looked at her and nodded. "The docks."

"But how can you be so sure? Do you have evidence against them? And when is this anything supposed to happen?"

"Slow down, Deidre. One question at a time," and he began to explain. "We have a reliable informant, and we're dead certain about who these men are and what they intend to do. We even know how they plan to bring the docks down. What we don't know is when it's going to happen."

"If you're so certain, why don't you arrest them now? According to what you're telling me, and if it's true, then you have enough on them to charge them with terrorist acts. What are you waiting for?" Deidre asked, incredulous.

"It's not as cut and dried as it may seem. First, we want to catch them committing the act so the warrant against them will carry more weight. We want to send them away for a long time. Second, we have been able to intercept their communications. There's only one cell tower that can be reached from the Brimson area. It's near Highland Lake, and all their calls run through that tower, making them easy to trace. We're trying to develop a data bank of all the communications going on between those five and the outside world."

Deidre had one last question. "Who is this informant you're so sure about?"

John looked away. "I don't know," he lied. He looked Deidre square in the eyes. "For security reasons, that knowledge is known to only a few within the department." Once again he looked away. "And I'm not one of them."

Deidre let the air escape from her lungs. "What am I supposed to do?" she wanted to know. "What are my deputies supposed to do?"

"What you've been doing. Now you're in the know, and I'll have more freedom to keep you in the loop. The ice has been broken, and I'm sure we can more easily work together from now on. We'll keep in touch," and he reached out and touched her shoulder. "My boss said he would have a directive for your mission drawn up for you in a few days. I'll get it to you as soon as it's done."

CHAPTER
TWENTY-SEVEN

IT WAS 5:00 IN THE MORNING WHEN THE BRIGHT RAYS of the rising sun streamed through a crack between the shade and the window frame next to where Zaim was sleeping. They found his eyes, and he jerked abruptly awake. He sat up in his bed and ran his hand over his arm. The ache was not too bad this morning.

He rolled out of the top bunk, gripped the side rail and lowered himself so his feet touched the floor.

"Come on, you four. Wake up," he urged.

"Jabril, Afu, get up. It's time we get our work done," Zaim demanded. He peeled the blankets off Murad.

"Imad, it's getting late, and we have a long hike before us today. Come on, Murad, fix some breakfast and get a lunch ready for us to take with."

The four men grumbled and cursed under their breath at Zaim, but they didn't linger in bed. Each stumbled outside and relieved himself behind the shack.

"At least this is one benefit of being so far out," Imad commented to the others as he zipped up his pants. The others ignored his optimism.

Murad busied himself at the kitchen counter and soon had a plate of scrambled eggs and toast ready for the group. In the increasing light from the rising sun, they ate in silence. Zaim was particularly sullen, and he barked at the others, "Don't be long. It will take us an hour to get to the bridge and then more time to set the charges. It is necessary to be ready at exactly 3:30 when the shift in the mine changes. I have timed the explosions, and they set off their blasts exactly on the second."

126

Not taking time to clean up the breakfast mess in the sink, the five men thrust their arms through backpack straps and headed outside. From there they followed Zaim as he strode down a narrow path that wended its way between jack pines, around patches of sedges, and eventually came to the Cloquet River. There, the trail they were using joined with another that followed the riverbank and they worked their way upstream, away from the hunting shack and the county road running past it.

There was no talking between them. Zaim moved forward with such determination that the others were breathless in a short time, sucking for air as their pack straps dug deeply into their shoulders.

After an hour of walking, they came to an abandoned railroad trestle that spanned the river. It was made of steel beams—large beams that at one time had supported the huge Mallet steam locomotives that pulled railroad car after railroad car of iron ore dug from the underground mines near Ely. Those mines had long since gone dead, depleted of the high grade ore running in drifts below the earth's surface.

Once the ore had stopped being mined, there was nothing to haul along the route, and the route had been abandoned. The railroad bed had soon begun to revert back to nature.

No longer needed, the rails of this particular run had been pulled and sent to steel mills that consumed scrap iron. Only the rail bed, partially overgrown with aspen saplings and the huge trestle remained. A few deer hunters who dared venture this far into the wilderness even knew of its presence, and no one really cared about it one way or the other.

"There it is," Zaim announced, "our target," and he smiled for the first time in several days.

Each man shed his pack and flopped down on the river bank. They inhaled the sweet smell of the river sedges, a pungent, almost perfume-like tang that hung in the air. As they wiped the sweat from their faces, a kingfisher dove into the water from a branch draped over the river's surface. A trout broke the surface and grabbed a dragonfly out of the air.

After a few minutes of rest, Zaim again began ordering the others into action.

"Today is a training day for us. We are going to practice taking down these steel girders with charges that will detonate simultaneously, causing the trestle to completely collapse. No one will miss it until the hunting season begins in three months, and only then if a hunter manages to get back this far.

"Carry the packs down to the river's edge, and pile them on that rock outcrop. They'll be dry there."

"Aren't you fearful that the blast will be heard? It's a long way back here, but certainly someone will hear," Jabril said as he fiddled with a loose thread on his pack.

Zaim looked at Jabril as though he should have been aware of something so obvious. "That is why we are going to detonate the explosives at exactly 3:30. If you haven't noticed, sound travels a long way out here," he said, his voice laced with impatience.

"Aren't you aware that you hear a distant blast every weekday at 3:30? Only twenty-five miles to the west is a mine pit, and everyday at exactly 3:30, when the day shift has left and before the afternoon shift has begun, they blast to loosen rock to be dug out."

"You are right, Zaim," Afu interrupted. "We've been here so long, the blasts have become routine. We don't even notice them anymore."

"And neither do any of the people who live up here," Zaim added. "The trees will muffle the sound of this blast, making it difficult to judge distances. If we time it to coincide with the mine blast, probably no one will pay attention."

Then he added, "Take another half hour to rest. I want you calm when you begin to strap the plastic explosives to the steel uprights and especially when you insert the detonators into the charges."

The five lay on their backs, staring at the blue sky and listening to the chirp of squirrels and the songs of warblers in the brush.

CHAPTER
TWENTY-EIGHT

HABITUALLY, DAVID WAS AN EARLY RISER. He seldom slept later than 6:00 a.m., but since the incident with the Latinos he had helped get out of the country, he usually woke with a start much earlier than that. This morning had been no exception, and he waited for daybreak.

After a second cup of coffee, David Craine could not take too much more of being cooped up in his stark, one-room apartment. It was light enough for him to see the ore docks materializing from the fog that was lifting from the harbor. He checked his watch—five-thirty.

David pulled on a heavy sweater to buffer him from the early morning chill and headed down the stairs to street level. He needed to move, to walk off his tension and pent-up energy, so he headed for the breakwater. There was an ore boat between docks two and three, and he wondered which one of the fleet it was. The sun was just beginning to break over the horizon, and everything at the docks was illuminated with a warm glow.

Turning right from his building, David walked briskly until he came to South Avenue, then turned left and continued for another two blocks. As he passed the Lake County Historical Society's museum, he noticed one of the sheriff's deputies sitting in his white SUV. He walked over to it.

"Well, hello, Jeff," he greeted the familiar deputy. "Looks like you've drawn the night shift again. Any excitement happen here last night."

"Hey, hi, David. How's it going?" Jeff answered with a genuine smile. He'd known David for several years, as had most people in Two Harbors, and the two made small talk for a few minutes.

129

Finally, David stepped back from the vehicle and waved his hand. "I've got to be moving. Like to put in a couple of miles this morning before the sun gets too high."

"Well, take care, David. I've got to get back to the office and file my report for the night. It's been a long one, and I need to get home and grab some sleep."

With that Jeff drove away, and David picked up the pace so he could get to the breakwater before the sun's rays lost their sunrise color.

He swung right on the street past the water treatment plant and strode across the parking lot of the DNR boat landing. That put him at the beginning of the breakwater, a quarter mile of concrete barrier that not only served to shield the docks from the waves, but also was a favorite walking surface for locals and tourists alike. He walked half way out and paused to lean on the safety cable that bordered the dock side of the wall. David leaned on it as he watched the steel chutes of the dock being lowered into the holds of the ship, and he read the boat's name, *Edgar Speer*.

Totally lost in thought, David was surprised to hear a voice behind him.

"Good morning, Mr. Craine." David cocked his head around and saw Ben VanGotten standing near him.

"Ben, how many times do I have to tell you, I'm not Mr. anymore, just plain Dave, or David if you prefer."

Ben looked David straight in the eye. "Mr. Craine, I've tried that, but it just doesn't work. To most of us who had you for a teacher, you'll always be Mr. Craine. No offense, but I think that's the way it is."

David laughed at this comment. "I was that tough, huh? Well, anyway Ben, it's nice to see you this morning. What are you doing down here so early?"

Ben leaned on the cable next to *Mr. Craine*. "I make a swing down here most mornings. The sun makes these old docks almost light up. Besides, it feels good on my shoulders when I catch the direct rays. How about you? How come you're up so early? I thought you retired people slept in every morning."

David turned and faced Ben. "I couldn't sleep this morning. Too much on my mind I guess. Enjoy the sunrise, Ben. I'm going to walk out to the end of the breakwater, and then go home. It'd be nice to get out on my boat today, but starting about noon, there are small craft warnings up."

As he walked away, Ben hollered after him, "Mr. Craine, take care of yourself."

David waved a hand, but he wondered to himself, *Seems everyone wants me to take care of myself. What else would I do?*

He walked briskly out to the signal light at the end of the pier, turned around, and almost jogged back to his apartment. Nothing had changed.

CHAPTER
TWENTY-NINE

THE FIVE MEN LYING ON THE BANKS OF THE Cloquet River revived quickly, and soon they were talking among themselves, discussing the planned destruction of the abandoned railroad trestle while they enjoyed the tranquility of the site.

"Time to begin," Zaim said, looking at his watch. "We have four hours to set the charges. We can make the final preparations and eat lunch afterward. Then we'll wait for three-thirty."

The men stood up, and they made their way down the river bank, where they shouldered their packs. Then they waded in thigh-deep water to the first steel upright.

"You've been through this in your training, but I want to make sure you haven't forgotten any of the details."

Zaim removed a block of material from his Duluth pack.

"Each charge must be molded to the I-beam like this," and Zaim shaped the formable material to fit in the channel of the beam. Then he picked up a handful of dirt and smeared it over the explosive. It almost blended perfectly with the rusted steel. "Plant the detonator carefully," and he made a hole in the charge with a sharpened stick, inserted a pencil sized rod with a wire hanging from one end.

He stepped back to admire his work.

"Good, it is almost invisible from a few feet away. In the shadow of darkness, no one would spot it."

He motioned to the others, "There are exactly enough charges for each of the upright girders. Make sure each has one stuck to it."

The five men worked in silence, each concentrating on the block they molded into place. To get from one piling to the other they waded in the clear water of the river. It was not an unpleasant experience. Each charge was fitted with a signal receiver that would be activated from a remote Zaim had carried in his pocket. Before they left the shack, he had removed its batteries to ensure the explosives couldn't be accidentally detonated. He had seen such accidents before from less experienced men, and he didn't want to lose even one member of his specially trained team.

Zaim looked at his watch. "It's ten to three," he announced as the last charge was set. "Let's go up on that ridge we crossed coming in. It has a clear line of sight to the bridge, and it's far enough away so we won't be injured.

"Those pine trees will give us shade, and the fallen needles are easy to lie on."

When they had climbed to the spot he had pointed out, he sprawled on the ground and rested his head back. After only a minute or so, a curious squirrel poked its head around a tree, then in jerky hops approached Zaim's motionless body. Zaim opened one eye, barely, and smiled at the little animal that was fearfully alert but at the same time attracted to this new thing in its woods.

Zaim made a chirping sound through his pursed lips and then smiled again as the squirrel sat upright, its ears perked to the sound. It tried to figure out if this thing on the ground was friend, foe, or just there. Zaim played his game with the little red-furred animal, for the moment forgetting his pain, his pent-up hatred, his desire for revenge. Then he realized time was passing.

He raised his arm to look at his watch. At that slight movement, the squirrel decided "enemy," scurried up a tree, and angrily scolded those below who had invaded his sanctuary.

To Zaim's amazement, almost a half hour had passed. He abruptly sat up.

"It's 3:25. Almost time," he announced to the others in a matter-of-fact voice.

The five waited for what seemed an hour, Zaim staring at the second hand of his watch, his other hand on the transmitter button. At exactly 3:30, he pushed the switch.

The forest sounds were instantly drowned out by the blast as each charge simultaneously detonated with the others. The trestle lifted ten feet in the air and hung as though suspended for just an instant. Then gravity did its job, and the entire structure crashed into the river, a tangle of twisted girders and steel rails. Water and smaller pieces of debris rained from the sky for a few seconds, and then there was silence. Not the kind of silence experienced on a calm day in the forest but a deathly silence known only as a total absence of sound.

To the five men, the blast in the mine pit near Aurora was so overpowered by their own explosion, they didn't hear it at all, and Zaim thought, *"Good news. The two blasts must have coincided perfectly."*

Several miles to the south, Eino Karinen was sitting at the bar at Big Jimbo's Tavern when the explosion occurred. He had been there most of the afternoon, and his glazed eyes belied the number of beers he had downed in those hours.

The country residents were so used to the customary 3:30 blast at the mine, the only thing that registered was when it did not happen, and that seldom occurred. Most folks, if only in their subconscious, felt something was different this time, but not all that different.

Eino looked up from his beer when the sound wave passed. "That was a big one," he slurred. "Must have been one of those hangfires where half the charges go off and lifts the bed rock, then the other half explodes in the air. I remember one time they threw room-size chunks of rock onto Main Street of the town."

The other patrons ignored him as they usually did. A couple shrugged, but all of them kept talking and drinking.

Zaim and the four others worked their way down to the wreckage. It was so complete that only a few of the bridge supports, now reduced to ragged stubs of steel, protruded from the river's surface. In an eddy by the river bank three or four trout thrashed belly up in the water, and the odor of spent explosives hung in the air. Zaim looked at the destruction with a smile of satisfaction on his face.

"If we can set our charges like that on the docks, this is what they will look like. If we time it right, we can catch an ore boat loading. There will be a locomotive and its string of gondola cars on the docks, and we'll bring the whole thing down together." He relished the image.

CHAPTER
THIRTY

SOMETIMES THE LAKE DIDN'T COOPERATE THE WAY DAVID would have liked. For five days the wind had blown steadily from the northeast, and it had pushed the water higher on the western end of the lake. That, coupled with the relentless push of the wind on the waves, created seven- to ten-foot crests that rolled over the breakwater of the harbor where the ore boats loaded. There had been small-craft warnings posted every day, and David had grown increasingly more restless as each day passed.

But late yesterday the weather front had finally passed, and by this morning the waves had subsided to long swells. The six o'clock weather report included the words he had been waiting for, the small craft warning had been lifted, and today he could take his boat out of the harbor. He thought he would head down the lake to Knife River, and then cut across the eighteen miles of open water to Cornucopia, a small town on the Wisconsin shore.

By six-fifteen, David was in his well-used Subaru. He headed out of town, up Highway 61. Ten miles from town, he crossed the bridge at Gooseberry Falls and glanced down the gorge carved through solid rock at the river spilling some one hundred feet below. Then he continued past the falls and on his way to the Silver Bay Marina and *Crusader, Too.*

His trip was not going to be a long journey, about thirty-five miles down to Knife River and then another eighteen across the lake, so he didn't have to provision his boat for days on the water. He planned to visit a friend in Cornucopia, stay a day or two, and then return to the North Shore.

When he turned onto the marina road, he was surprised when he looked in his rear-view mirror and spotted a sheriff deputy's car close behind. Reflexively, his eyes turned downward to his speedometer, but he was well below the twenty-mile-per-hour posted speed limit. He swung into a parking space reserved for overnight stays. The deputy took the slot next to him, and they exited their vehicles at the same time.

"Hey, Ben, how's it going?" David asked, recognizing his former student.

"Great, Mr. Craine. Looks like the lake has settled down a little. You going out today?"

David answered, "I've been in my apartment for five days, and it's almost driven me nuts. Time to get on the water and clean out the injectors on *Crusader, Too*'s engines. I'm heading to Cornucopia. If you weren't on duty, I'd ask you to ride along."

Ben put his hand on David's shoulder. "Some other time would be great. Be careful now, and don't take any dumb chances."

"*There it is again,*" David thinks. "*What do they know that I don't?*" He answered, "Sure won't. Have a good day, Ben. I'll be back day after tomorrow at the latest."

With that David gave a wave over his shoulder and hurried down to his boat. After topping off her tanks with gas, he started *Crusader, Too*'s two Chevy engines and slowly left the marina, careful to not create a wake that could damage other boats. Once in open water, he headed southwest, and opened both throttles. The boat sprang forward like a race horse that had just felt the quirt, and the wind riffled through David's thinning hair.

The sky was chicory blue, the waves had all but subsided, and David felt carefree as he hadn't for days. He turned slightly southwest around the point of land protruding out into the lake at Castle Danger and softly hummed a mindless tune.

Suddenly *Crusader, Too* lurched as though she had been torpedoed. Her bow leaped from the water, and David heard a sickening grinding sound followed by a metallic clang, then silence. The impact threw David forward, and he was bruised when his shoulder and chest slammed into the bulwark of his craft. It took a few seconds for his head to clear and for the realization of what had happened to sink into his conscious.

At that instant, David realized he had made the same disastrous mistake so many other captains had made. He had come too close to the shoals after which this community was named, Castle Danger. *Crusader, Too* sat half out of the water, listing to her port side.

David rushed below deck to check if water was gushing in through a hole, but after only a minute or two he decided the hull must be intact. By now the boat would be filled with water if there were a hole in its shell. It wasn't. That was some good news, anyway.

He sent out a call over his radio and made contact with the Coast Guard.

"This is David Craine, captain of the cruiser *Crusader, Too* out of Silver Bay. I've run aground on the shoals off Castle Danger and am in immediate need of assistance."

After a few seconds, the dispatcher's voice on the other end answered. "We read you, Captain Craine. What's the size of your craft?

"I'm on a thirty-four-foot cruiser powered by twin 454 Chevy engines. I scraped the rock shelf roughly three-quarters of a mile off Castle Danger, and I'm grounded. I'm pretty sure I've taken out my props and possibly the drive shafts. The engines are running, but there's no response from the props. The engines sound like they aren't running under a load and are freewheeling."

Again the dispatcher came on the line. "Do you have any passengers with you, and are there any injuries?"

"Negative on both counts," David replied, amazed at how calm his voice sounded in his own ears.

"I think our best response is to alert the Lake County Search and Rescue Team. They can make it up to you in about twenty minutes. We'd have to come from Duluth. Keep your radio open, and their dispatcher will be with you in seconds. Good luck, Captain."

David heard a click as the Coast Guard dispatcher switched him over. He was reassured to hear the familiar voice of a lady who had been a seventh-grade student in his class during the first year he had taught in Two Harbors.

"Hi, David. The call has already gone out, and the crew is on their way to you. They've got their Zodiac in tow and will land it at the DNR site. It shouldn't take long. How are you doing, taking any water?"

"No, everything's sound—but for the drive train."

"Well, take care, David. I've got to keep this line clear."

Search and Rescue arrived a half-hour later, and David was surprised to see Ben standing in the bow, a hawser in his hand.

"Hey, Mr. Craine, need a hand?" he hollered over the motor's growl, and he threw the rope to David.

CHAPTER
THIRTY-ONE

DAVID TIED THE LINE OFF ON THE STERN OF *Crusader, Too* and the Search and Rescue craft slowly backed away. The line became taut, and the grounded boat began to slowly move backward off the reef. The scraping and metallic screeching resounded through the craft's hull and sent shivers up David's spine. He imagined the bottom-side of his boat being left on the rough basalt rocks that lay only a foot or two under the water.

Then there was silence, and *Crusader, Too* rocked in the gentle waves that lapped against her side. David rushed below deck, afraid he would find water gushing through a man-sized hole in her hull. To his immense relief, all was well. No water filled his craft, no fumes vaporized from the gas tank, and the craft gently rocked back and forth. He returned to the deck.

"Everything all right?" Ben bellowed across the water.

"No apparent leaks," David shouted back. "But I don't know if I have any power."

He reached for the starter switch, and the two Chevy engines fired up. To David's ears they seemed to be making their familiar deep throated purr, the exhaust coughing now and then when a wave splashed into the exhaust port.

"Can you shift it into gear," Ben wanted to know.

It would be good if he could limp back to the Knife River Marina rather than them having to tow him all the way.

David shifted the boat into reverse. The engines continued their quiet beat with no indication of an added work load. The boat didn't move other than its drift before the light breeze. Nothing.

David shifted into neutral, then to forward. Again, no change in the tempo of the engines' strokes, and again the boat showed no sign of response.

"I think I knocked the props off or broke the drive shafts. It sounds and feels like both engines are just free-wheeling. I'm afraid I need a tow into Knife River. Theirs is the only marina nearby equipped for this size boat."

Ben checked the towline to the rescue boat, and David made sure his end was fast to his boat's prow. The trip back to Knife River was slow, and it took the remainder of the day for the two boats to make harbor.

"Hi, David, Ben," Jimmy, the manager and primary mechanic at the marina, greeted them as they pulled into docking spaces five, six, and seven. "Took you longer than I thought it would. I heard your call over the radio this morning and expected you by mid-afternoon."

"I must have lost my rudders," David hollered from his boat. "We had to go slow, because the boat kept slewing back and forth, and it didn't respond to the wheel at all."

By this time, Ben and the others in the rescue boat had secured David's boat to the dock and were on their way out of the harbor. David climbed up on the walkway and slowly made his way to where Jimmy stood waiting.

"How soon can you get to this, Jim?" he wanted to know.

Jimmy playfully jabbed at his ribs. "I knew you'd be in a hurry. I've already got the slings set up. All we have to do is tow *Crusader, Too* over to the landing berth, and we can lift her out of the water. I'd guess we're going to be looking at significant damage. Those rocky shoals can really do a job on the drive mechanisms, you know."

After an hour of maneuvering and jostling the boat into position, the two men were ready to lift the disabled *Crusader, Too* from the water. Slowly the cables on the crane tightened, and the hull came clear of the water. David stood back, his spirits sagging as he saw the damage.

"Well, you can see right away that both props are gone, but I don't think that is the worst of it," Jimmy said without a lot of emotion.

He swung the boom of the crane so that *Crusader, Too* was suspended over dry ground. Then he climbed out of the crane's cab, and both he and David walked under the boat's belly to inspect it more closely.

"Yep, just what I was afraid of," Jimmy intoned, once again trying not create too much despair. "You see up there? The ends of your shafts are missing. My guess is that when you hit the shoal, you were traveling at a pretty good clip. Must have snapped both shafts completely off and then they pulled out of their housings. They're laying on the bottom of the lake now." He couldn't help but shake his head, and David wondered if he was shaking it because he felt sorry for him or couldn't believe his stupidity.

Jimmy continued. "Completely knocked both rudders off, too."

All David could do was stare for a couple of minutes, then he asked the question.

"How long?"

"Two weeks, at least," Jimmy answered. "I'll do what I can from this end, but we have a lot of parts to order. We're a small operation here compared to places like Bayfield. We have to wait our turn, but I'll see what I can do to speed things up. Sorry about that."

Up to this time, it hadn't occurred to David that he had no way to get home. His car was still parked at the Silver Bay marina. That would be a long walk.

"Hey, Jim," he hollered at Jimmy's retreating figure. "What time are you off today? I could use a ride into Two Harbors."

Jimmy turned and smiled. "I thought you might. I'm on overtime right now, so let's go. I suppose your car is up at the other marina. I'll give you a ride up there. It'll be good to have an excuse to go up and scout out the competition," and he smiled again.

CHAPTER
THIRTY-TWO

AFTER THE SUCCESSFUL TEST RUN AT THE OLD RAILROAD TRESTLE, Zaim and his four companions stayed close to their wilderness shack. A week passed, and no one came calling. It was obvious that their explosion had gone undetected.

"Tomorrow, we are going fishing," he announced to his cohorts.

"Fishing?" Murad was surprised by Zaim's announcement. "What has fishing got to do with anything? Last week it was blowing up a bridge in the woods, now it's fishing. When do we act?"

"Easy, Murad. We are getting close. Tomorrow we will act the part of trout fishermen. The weather is supposed to be calm, and there will be many boats being launched at the DNR landing in Two Harbors. I've got an open boat rented. We'll leave the marina in Knife River and motor up to Two Harbors. We can enter the harbor, and if we act like we're fishing, we can scout the docks.

The final plan will be to approach the docks in the dark, using the same kind of open boat. This is just a test run in the daylight."

Murad was appeased, and began preparing supper for the group. He thought, *When the time comes, I'll show them I can do more than cook.*

FOUR-THIRTY THE NEXT MORNING, ZAIM WOKE THE OTHERS and ignored their grumbling. After a hasty breakfast of strong, black coffee, bread, and cheese, they headed toward Two Harbors in the silver Land Cruiser that the four men had used before Zaim's arrival. They motored through the small town to the burg of Knife River, and Zaim turned onto the road leading to the marina. There, they were greeted by the marina manager.

143

"Good morning," Zaim said with a warm smile. "I have an eighteen-foot boat rented for the day. We plan to do a little trout fishing near the Two Harbors breakwater. Is the boat ready?"

Jimmy, the manager, looked at the group with curiosity.

"It's ready. The day should be calm and sunny. No weather in the forecast. Have you been on the lake before?" he asked.

Zaim answered, "Oh, yes, many times. The fishing is always good off the breakwater." The other men looked away to hide their faces at his comments.

Jimmy helped them down to the boat, noticing that their fishing rods were more suited for ponds and small lakes, and that the lures attached to and wound around the poles in rat's nests of monofilament were floating Rappalas, not something you'd ever use on Lake Superior.

As the five motored out of the harbor, Jimmy had to smile. *Well, the trout will be safe today, at least from that bunch.*

Once clear of the harbor, the boat encountered smooth, regularly spaced swells that rhythmically lifted and then dropped the boat every few seconds. Murad leaned over the boat's gunwale and lost his breakfast.

"It is bad enough that we are stranded up in the woods," he complained "but now we have to endure this torture. And for what?" he demanded.

"When the time comes, we will be entering the harbor during the night," Zaim reminded him. "Then you will appreciate what we are doing today. Anyway, get used to this. The night we move may be rougher than this. Then what are you going to do, Murad?"

The other three men took no pity on Murad. They were not experiencing the churning stomach and reeling head associated with seasickness, and they found it fun to add to his miseries with comments about the up and down motion.

As they neared the entrance to the harbor where the ore docks were located, Zaim said "Okay, each of you pick up a rod. Cast out the lure and appear to be fishing. We're going to see how close we can get to the base of the docks in broad daylight. It shouldn't be too difficult. There are two other boats trolling near there."

Each man picked up a rod and attempted to unravel the puzzle of tangled line, and Zaim slowed the motor to almost no speed. The boat glided into the calm water of the harbor.

CHAPTER
THIRTY-THREE

INCLUDING THE WEEK BEFORE HIS ACCIDENT when small craft advisories were up and the week since David ran his boat onto the rock shoal in Castle Danger, he had been on the water one hour out of the past fifteen days. He was tired of being stranded on land, but Jimmy had said it would be another day or so before his boat was ready for the water. His tiny apartment was too cramped, and the Twins baseball team was on a losing streak. He wanted to get on the water again, maybe take the trip to Cornucopia, Wisconsin, he had planned before grounding *Crusader, Too.*

At sunrise, he decided to take a walk to the breakwater, and he picked up his binoculars from their shelf. He figured he might as well see if there was any action on the docks that morning. The *Edgar Speere* was supposed to be in port again today to take on a load of ore pellets.

As he walked to the DNR landing, he passed by *Crusader*, his boat's namesake, and ran his hands over the cypress planking of her hull. She was a museum piece now, propped up on dry land, never to return to the water. The boat was forty feet long with a covered deck and a pilothouse perched at the very rear, and he wondered what it must have been like to work on a boat like that during the heyday of herring fishing on the lake.

She had been out of Knife River then, and each day from ice out to freeze up her owner and his family would take her onto the cold waters of Lake Superior. They would travel up to three miles from shore, in rain, snow, sunshine, or if the lake was calm or churning. There they would locate the buoys marking their set nets and would begin hauling them over the boat's transom, stripping the sil-

146

very, blue-finned herring that were hung up by their gills entwined in the mesh.

Sometimes they would return to shore with as much as a ton of fish, and then they would begin cleaning and salting them, readying them for market. David wondered if he could have done that, or would it have been too much for his physical makeup.

He continued on to the breakwater, stopping where the concrete barrier jettied out into the lake, and he looked down at the algae-covered rocks. He was mesmerized by how the dark-green filaments waved back and forth in the water like green hair. He remembered that the biology teacher in the school where he had taught had told him it was one of the few places where he could get a pure sample of *Ulothrix*, and he wondered why he remembered such inconsequential trivia as that.

David continued his unhurried stroll out onto the breakwater until he reached the small building on stilts at the end of the concrete that housed the warning light and horn. He sat down and began to scope the docks, wondering if he would recognize any of the workers emptying the railroad cars into hoppers atop the massive steel structure.

When he put the glasses down, he took in the panoramic scene. There were four fishing boats circling back and forth in the dock's shadow, and one of them caught his attention. Its five occupants seemed to be having a difficult time, and it was apparent to David that they had no idea what they were doing. He lifted his glasses to get a better view.

Jibril had gotten tired of what some people might call fishing. He couldn't seem to keep the line from getting wound around the eyes of his rod, and because the lure continually skipped across the surface of the lake, it spiraled in a pattern that twisted his line into kinks and coils. He reeled in the lure as best he could, and picked up his binoculars. He thought he might as well amuse himself by watching the tourists on the breakwater through his binoculars.

Just before Jibril lifted the glasses to his eyes, David brought his own binoculars to focus on the open boat and its occupants. At that instant, Jibril's face was clearly visible, and a hot streak like an electric shock jolted up David's back. He instantly recognized the make-believe fisherman as one of the people he had smuggled out of the country almost three months ago. He dropped his glasses in disbelief.

Almost simultaneously, Jabril spotted David on the breakwater. Recognition was immediate. Together, they raised their glasses again, and the image they each saw would have been comical if it weren't so serious. There was no doubt each knew the other had seen and recognized him.

"It's him! It's the captain who dropped me off on the Canadian shore!" Jabril excitedly shouted to Zaim.

"What are you talking about?" Zaim demanded.

"The captain of the boat that took us to Cananda, he's standing on the breakwater. I saw him!"

"So he's there. So what?" Zaim questioned. "He lives here. I'd expect him to be around."

"No, no," Jabril exclaimed in a state of panic. "He saw me. He recognized me. I know it. He was looking at me through binoculars just before I put mine to my eyes. He dropped them down, and then brought them up in a hurry. We were looking at each other face to face. I could tell by his expression he recognized me. He was shocked. I know it."

Zaim was clearly troubled by what Jabril said.

"We can't leave in a hurry. That would be a clear tip off, but now I wonder how much he knows. Let's make one more pass by the docks as though we are fishing. I've seen what I wanted to see, so we can leave. We'll not hurry, and it will give me time to think."

CHAPTER
THIRTY-FOUR

WHEN DEIDRE OPENED HER EYES AT 5:30 A.M., her first thought was of the conversation she had last week with Agent Erickson. She wondered why she hadn't heard from him for several days, and even before she rolled out of bed, she resolved to call his office after the deputies had presented the usual morning report.

After her mandatory first cup of black coffee and two pieces of whole wheat toast, she made her way to the office. The morning reports were what might be expected for a small town: a complaint of teenagers loitering under a street light at 11:30 last night, a barking dog creating a nuisance, old Charlie needing a ride to jail so he could sleep off his drunk, and a report of a suspicious person walking in the alley between Fifth Avenue and Sixth Street. It turned out to be Judge Henry looking for his Siamese cat that had made a run for it.

"Are there any other issues that came up last night," she asked her deputies.

"I think I spotted something that might be of more interest than Judge Henry's cat," Ben said, his face serious.

"Just before I came in, I stopped near the breakwater and spotted something we should note." He went on to relay to them what he saw.

"The lake was calm this morning, and I wanted to see the sunrise. The trout must be biting after the big blow we had a week ago, because the parking lot was full of boat trailers and pickups.

"A few of the fishermen were trolling past the docks on their way out to the big lake, except for one boat. It kept weaving in and out of the slips between the docks. The men in the boat were the worst fishermen I've ever seen. It was almost like a cartoon, but I

149

don't think they were interested in catching anything. They weren't breaking any laws, but they sure didn't belong out there."

"Thanks, Ben. I'll relay that information to my contact at the FBI."

Deidre took the reports into her office, not in too much of a hurry to re-examine the details other than what Ben had reported. She was about to dial the FBI office in Duluth, had her hand on the phone, when it rang.

"This is Sheriff Johnson," she answered.

"Hey, Deidre. That was quick. You must have been sitting with your hand on the phone, waiting for me to call."

In a moment of playfulness, Deidre asked, "To whom am I speaking, please?"

There was a long pause on the other end of the line. "This is John, John Erickson, Special Agent John Erickson."

Deidre let out a giggle. "Hi, John. As a matter of fact, I did have my hand on the phone. It's been awhile since we talked, and I'm wondering if anything's happening we should know about on this end."

"Have your deputies noticed anything that might make you wonder if something's going on?" John wanted to know.

"Well, that's what we needed to talk about. One deputy reported that he saw men early this morning who match the description of those up in Brimson. They were in an open fishing boat down by the docks. Seems they weren't having too much luck with their floating lures and pan-fish rods."

"Did the guys in the boat see your deputy watching them? That would throw up a red flag right away."

"No. It was Ben who saw them first. Lately, he's turned out to be one of my best people on this case. He stayed well away from the shoreline the whole time, used his binoculars, and kept an eye on them. He said there never was a time when they looked up to where he was sitting, said they were more concerned about the people on the breakwater than anything else."

Deidre heard an audible escape of air from John's mouth, then a pause.

"My boss talked to our informant this morning. Evidently, he saw the same fishermen Ben did, and he said the same thing you've told me. They really weren't fishing, hardly knew which end of the rod to hold. We're sure they were making a trial run in the daylight. When they carry out their plans, it'll most certainly be at night. The word I get is that whatever's going to happen is going to happen sooner rather than later."

"John, can't you tell me who this informant is? He must have a room or something in the area if he has been able to observe the docks. It'd help us to know."

Without hesitation, John lied. "I don't know who he is. The upper level won't share that information with me, because they say their source is too vital to this operation, and they don't want his cover blown. Sorry."

Deidre knew it was no use pushing any further.

She was about to say goodbye when John asked, "Have you been keeping David Craine in your sights. We have an idea of what he's up to, but we want to make sure you don't get so involved with this other issue that you let him slip away."

That was a sensitive issue with Deidre. "We have a close watch on him. Don't worry. It's been pretty easy lately. He piled his boat up a week or so ago, and it's in dry dock in Knife River. About all he does is hang out down by the breakwater and have a beer or two at Dunnigan's."

"Good," John responded matter-of-factly. "Just make sure you know where he is."

Deidre didn't like the sound of that, but there was nothing she could do.

"John, I have to go. I've got a couple of meetings with board members this morning. Keep in touch, please."

"Sure will," John replied. "Say, any chance we could meet for supper sometime after work? Maybe the place that served those great hamburgers," and he chortled.

"That'd be nice. Let's do that sometime. We'll talk later." And Deidre hung up the phone.

She leaned her elbows on her desk, resting her head in her hands for many minutes. With all that was going on in her usually quiet county, she felt like a piece of driftwood being carried downstream, and she realized there was little she could do except go with the flow, keep her guard up, and be ready to react to whatever developed. She wished she could go on the offensive, make the first move. This idea of waiting for the shoe to fall and then reacting was unnerving.

CHAPTER
THIRTY-FIVE

ZAIM AND HIS CREW OF WOULD-BE FISHERMEN returned to the Knife River Marina. Jimmy met them at the dock.

"Hi, fellas, any luck?" Jimmy always seemed to be upbeat and was known for his banter with fishermen when they return to his dock. The information he gathered usually was passed on to others, and he was known for his knowledge of what was happening on the lake.

"No, nothing," Zaim snapped back. "Will you please help us unload? We are very much in a hurry."

Jimmy jumped to help them. It was evident they were not in the mood to talk, but he thought perhaps he could give them some pointers that might create a return customer.

"Say, I happened to notice your fishing rigs. They seem to be a little light for the kind of fishing we do here. And your lures, nothing is going to strike on the surface in these waters. Most people use spoons or sinking lures. Trout are deep-water fish. You know, there are several experienced fishing guides who live nearby. I could line one of them up for you, if you'd want."

Zaim glared at Jimmy. "We'll remember that the next time. Help us load our gear in the car, and we'll be on our way."

Jimmy wasn't one to be easily dissuaded.

"Where you off to, anyway? Staying around here?"

Zaim looked at him, annoyed by the man's persistence. "No, we are from a way off. We'll not be here much longer." He turned to the others. "Hurry, we want to be home by dark."

The five men hurriedly climbed into the SUV and sped away, leaving Jimmy waving the dust from in front of his face.

Away from the marina, Zaim became progressively more agitated.

"Everywhere, questions. What is it with these people that they can't mind their own business? The time can't come soon enough when we can return to our land and our people."

ON THE WAY HOME FROM THE MARINA, Zaim was quieter than usual. His perpetual scowl deepened and he was lost in thought. The others caught the clue that this would not be the time to complain about the backwoods, the mosquitoes, or the lack of decent food. They rode in silence.

Zaim was deeply troubled by what had occurred in the harbor. Had this captain forgotten about the men he had ferried out of the country? What if seeing Jabril had brought back the memory of that night? What if he had found the lost flash drive and not reported it? Surely, if he had their operation would have been shut down by now. What if the captain had opened the drive and now realized its significance? What if he was getting ready to report the whole affaire to the authorities?

These and what seemed like a hundred other scenarios ran through Zaim's mind as he slid the SUV around the loose gravel-coated corners of the dirt road in Brimson. By the time he reached the hunting shack, he had made a decision.

The men trooped into the confines of the building and threw their odd array of fishing gear in a corner. The lines were completely entangled and some of the hooks hung loose, swaying from side to side like pendulums ticking off time. It would take hours for an experienced angler to untangle the mess, but it didn't matter. Zaim and his men would not go fishing again.

"Sit down," he ordered. "We must talk about an action now. I don't think we can ignore this captain any longer. Although we don't know exactly how much he knows about us, I think we have to take him out, just as we did that man, Herminio. It shouldn't be too diffi-

154

cult. There are five of us and only one of him. When we saw him he was alone."

"We don't know his name, Zaim, let alone where he lives. Do you have information we don't know about?" Jabril asked, a serious look on his face.

"No, but Two Harbors is a small community. Jabril, do you remember the name of the boat on which you were taken out of this country?"

Jabril looked at Zaim, and his eyes narrowed.

"How could I forget. It was *Crusader, Too.* They name even their boats to honor those who slaughtered out ancestors."

"I'm going back to the marina tomorrow morning and see if I can get the information we need from its operator. He seemed anxious to talk when we left. Perhaps he will still be in a talkative mood, and I'll be able to find out something about this captain. Murad, get supper ready. I've got to have some time to think this out."

ZAIM SPENT A SLEEPLESS NIGHT. They were so close to completing their mission, and now, this captain could upset all of their plans if he went to the authorities with what he knew. Zaim was quite sure he hadn't already done that, because no one had yet confronted them.

He drifted off to sleep sometime before sunrise, and the sun was already high in the sky when he awoke. After a quick cup of traditional thick, black coffee and a biscuit, Zaim climbed into his Ford SUV and headed back to Knife River.

It was about a forty-minute drive to the marina from their camp, and Zaim drove the speed limit. He saw no reason to speed and risk being stopped by a zealous deputy. He pulled into the marina parking lot at 11:00 a.m. as if he had all the time in the world. Jimmy came out of his office.

"Did you forget something yesterday?" Jimmy asked Zaim, not quite sure how his question would be answered.

Zaim was all charm. "No, but I have been thinking about your offer yesterday to help us learn to fish. It must have been obvious to you that we know nothing about that subject," and he smiled a broad smile.

"Hey, great! The first thing I'd recommend is hiring a charter captain to take you out on the lake. There are a few out of this harbor who would be happy to teach you the ropes."

Just then Zaim noticed a boat near where they stood. It was moored in one of the berths, pointing toward the lake as if it were ready to sail at a moment's notice. Across its stern was its name, *Crusader, Too.*

"That would be so very helpful," Zaim answered Jimmy with enthusiasm. Then he added, "I would like to go on a large boat, like that one over there sometime. Does its captain take fishing trips?"

"Oh, you mean the captain of *Crusader, Too.* No, that would be David Craine. He doesn't fish, just runs around the lakes in his boat. He stops here and there, loves the water and mostly lives on his boat all season long. Going on two weeks ago, he ran his boat aground, and I finished the repair work this morning," Jimmy volunteered.

"Does he ever take passengers?" Zaim pressed.

"Only close friends once in a while. Mostly, he stays to himself. David isn't what you'd call a loner, but he likes to be alone on his boat most of the time. Actually, he likes being alone a lot, I guess. He stays in a small apartment above Dunnigan's bar in Two Harbors when he can't be on the water."

"This David Craine must be an interesting man. Pity he doesn't take on charters. I'd like to have experienced his love for the water," Zaim lied. "His boat is here now. That must mean he is at his home. Do you think he could be persuaded?"

Jimmy shook his head. "The only reason his boat is here now is that I just finished repairing it. He's coming for it first thing in the morning. I know he won't be talked into taking on a charter."

"Then do you have a listing of other captains I might contact?"

Jimmy pulled a folded flyer from his back pocket and thrust it at Zaim. "Here, take this with you. It lists all of the charter captains who use this harbor, along with their phone numbers. Any one of them would be great."

"Perhaps in a few days I and my friends will come back. Thank you for your advice. You have been very kind and helpful."

Zaim extended his hand to Jimmy, then climbed into his SUV and left Jimmy standing on the beach, confused at the abrupt change in the man's attitude.

CHAPTER
THIRTY-SIX

THE DAY AFTER HIS SURPRISE SIGHTING OF JABRIL, the same day that Zaim paid his visit to Jimmy, David sat on the far side of the point of land jutting out into Lake Superior, the side away from the ore docks, and rested his face in his hands. The concrete bench placed in memory of some forgotten person was cold beneath his butt, and he shivered a little. The sun breaking above the lake's distant horizon always fascinated him. He relished that moment before the sun actually became visible when the lake and the sky were separated by a faint line that, if he used his imagination, appeared to reveal the slight curvature of the earth's surface. Then, as if by the stroke of an artist's brush, the sky first turned pink, a rose-colored fire ball rose, its rays warming everything upon which they fell. David never tired of this magnificent display of nature, and he wondered why amid this beauty so much hatred and pain filled the world.

He rested at that spot for as long as it took the sun to rise several degrees above the horizon. Slowly, he stood, feeling old for the first time he could remember. Too much had happened to him, he thought. It seemed as if his life had been filled with peaks of unbounded joy, only to have had that joy shattered every time.

During that quiet time, when peace was so close he thought he could reach out and touch it, he was acutely aware that peace always had seemed to elude him. Even as a child he saw the glass as half empty rather than half full. He wondered how his childhood played into that, the poverty in which he had been raised, the fact that he had grown up in a wilderness setting with no playmates. He was aware that throughout his whole life he had seen the dark side of life rather than the sunny side.

David replayed the happiness of having graduated from college with a teaching degree, then the disappointment of discovering he couldn't save the world. He remembered how discouraged he was to first discover that too many members of society held his profession in such low esteem. This, of course, spilled over into their children's, his students', respect for education, and he remembered wondering at the end of every school year if he had made any difference at all in their lives.

He replayed the joy of meeting Alicia, of falling in love, of their wedding, and he remembered the anguish of mourning her death. He still hadn't shed the pain of the day the highway patrol officer came to his home to inform him of her accident and death. And David wondered how different his life would have been if life's circumstances had been different.

He remembered the freedom of sailing the Great Lakes, the joy of having the wind blow through his thinning hair, the freedom of moving from place to place, the peace of being rocked to sleep by the gentle rocking of his boat at its mooring.

He wondered where all of this mess he was embroiled in was going to end.

He had been so deep in thought, David suddenly realized he had followed the rocky trail completely around the point and was now standing near the parking lot opposite the ore docks. He abruptly changed direction and headed for his apartment. There, he poured a cup of stale coffee and looked out the window at Main Street. Businesses, what few there were remaining in his depressed town, were being prepared to open, and people were beginning to follow their routines.

He took his cell phone from his pocket and hit the speed dial.

"Hello, Jimmy? This is David."

"Well, hello," he heard Jimmy's cheerful voice. "I was getting ready to call you. Worked late last night on *Crusader, Too*. She's set to go. Why don't you come down this morning, say 9:30. We'll set her in the slip and see how she floats. The two of us can take her for a spin on the lake, see how she handles. Okay?"

"Hey, Jim. This is the best news I've had in a long while. See you then."

David pulled into the Knife River Marina's parking lot. There sat his beloved boat on wooden blocking, ready to have the slings placed under her belly, ready to be lifted and then set into the water.

"David, you're early! But then I guess this has been a long wait for you. I've got to help those guys over there back down and unload their fishing boat. Then we can get at *Crusader, Too.*"

David watched as Jimmy expertly wheeled the twenty-foot boat on its trailer down the ramp and the four fishermen loaded their gear into it. Their motor started without a hitch, and they were off. Soon they were out of sight, and Jimmy began to unroll the straps of the sling. He attached their ends to the hook on a cable swinging from the boom of the crane,

When all was prepared, Jimmy climbed into its cab and started the engine of the crane. Slowly the cable tightened, and the slings cinched together tightly under the boat's hull. David saw a small crack of daylight appear between his boat and its blocking, and she was raised high enough that Jimmy could swing her out over the water.

He concentrated on every move, ignoring David, the sea gulls that looped around, the boat that motored into the harbor, and he rotated the crane on its base. *Crusader, Too* was perched over the water, ready to be lowered into her element.

With a gentle splash, she was home.

David jumped from the edge of the slip onto her deck, moved to the wheelhouse, and turned the keys, first to one engine, then to the other. The sound they made was pure music to his ears.

By this time Jimmy had climbed down from the cab of the crane and was ready to jump on board. Before *Crusader, Too* had a chance to rub against the worn tire bumpers of the pier, he leaped and lightly landed on the deck.

"Let me take the controls for a bit," he said to David. "I want to see what she feels like, check for any vibration. That was quite the collision you had with the reef off Castle Danger. Bent the shafts pretty bad."

David turned the helm over to Jimmy without a word. He was almost jealous because someone else was touching his prize, and Jimmy eased the boat out of the harbor. Out on the big lake, he slowly ratcheted up the throttles until *Crusader, Too* was spewing a rooster-tail wake behind her.

"Feels good to me," he yelled over the roar of the engines and the wind whipping by their ears. "I can't feel any vibes at all. Smooth as all get out."

He throttled back to half speed. "Here, you take it and tell me what you think." David took the wheel. He, too, opened up the throttles and felt the surge of power. After making several wide turns, one way and then the other, David tightened the radius until he was satisfied that all of the controls were functioning.

"Jimmy, you're a genius. I think she handles better than when she was new. I can't thank you enough."

Jimmy smiled a crooked grin. "You haven't got my bill yet."

"Tell you what, whatever it is, it's worth it. I'll be back tomorrow to square up with you and to take *Crusader* back to Silver Bay. I think it's time for me to take a trip to the other side of the lake, Cornucopia maybe. I've got some things to straighten out in my mind, and I need some time away."

With that he turned his boat's prow toward Knife Island and the harbor behind it.

CHAPTER
THIRTY-SEVEN

DEIDRE REALIZED THERE WAS NO WORSE STRESS-INDUCING situation than having immense responsibility and having little control over the circumstances, and the weight of her job was beginning to take its toll. She was caught between too many factions: the FBI, the men holed up in the shack in Brimson, and David Craine. What was causing her to lose sleep was that she didn't know enough about the men up north, she was close to David, and she didn't quite know what to make of Special Agent John Erickson.

That night she sat, trying to relax with a vodka tonic, but it wasn't working. She felt like a wound-up spring that was about to be released with no restraints. Her phone on the counter rang, and she lunged up from her chair to answer.

"Deidre Johnson speaking," she barked into the mouthpiece. She was surprised to hear John on the other end.

"Hi, Deidre. Just wanted to call to see how things are going for you. I'm wondering if everything is still calm on your end."

Deidre felt an unexpected wave of relief flow over her at the sound of John's voice, and she wasn't used to feeling that response.

"John, I don't know what it is, but I simply can't let go of this idea that something not good is going to rear its head, and soon. Do you have any inkling of what's going to happen, and when?"

"Deidre, I don't think anyone knows what exactly is going to take place, or when for that matter. All we can do is be ready for it. I'll say, though, things are getting a little harried here at the office in Duluth. Something is in the wind. I have a meeting labeled urgent with that old goat, Enos Pratt, first thing in the morning. I might have more to share with you by the time it is over. Would you like to do lunch someplace on the shore? We can talk then."

The invitation sounded exceptionally welcome to Deidre, and she hoped her acceptance didn't sound too eager. "I'd love that," she blurted out. "How about that place that makes beef belly bombs? You seemed to survive the last time," and she laughed.

"That'll be fine. I'll see you there at 12:30. You'll recognize me. I'll be the guy who looks like an FBI agent," and he laughed too.

AT TWENTY MINUTES AFTER TWELVE, Deidre pulled into the parking lot of the restaurant. She recognized John's car in the lot, and she also recognized the same feeling of mixed relief and anticipation she experienced last night on the phone.

She entered the dining area and saw John sitting at a table in the far corner. It surprised her that her breath caught slightly in her throat as she crossed the floor toward their table. John stood and pulled out one of the chairs for Deidre. She sat and he helped her pull it up to the table's edge.

"John, it's so nice to see you. I find myself more and more restless and apprehensive these days. It's like I know something's going to explode, but I don't know what or when."

John reached under his chair and pulled out a brown manila envelope.

"Believe it or not, Director Pratt gave this to me to go over with you. I think you may finally get some of the answers you've been searching for."

Deidre took the envelope from him and began to open the seal.

"You can look this over right now if you'd like, but I don't think we should discuss it here. This is such sensitive information that I wouldn't want anyone to get even a piece of it. Why don't you browse through while we wait for our food, and then maybe we can return to your office? I'll try to answer any questions you might have. I think after you've read the pages, you'll agree that we must begin to move our assets into place."

Just then the waiter came to their table. Suddenly Deidre had lost her appetite, but she ordered a cold tuna-macaroni salad. John ordered a hamburger, well done, and fries. The waiter left with their order and Deidre began to read:

CONFIDENTIAL MESSAGE: Sheriff Deidre Johnson

From Enos Pratt, Director of Duluth Offices
Federal Bureau of Investigation
August 23, 2011

For the past several months our department has been aware of a terrorist cell inhabiting an abandoned building some twenty miles north of Two Harbors, Minnesota. Based on credible information from an involved informant, there is sufficient cause to believe that the ore docks in Two Harbors will be subject to an attack in the very near future.

If this action is successful the terrorists will accomplish at least three objectives: (1) They will effectively shut down a significant link in the flow of raw materials from the Iron Range to the eastern steel mills. (2) They will demonstrate to our citizenry that not only are our largest cities vulnerable, but also our rural, out-of-the way villages, striking uncertainty into people across the country. (3) If successful, they will be emboldened to carry out more attacks of this nature.

For these reasons, it is necessary that they be thwarted in their efforts. Therefore, I am appointing Special Agent John Erickson as liaison between our office and the sheriff's office of Lake County.

Sheriff Johnson will designate however many of her personnel as necessary to provide around-the-clock surveillance of the ore docks and to report any suspicious activity to Agent Erickson. He will be housed, anonymously, in one of the local motels.

Sheriff Johnson will continue to keep David Craine under surveillance, reporting to Agent Erickson any unusual contact he has with persons recognized as being unfamiliar in the area.

Under no circumstances is Sheriff Johnson to attempt to apprehend the suspects or anyone directly connected to this case. All matters will remain under the jurisdiction of the FBI.

Agent Erickson is authorized to share information as it relates to this case and as he deems necessary for Sheriff Johnson to carry out her mandate.

Signed Enos Pratt, Director

By the time Deidre had finished reading the report, or as she thought, directive, she could hardly touch her food when it was placed before her. John had eaten all of his burger and was in the process of mopping up ketchup with his last French fries. He finished his iced tea.

"Well, what do you think?" he asked.

"I think I should get back to my office," and she pushed her untouched food away and stood up, the manila folder in her hand.

CHAPTER
THIRTY-EIGHT

DAVID WANTED TO GET HIS LIFE BACK ON TRACK, to live peacefully on his boat, to have the freedom to travel the Great Lakes as he had in past years. As he arrived back at his apartment after being on the lake with Jimmy, David wondered when that day would arrive, if ever.

One laborious step at a time, he climbed the back stairs leading to the second floor. He couldn't remember feeling this tired ever before, and he chocked it up to all that had been going on in his life of late. First, it was the business of Herminio contacting him and talking him into make a decision the he regretted. Then it was Herminio's phone call and his subsequent murder.

As David climbed the stairs, he stopped, not because he was out of breath, but because he was so deep in thought that his feet didn't receive the message from his brain to move. He thought about the flash drive found on his boat after ferrying the Latinos north, and with that thought, drops of perspiration formed on his forehead. He wiped them away with his shirt sleeve.

The grinding image of his boat being run aground on the reef off Castle Danger caused his stomach to knot. That moment of inattentiveness could have ended much worse than it did, and David knew how lucky he was to have escaped with only significant damage to his *Crusader, Too*. She could have been totally wrecked. Worse yet, he could have been killed.

Then two days ago, the sighting in the harbor of one of the six illegals he had taken to Canada was more than he could fathom, especially in light of what he knew was on the flash drive. David realized something was going to have to be done, and soon.

166

He forced himself to continue to the top of the stairs, and he turned down the hall to the left, to his door. The ancient wood flooring creaked underfoot, and he reached out for the door knob. He was brought to an abrupt halt. The door to his apartment was open a crack, only a fraction of an inch, but he could tell it was not latched. His mind spun as he tried to remember if he had locked it on his way out. He couldn't remember if he had or hadn't.

With his heart in his throat, David thrust the door open and stepped back, ready to run—from what he was not sure. No one burst out at him. The room was well lit by the bright sun from outside, and he could see that it was empty. Nevertheless, he almost tiptoed inside.

After carefully looking around, he concluded that nothing was missing and that he had forgotten to close the door completely when he left. To David, this was another sign that the pressure of his situation was finally wearing him down. He picked up his cell phone and dialed Jimmy at the marina.

"Hey, Jimmy," he said into the speaker, glad to hear his friend's voice. "Any chance you can have my boat fueled and ready to go early tomorrow, say about 7:00? I'd like to move her up to the Silver Bay Marina."

"Better yet, Dave, you could help me out. There's a boat up there that needs some major engine work. The owners have asked me to take a look at it. It'll probably have to be towed down here to Knife River, but they want an estimate of what it's going to cost them before we start the job.

"How about I run your boat up to Silver Bay for you today? It's still early. You can drive up, meet me at the marina, and then give me a lift back home."

At that point any reason to get away from his apartment was good news to David.

"Sounds good to me, Jim. What time should I be there? I don't want to sit around the marina office too long. I don't feel like chitchatting with strangers today."

"Let's see. It's 2:00 now. Give me a half hour to get things cleared up here, and to be on the conservative side, give me another two hours to make it to Silver Bay by boat. Say I'll meet you at the marina at 4:30. On the way back we can stop at one of the restaurants along the shore for dinner."

David thought the idea a good one. The one thing he hated about being alone was meal time, and it would be good to have someone to visit with. "Great," he answered. "See you then."

But before he could hang up, Jimmy threw a friendly jab. "Don't worry. Davy Boy, I'll steer clear of Castle Danger." He guffawed and hung up before David could answer.

David grabbed his tattered Minnesota Twins hat from where it hung on the back of one of his kitchen chairs and jammed it on his head. When he left his apartment, he made sure to close the door and double checked that it was locked.

AT 3:50 IN THE AFTERNOON, DAVID GOT IN HIS CAR, buckled his seat belt and turned the ignition key. The car started, but David wondered how much longer the old wreck would continue to run. He never had been much of a car guy and hadn't always serviced it on time. He shrugged and pulled out of his parking space, left Two Harbors, and headed up Highway 61 to Silver Bay.

David couldn't help but notice the natural beauty, the rugged shore line of Lake Superior's north shore, the rocky crags split by deep fissures, the streams at the bottoms of deep cuts, all of them making for a wonderful but formidable landscape.

David was lost in his thoughts as he wound along the curvy and sometimes treacherous two-lane road until he reached the bridge at the Gooseberry River. The entrance to a state park was just before that bridge, and that time of year there were always pedestrians wandering around, usually not being attentive to approaching traffic. David slowed a bit. He had experienced enough traumas in his life lately without running some tourist down.

From the Gooseberry River it was only a few minutes to the marina in Silver Bay. When he arrived he was grateful to see Jimmy standing by the office, a can of Coke in his hand and a smile on his face. Nearby, *Crusader, Too* rocked in her berth.

Jimmy ambled over to David's car and climbed in without an invitation.

"Hi ya, Davy Boy," he said with a grin. "I made good time, didn't even get hung up at Castle Danger," and he snorted out loud.

"That's a good thing," David shot back. "Otherwise the next repair bill would have been on you," and the men chuckled as David wheeled out of the parking lot and onto the highway.

"I made sure that *Crusader, Too* was gassed up full after I docked. She's all set for you to take off tomorrow. You're pretty low on food and wine though. I thought I'd have a glass or two on the way up here, but couldn't find a drop. Next time, think of me will you?" Jimmy chortled again. Of course Jimmy laughed at almost anything.

David glanced over at Jimmy and saw the mirth in his eyes. "What say we stop at Beaver Bay. There's a new restaurant there. We can have a decent meal, and you can have all the wine or whatever you want. I'm driving and paying so you don't have to worry."

"Can't argue with that."

David pulled over at Beaver Bay, and the two men walked into a nearly deserted room. The sign said "PLEASE WAIT TO BE SEATED," but there was no hostess to be seen. They seated themselves, and in a minute or two she emerged from the kitchen.

"Sorry about that, guys," the young lady apologized. "I'm wearing about three hats today. Word isn't out yet that we're open, and it's kind of slow." She smiled at them and said, "My name's Mary. I'll be your hostess, your waitress, and your bartender today," and she giggled a little, her eyes meeting Jimmy's.

Mary asked if they would like anything to drink. David ordered a glass of water with a lemon slice in it. Jimmy ordered a double vodka tonic. She left two menus before she walked away.

Jimmy shrugged. "Well, you offered," and he laughed.

"Look at these prices. They must be trying to get people in the habit of coming, and then in a few weeks they'll jack them up. Might as well take advantage while we can," he added.

He was right. David hadn't seen that kind of food offered for those kinds of prices in a long time.

"What do you think, Jimmy? The steak and shrimp looks awfully good to me."

"Naw, I like the looks of the walleye dinner. Haven't had that for ages, and maybe another tonic or two before we leave."

Mary emerged from the kitchen.

"Say, you aren't the chef, too?" Jimmy asked.

"No," Mary answered, again seeming to find humor in what Jimmy said. "We do have an excellent chef though. He worked for a big corporate chain before getting sick of the rush and expectations. He's from New York, came here looking for a slower paced life, and found it. Once his reputation gets out, we expect business to boom. Well, what'll you boys have?"

David thought Mary was going to have to class up her act a little if she expected to draw the well-heeled from up and down the Shore.

"I'll have the steak and shrimp, medium rare on the steak, baked potato with sour cream, and salad—balsamic vinaigrette dressing, please."

Mary turned to Jimmy. "Walleye, fried onion rings, cream of wild rice soup, and add a salad, too—both French and bleu cheese dressing, lots of it. Thanks," he said.

David wrinkled his nose. "Why don't you just drive a stake into your heart? There's enough cholesterol there to plug up the water works in Two Harbors." He chastised Jimmy.

Jimmy snorted. "I don't worry about tomorrow, only when my next meal will come. Look at me, skinny as a rail. I can't put on weight even if I want to, just lucky, I guess."

The two men bantered for the next twenty minutes, Jimmy doing a good job of downing his drink and David sipping his water.

He signaled Mary over and ordered a large iced tea with lemon and reclined in the booth.

"This is the first time in ages I've felt relaxed and happy. I've had a lot on my mind lately."

"Oh?" Jimmy asked. "What's getting you down? I haven't noticed you uptight or anything?"

Before David could answer, Mary came from the kitchen, her arms laden with platters of food which she began to dole out at their table.

"Here it is, boys, a meal fit for a king. Dig in."

David sampled one of the shrimp and was struck by how delicious it was. "Mary's right. This chef's great. I don't know what he put on this, but I've never tasted anything like it before. How's your walleye?"

"Absolutely great. Word gets out about this food, and they'll have plenty of business."

The two men ate in silence for a minute or two, and then Jimmy remembered something he was going to tell David.

"I almost forgot. Yesterday five guys came in and rented an eighteen-foot fishing boat from the marina. I'll tell you, they were the worst greenhorns I've had in for a long time. Said they wanted to go trout fishing up around Two Harbors breakwater, but they didn't know which way was up as far as fishing. They had a handful of ultra light rods you and I would use for pan fish and a few floating lures. I offered some advice, but they brushed me off. Naturally, when they came back, they hadn't caught anything, but this time I could tell they were in a different mood, in a hurry and not saying much at all, even to each other.

Then, this morning one of them came back right after we dropped your boat in the water and you'd left. His whole attitude had changed. He wanted to charter a boat to go fishing and singled out *Crusader, Too*. I told him you didn't do charters, but he asked a few more questions about you. I told him where you live, but that you'd probably not be interested. Thought I'd give you a heads up incase he decides to try to talk you into it."

David had a mouthful of steak halfway to his mouth and stopped mid-movement. A knot instantaneously formed in his gut and he could feel sweat form and run down his back.

"What did this guy look like," he demanded of Jimmy.

Jimmy's eyes widened as he instantly picked up on the change in his friend demeanor.

"I don't know. He was just a guy, tall, black hair. I suppose kind of darker skin than most around here."

"Did he have an accent?"

"Yeah, he did speak a little differently, but I don't usually notice those things. We get all kinds of people coming and going at the marina. I just don't pay much attention."

"What was his attitude like when he came back, nervous, agitated?" David pressed on.

By this time, Jimmy knew something wasn't right with his dinner partner. "That's what was strange. The day before this guy didn't want anything to do with me. In fact, I'd say he was just plain rude. He seemed to be the leader, giving orders, and trying to hurry the others. Now, today, he comes back all full of charm and smiles. I don't know if he was on something or what, but he was sure a lot calmer and smoother this morning than yesterday."

There was a moment of total silence. Jimmy spoke again. "Come on, Davey. What the heck's happening? I can tell something's eating at you. What is it?"

David shoved the bite of steak in his mouth. "Nothing. Nothing's going on. Just forget it, and let's finish our meal."

The two men ate in silence, David's food suddenly having lost its taste.

RETURNING TO HER OFFICE AFTER HAVING MET WITH JOHN, Deidre was more confused than ever, confused over the letter from Enos Pratt, the FBI director in Duluth, but almost more confused over her feelings about John having been moved to a hotel in Two

Harbors and the directive stating she was to work closely with him.

Somehow, that directive provided instant comfort to her, and she was a little perturbed at herself for feeling that way. It was as though her independence and self-assurance were being eroded one small piece at a time. She didn't like that.

Deidre opened the envelope from Director Pratt, slowly read it one more time, and tried to find any kind of clue she had missed in her first reading.

She could understand the bit about the terrorist threat to the docks. Ever since 9/11 her department had been on a higher alert concerning those towering steel structures that were vital not only to her community, but also to the nation's steel producing capabilities. It didn't come as a surprise to her that terrorists would see them as a potential target. However, she couldn't understand why the Department of Homeland Security hadn't stepped in to arrest those men holed up in a hunting shack north of the town. It seemed to her that would end the threat in its tracks. Of course there was the argument that data was being gathered from them as long as they kept communicating over the cell phone towers.

She wished she knew more about the logistics of the situation. How had the FBI learned about the impending attack? How had they acquired enough information to be certain this was happening, and how did they know the action was going to be imminent?

These questions weighed heavily on Deidre's mind, but not nearly as heavily as the order to keep David Craine under constant surveillance. What had he done to warrant such close observation, she wondered.

Deidre's memory took a trip back to that day when Mr. Craine had summoned her to his office and had intervened in the hellish life she was enduring. She remembered sharing with him what her home life was like, the threats from her stepfather, the abuse her mother had endured, and finally, the drunken rage that had led to her mother taking them to the women's shelter in Two Harbors.

She remembered her decision to become a law enforcement officer who would make a difference in the lives of those who were beyond helping themselves. She remembered Mr. Craine and his gentle guidance.

Whatever could he have done to plant himself in the scenario outlined in the directive she was studying? It was evident to her that he was somehow entangled in situation, but how? Certainly he could not be considered a terrorist by any stretch of the imagination, and most certainly he had not willingly joined a cell. The thought crossed her mind that he was an agent of some kind working with the FBI, but she thought it not probable at all. At his age, he couldn't possibly meet the requirements of that group.

Deidre placed the letter from Director Pratt back in its envelope and locked it in her desk. She picked up her phone and dialed the number of the Country Inn motel.

"Yes," she said in response to the person who answered. "Will you please connect me to room 210."

CHAPTER
THIRTY-NINE

As ZAIM STEERED HIS VEHICLE AROUND THE dirt curves of the country road, he passed a deputy in his squad car, traveling the opposite direction. Both men nodded to each other. Zaim smiled to himself, thinking if only the officer knew how close he was to being a hero or a dead man.

After the many weeks they had stayed at this location, the dusty driveway was a familiar path for him to follow, and he wheeled up to the ancient building with its flaking logs and falling-out chinking. The dust cloud he stirred up followed him.

Afu and Jibril were sitting in the screened porch, looking bored, and they walked out to meet Zaim.

"Hey, man, that didn't take as long as we thought it would. Did you get any answers?"

Zaim brushed off the question. "Where are the others? We need to talk right now and make a plan. Where are they?"

Zaim had not broken stride and was heading into the house.

"We didn't expect you back this soon, Zaim. Murad and Imad decided to walk down to the river for something to do. They left about twenty minutes ago."

"Jibril, run and catch those two. Are they going native on us, walking down to the river when they should be on the alert incase something were to happen?"

Jibril knew not to argue, and he set off at a trot to retrieve his cabin mates. Zaim spun around to face Afu.

"Get out five of our hand guns. Make sure they are cleaned and that there is a supply of ammunition for each man." Afu didn't wait for more instructions and began to remove the wall board that concealed the hiding place for the weapons.

175

"Bring out four rifles with ammunition as well. We may have to take a long shot if we are not lucky," Zaim directed Afu as he worked assembling an arsenal.

Zaim mumbled, "Where are those three? I told Jibril to run after them." His agitation was clearly visible to Afu, and in his haste he fumbled to ready the guns.

"Afu, watch what you are doing. If you are clumsy like that now, what will you do when we need you to act?"

"Incompetent idiots. Why do we even bother to train them? It doesn't help," he berated under his breath.

Just then Jibril, Murad, and Imad burst through the door, too out of breath to even address Zaim.

"Where have you two been? All you had to do was to be alert and ready, and you couldn't even do that? I said to be ready when I returned, and where were you? Gone off on some nature hike. Why do you think we are here? Why do you think the organization has spent hundreds of thousands of precious dollars on you, training you, preparing you for a mission important to our cause, so you can commune with the birds? Get your heads back into why we are here, or by the blood of my ancestors, I will make you wish you had obeyed."

The four underlings withstood the verbal abuse in silence. Now was not the time to respond or to show any sign of rebellion. They knew Zaim and his single-mindedness. They knew that he was driven beyond what any of them were, and they knew their duty was to follow, no matter what the consequences.

"Sit down. We have important business to discuss. Murad, hand me that tablet of paper and a pen. Do you think you can do that task without forgetting what it is?"

Murad moved quickly to retrieve a pen and legal tablet from the counter. He gave them to Zaim, avoiding eye contact, and took his place at the table with the others.

"I have decided we must do away with the captain of *Crusader, Too* tonight. He knows more about us than he should, possibly more than we can guess. Even if it is only that he recognized you, Jibril, that is enough. Here is what I found out from the manager at the marina in Knife River.

"The captain's name is David Craine. He lives in Two Harbors when he is not on his boat, which I gather is not often. However, his boat is at the marina today, and he will not be leaving until tomorrow morning. That gives us tonight to act.

"He lives above Dunnigan's Pub on First Avenue. Do you remember where that is?"

The others nodded in affirmation, too cowed to speak. Finally Murad responded.

"I believe that is next to the hardware store and across from the post office. Am I correct?"

Zaim fixed him with a stare. "Yes, that is the place."

He began to sketch on the tablet. "Waterfront Drive is the street that runs down to the lake. Here, on the corner, is Dunnigan's. This door on the side, the one facing Waterfront, is the entrance he uses. Inside and to the left is a door to a small cafe, but straight ahead and then to the right is the landing to a stairway that leads up to his apartment. There are two apartments upstairs. His is the one to the left and then straight back.

"I took a chance on the way home and stopped to look. I walked up the stairs, saw where his apartment was located, and quickly left. He may have been home or not. I don't know."

Zaim's impatience seemed to be diminishing enough that the others were a little more at ease.

"So what is your plan, Zaim?" Afu ventured to question.

"Tonight, after everything quiets down and the tavern closes, we are going to pay Captain Craine a visit." Zaim's eyes lit up for the first time since he returned from town.

CHAPTER
FORTY

DAVID AND HIS FRIEND JIMMY LEFT MONEY at the table to cover the bill and a healthy tip for Mary. Then they walked out the door and down the newly painted entrance stairs.

"We'll have to come back here soon," Jimmy said, trying to start up a conversation again.

David didn't seem to hear him at first. "Huh, oh, yeah, that'll be a good idea. It was pretty good."

"Pretty good! The food was great. What's wrong, Davy? Something set you off, and I want to know what the heck's going on."

Before David could answer, the two men almost bumped into a Lake County deputy coming up the steps.

"Hey, David, how're you doing? Staying out of trouble, I hope."

"Oh, hi, Ben. Sorry I almost ran into you. My mind was somewhere else I guess. How are you doing? It seems that I run into you wherever I go. You aren't following me, are you?"

Ben laughed and patted David on the back. "No way. I had enough of you when I was in school.

"We've been drawing some crazy shifts lately, sometimes here, sometimes there. I suppose its just coincidence that we seem to be following the same routes these days. Say, how's the food here? I heard it's pretty good."

"Pretty good!" Jimmy interrupted. "It's about the best I've had around here. You can't go wrong as far as I'm concerned. Order the walleye!"

Ben finished climbing the stairs and went inside. David and Jimmy climbed into David's car, and they started their ride back to Two Harbors.

"Look, Jim. I admit I was a little rattled back there in the restaurant, but it's nothing, at least nothing I want to talk about right now. Maybe

178

someday we can take a few beers out on the lake, and I'll tell you all about it, but for now just let it drop. I'd appreciate that."

As if to change the subject, David's old Subaru gave a cough and a jerk, then it wheezed a gasp and straightened out its ways.

"Geeze, Davey. If you took care of your boat the way you do your car, it would have sunk years ago. When was the last time you changed oil and had the filters changed?"

David looked at Jimmy, mock surprise on his face. "You mean you're supposed to do that? I thought these modern cars were supposed to be maintenance free." The two men continue bantering about how to treat a vehicle.

This made time go faster, and, in what seemed only a few miles, they were at the marina back in Knife River.

"Jim, thanks for all you have done. I mean it. I'll think of you and appreciate you tomorrow morning when I'm on my way to Cornucopia. I hope to spend a couple of weeks there, and maybe when I return I'll have my head screwed on right. See you, friend."

Jimmy slammed the door shut, and something rattled as though part of the car was going to fall off. David put the Subaru in gear and pulled out of the parking lot, turned right on Old Highway 61, and headed back the eight miles to Two Harbors.

A very large wedding party was in full swing when he arrived, and when David tried to park behind his apartment, he found that all of the spaces were filled. Peeved, he swung his car back onto the street, and as he did, the driver of a car parked squarely in front of his apartment entrance pulled away from the curb. Without hesitation, David parked his old Subaru in the vacated space. The thought crossed his mind that this would make it easier for him to get out in the morning. Because he wouldn't have to back up, no one would be able to box him in.

David cautiously walked up the stairs and quietly checked his door to determine if it was still locked. It was, and he entered what was once his safe place.

Below, Dunnigan's was going full tilt, and the raucous voices of its patrons having a wild time drowned out any other noise.

CHAPTER
FORTY-ONE

AGENT ERICKSON PAUSED A MOMENT BEFORE ANSWERING the phone in his hotel room. Only two people knew he was there—his boss, Enos Pratt, and Deidre. He hoped it wasn't Enos.

"Hello, John speaking."

"Hi, John. This isn't exactly an emergency, but I thought you might be looking for a place to eat supper tonight, unless you packed a week's worth of meals to store in your room." Deidre said with a lilt to her voice.

"Well, Deidre. I was hoping it was you and not Enos. You're right, I was just wondering how I was going to keep a low profile when there are only two cafes in town. After three or four meals, I think people would begin to recognize me. Of course I could use my Jiffy FBI Disguise Kit."

It felt good, John thought, to banter rather than be serious with her.

"That's what I was thinking. How about you come over to my place for supper tonight? It won't be fancy, but I can fill our bellies with something. Do you like beef stroganoff? I've got a recipe that takes only a few minutes to throw together, and it's pretty good."

"Sounds great to me," John answered. "Do you need any help? I'm not too bad in the kitchen. At least I can boil water without burning it too badly." He liked the sound of Deidre's laugh on the other end of the call.

"Sure. I can't start it until I get home from work, and we can throw it together. You're the elected onion chopper. I hate that job, makes me cry every time.

"I'll stop and pick up a bottle of red wine on my way home. My address is 814 Ninth Street. If you turn up the alley between Eighth and Ninth, you can park behind my house and come in the back way. It's pretty hidden, and the neighbors won't notice you—except for old Mrs. Olson who doesn't miss a thing. But she's pretty harmless. It'll give her something to think about tonight."

Again, John realized it was nice to hear her laugh.

"Come about six. See you then."

John parked his car alongside Deidre's sheriff's vehicle. Before opening the gate to her backyard, he instinctively glanced to his left and to his right just in time to see a gray-haired lady holding back the curtain of her kitchen window. He waved, and she hurriedly dropped the curtain. John said to himself. "Glad to meet you, Mrs. Olson."

The sidewalk leading to Deidre's back door wended its way through neatly kept flowers. The day lilies were in bloom, and he was taken by the large variety that Deidre has accumulated. He couldn't help but stop and admire the scene.

Deidre opened the door and stepped out.

"Hi, you," she said. "Now you've seen my feminine side. I love growing these flowers. It's one way I keep my sanity in this crazy world.

"Come on in. We don't want the whole world to see you out here. People will begin to talk," and she laughed the laugh John was becoming accustomed to hearing.

As they stepped into her home, John said, "I've already met your Mrs. Olson, kind of anyway. Does she always keep tabs on you this way?"

"She keeps tabs on the whole neighborhood, but, you know, I've never heard her gossip about anyone. She's quite a lady."

Deidre's home was one of those places that when you entered it an immediate feeling of well being took over. Bouquets of flowers from her garden decorated the kitchen and dining room. John expected that was true of the other rooms as well. He immediately felt at home.

"Where are those dastardly onions that make you cry? I might as well attack them right away and get it over with."

Deidre turned to her stove where slices of sirloin steak were browning in a fry pan, and she said over her shoulder, "They're on the counter. Use that cutting board they're sitting on. I can't stand getting onion smell on everything. That's my onion board.

"Better get them done fast. It's almost time to add them to the meat."

John picked up the knife and began dicing the tear-inducing vegetable. It took him less than a minute, and he carried the board over to the stove, dumped the chopped onions into the skillet and heard the spatter as the liquid in the onions met the hot grease.

"Careful, John, I don't want you ruining dinner by getting burned," and Deidre muscled him out of the way as she shook the fry pan, mixing the browned meat with the now sizzling onions.

Deidre added a carton of sour cream, some ketchup, a can of mushroom pieces, and stirred them together. In an instant she dumped a pot of boiling noodles into a colander and supper was ready to be served.

The two of them sat down to a meal that John judged as far more than adequate. He poured a glass of wine for each of them.

"Here's to a delightful evening," John toasted as he lifted his glass. Deidre did the same and, they gently clinked the goblets together.

"To a delightful evening," Deidre echoed.

Deidre realized that she knew hardly anything about the man with whom she was sharing a meal. As they talked, the two began to share some of their personal history. She told him about the force that had caused her to want to go into law enforcement, and as she related the events that led to her, her siblings, and her mother having been taken in by the women's shelter, John's eyes teared up.

"That must have been a terrible time for you," he empathized. "How did you ever make it through?"

"I don't think I would have if it hadn't been for David Craine and his wife. They took me in as though I was their own child. Without their support and help, I know I wouldn't be where I am today.

I owe him in so many ways. His wife was killed in a car accident a few years ago. Now he's so alone, I wish there was some way I could pay him back."

John couldn't help but think of what was going on in David Craine's life at the present.

"I'm sure the time will come when you'll be able to repay him. Maybe you already have. Every time he sees you, he must be proud of what you have done with your life. I'm sure that's quite a reward in itself.

"By the way, have your people been keeping an eye on him. I haven't heard much about him these past couple of weeks."

John's words had a way of changing the mood of the moment, and Deidre sat up straight in her chair. John wished he hadn't said anything.

"He piled his boat up on a reef about two weeks ago. No one was injured, but it did a number on his boat's underside. He's been unable to be on the lake while the boat was being repaired.

"Ben, one of my deputies, saw him in Beaver Bay today. He told Ben that *Crusader, Too* is seaworthy again and that he'll be taking a short trip across the lake tomorrow morning. Plans to stay over at Cornucopia for a week or so.

"If you want to continue surveillance on him, you'd better contact the Bayfield County sheriff. That's way out of our jurisdiction."

John wished he hadn't brought up the subject. "I know he's special to you. Take care of him while he's in the area, and let others see to him when he leaves."

Deidre stood and began to clean up. She put the dishes in the washer and rinsed out the wine goblets.

"John, I don't know why you can't tell me what David's involvement is in this operation. It's evident he's somehow mixed up in the terrorist threat. Is he involved in the organization up in the Brimson area? If you think he'd be a part of any violent plot, you've got another think coming. He's the kindest, gentlest man I know, and I've known him for a long time. I think I deserve to know his involvement, if for no other reason than I'm responsible for his well-being. Not only that, he's a dear friend."

"Look, Deidre, I know it doesn't make sense. I don't think it does either, but Enos won't clear me to give you the complete story. He's one bullheaded old duck, and once he gets an idea in his thick head, it's lodged there until something kicks it out. If word got out that I leaked information about Craine, I could kiss my job goodbye, and I'm not willing to take that chance, not even for you."

Deidre looked at him with steely eyes. "Perhaps we better call it a night. We both have work in the morning, and I need to be sharp. Maybe we can do this again sometime."

John rose from his chair and extended his hand to Deidre. "I suppose you're right. I want you to know I enjoyed the evening very much, at least until we started talking work."

Deidre followed him to the door, already regretting what she had said.

"Good night, John. Again sometime," and she closed the door behind him.

John walked past the flowers, now colorless in the dark. He noticed the curtain of the neighbor's window pulled back a crack.

"Good night, Mrs. Olson," he said out loud, although he knew she couldn't hear him, and as he slid into the driver's seat of his car, he glanced at the window looking out the back of Deidre's house. She was there, watching him leave.

CHAPTER
FORTY-TWO

"MY PLAN IS THAT WE DRIVE INTO TWO HARBORS after dark tonight," Zaim said. "Surely Captain Craine will be spending the night in his apartment. His boat was in the water this morning when I visited the marina, but the operator said he was not going to be leaving until morning."

Zaim turned his drawing so the others could better look at it.

"We will park our SUV over here, by the old train engine. It almost totally blocks the street light, and in the deep shadows, our black vehicle should be hidden quite well. Imad, you will stay in the vehicle in case we must make a hasty retreat. Do you think you can be ready for that, or will you have to take a walk to relieve your boredom?" Zaim asked with a sneer.

"I will be ready," Imad promised, his eyes averted to the floor.

"Murad, you will position yourself in the back, near where the parking spaces for the apartments are located. I don't want you to be by Captain Craine's car, though. We don't want a village police patrol to see you there for no apparent reason. They might stop to question you as to your purpose for being in the alley that time of night."

On his makeshift map, he pointed to a particular location. "There is an alcove next door that is the entrance to the hardware store. It has no light near it, and if you crouch down inside it, you will be able to spot anyone coming or going from the apartment and not be seen yourself.

"Jibril, you will position yourself across the street. Once again, there is a part of a building that juts out toward the alley opposite Captain Craine's apartment. You will be well hidden there but with a view of the street and the entrance to his building.

"Afu, you will come with me. If we can make our way up the stairs without being detected, perhaps we can surprise Captain Craine in his bed."

The four men sat in silence for a few seconds, digesting what Zaim had laid out for them. They fidgeted. Finally, Zaim broke the silence. "Well, what is it. Do you not approve of what I have said?"

"Oh, not that at all," Afu was quick to respond. The others were quick to shake their heads in unison.

"What are we going to do when we find him? Shoot him?"

"What is wrong with your thinking?" Zaim snapped back. "One gunshot in that room and the whole town would be awake. Our best bet is to subdue him and escort him out of the building. Then we can take care of him like we did Herminio. They can find his body in a gravel pit in a couple of days. By then we will have carried out our plan.

"Imad, just be ready to drive away when we have him in the SUV. If we act quickly, no one will be any the wiser."

The others looked at Zaim's sketch of the streets and alleyways near David's room. They asked a few inane questions to appease Zaim.

"It is best that we get some rest this afternoon. It is going to be a long night, and we want to be alert. We leave at ten o'clock tonight, which will get us to our spots no later than 10:45. Then we will wait for our opportunity."

Each man lay down on his bunk. Afu and Imad fell asleep immediately, Murad tossed and turned for a few minutes, and eventually Zaim heard their rhythmic breathing. He did not sleep but rested on his bunk, thinking of a time and place far removed from where he was now.

CHAPTER
FORTY-THREE

DAVID CLIMBED THE STAIRS TO HIS ROOM, placed one foot on the tread and brought the other up beside it, then paused a second to listen for any out-of-place sound. Dunnigan's was erupting with music, laughter, every patron shouting, trying to make him or her self heard over the din. He strained to hear, but it was impossible to pick up any hint of someone else being in the hall above.

He reached the upper landing and slowly moved along the wall to his door. He reached out and firmly grasped the doorknob and turned it without making a sound. David was aware that anyone inside would see the knob turn, but he could think of no other way to test if the door was locked or not without inserting his key, an action that would have surely made a scraping sound.

The knob turned without a sound, and David gently pushed on the door, half expecting it to swing inward and being ready to turn and race back down the stairs. To his relief, the door moved only a millimeter, and then he felt the deadbolt press up against the striker plate. He breathed a sigh of relief, knowing that the door was still locked. David inserted the key in the lock, released the bolt, and opened the door.

His one room never looked so good to him, like an old friend greeting him at the end of a long day, and he closed the door behind him, making sure to turn the lock.

He had a lamp with a low setting, and when he turned it on, it hardly lit the room, casting dim shadows on the wall. David didn't want bright lights that might outline his shadow on the shades. He thought it would be best if no one outside could see his silhouette.

Having choked down most of his steak at the restaurant in Beaver Bay, he wasn't the least bit hungry. His stomach seemed to have quit working, and his late afternoon meal was a lump in his belly. He went to the refrigerator, which was making its usual loud humming noise as it labored to keep its contents cold, and took out a can of beer.

David popped the opener tab and took a sip of the brew. Immediately, he hiccupped and for an instant thought he has made a bad mistake. But then the carbonation welled up inside and he burped a most satisfying belch. He felt better.

David sat down in his comfortable chair and turned on the sports channel that broadcast his Minnesota Twins. They were having a tough summer, almost as tough as he was, he thought. The score flashed on the screen—bottom of the ninth and Kansas City was up, seven to one.

He downed the rest of the beer, turned the TV off, and sat in the dim glow of the table lamp. David cupped his face in his hands and looked at the far wall.

Eventually he stood up and walked over to his dresser. He had never wanted to do this, but if there was ever going to be a time it was now. He reached in and fumbled under a pile of unmatched socks and felt the cold metal of a pistol.

David had always been a pacifist but not one who refused to defend himself. That was why years ago he had bought this nine-millimeter Glock. He had intended to keep it on his boat, but after only a short time he had come to think he was a greater danger to himself than was any hypothetical marauder. The pistol had remained hidden in his drawer all these years, and now he wondered if he even remembered how to use it, or if he was forced, would he have the will to pull the trigger if it was aimed at another human being.

As a safety precaution, he had always kept the bullets for his pistol in a separate spot, and David rummaged in his closet before he found the ammunition box tucked away behind some time-worn sweaters on an upper shelf.

The box was heavy in his hand, ominous to his touch, and he opened the lid and examined the glint of the bullets' copper jackets before removing a handful. He couldn't remember how many the gun held.

David systematically pushed the cartridges into the clip and felt the restraint of the spring increase with the addition of each bullet. He shoved the clip into the handle of the pistol and heard it click into place, laid the loaded weapon on his table, and went to bed to await the sunrise. He knew he wouldn't sleep well.

CHAPTER
FORTY-FOUR

WHEN SHE HAD WATCHED JOHN OPEN HIS CAR DOOR and climb into the driver's seat, Deidre wanted to run out and holler, "Wait," but she couldn't do it. She knew she wanted him to stay longer, but she couldn't get herself to call out to him.

Dejectedly, she stepped to the kitchen sink and finished cleaning up after their meal, and she wished she weren't so defensive and protective of Mr. Craine. After all, she told herself, he was a grown adult who should know the difference between right and wrong, and if he was involved in something wrong, that would be his problem, not hers.

But at the same time she couldn't make herself believe that her friend was in any way involved in any activity that the FBI would consider to be subversive.

To herself she muttered, "David Craine, whatever it is you've gotten your tail in a ringer over, you'll have to get it out yourself, because there are some things I just can't fix."

Deidre rattled around inside her house, trying to fill the evening hours, but it wasn't working. She was restless and at odd's end. Even another glass of wine failed to calm her to the point where she could sit and relax. Finally she gave in to what was causing her unrest, reached for her phone, and dialed John's cell phone number.

She heard the phone ring, expecting him to answer, but to her chagrin, the ringing continued until she heard a click at the end of the line and then the message.

"You have reached the voice mail of John Erickson. I am not available to take your call right now. If you leave your name and phone number, I will return your call as soon as possible."

190

Deidre's response was a feeling of immediate rejection. She pictured John picking up his cell phone, looking at the caller ID, and then closing the lid. Surely, she thought to herself that he must not want to talk to her after she virtually had kicked him out. She pressed the "END" button without leaving a message, forgetting that the call would register on his phone as a "missed call."

She slumped in a chair in her living room and tried to sort out what she was feeling. Deidre had vowed as a teenager that she would never get romantically involved with a man. When she was a toddler, long before she could remember him, her biological father had deserted his family. He had never tried to contact them. He had never contributed one cent toward their living expenses. All she could remember was a nagging question, "*Why?*"

Then she had seen the result of her mother's entanglement with her stepfather, a marriage that should never have had happened, one that was filled with abuse and belittlement for them all. It wasn't that Deidre disliked men. She simply couldn't trust them.

That was why her emotions tonight confused her so. Why did it matter to her at all whether John ignored her or not? She had no intentions of getting involved. But there was a wound inside her that had been suddenly reopened, the wound of rejection, and she was angered that she had placed herself in the position to be hurt again.

But at the same time she found herself wanting to cry, an emotion she seldom had allowed to spill out. Almost as if she was praying, Deidre held her phone in both hands as tears welled up in her eyes. She jolted when the phone rang.

Opening the cover, she answered without looking at the name of the caller.

"Hello," she blurted into the phone.

"Hey, what's up?" Deidre heard John's voice on the other end of the call. "I was in the shower when you called a few minutes ago and didn't hear the phone ring. Is everything all right?"

Deidre was totally flummoxed, because she had no real reason to have called John, and a long silence ensued while her brain spun.

She groped for words. Finally she said, "John, I'm really sorry for the way I reacted tonight. I was totally out of line, and I ruined what was a very enjoyable evening. I'm sorry."

"I must say, I was a little taken aback by the way the evening ended, and I apologize for bringing up work when I did. I'm sorry if I treated our date as a business meeting."

John was shocked by what he had just said. Deidre sat bolt upright in her chair at the word "date." She had never been on one in her life, and it hadn't even dawned on her that she had scheduled a real and true date with a man.

John stuttered into the receiver, "I, I suppose you might not have considered it a date. That was a poor choice of words on my part." Then he paused. "I think I'll shut up now. I'm digging myself into a deep hole here, and I don't want to mess this call up like I did our evening."

For the first time, Deidre could laugh. "So you thought you were on a date, huh? Well, that sounds pretty good to me. And it wasn't you who messed up the evening. I'll take full responsibility for that."

"No, no, I'll take the responsibility for that. But this could go on all night. The question is, where do we go from here? I'd definitely like to see you again, in a non-working way, a date if we can call it that."

Deidre could feel her face getting flushed, but she regained her composer. "What would you say to another try again tomorrow night? I have another quick recipe we can put together for a semi-elegant meal. Same time as tonight?"

John relaxed. "Same time. Oh, and warn Mrs. Olson that I'm coming. That way she won't have to stand at her window, waiting."

They both laughed at the thought.

"Good night, John."

"Good night, Deidre. Sleep well."

CHAPTER
FORTY-FIVE

IT WAS 9:00 IN THE EVENING, AND ZAIM HAD NOT SLEPT, although he lay quietly the whole time, his eyes closed as though he were sleeping. He got up from the bed, not able to stay still any longer and started to rouse the others.

Murad, a light sleeper, heard Zaim swing his feet to the floor and scuffle putting on his shoes. The others slept more soundly, and Zaim first grabbed Jibril and then Afu by their shoulders and roughly shook them awake.

"Put your shoes on. It is time for us to leave. Jibril, you are in charge of making sure the extra ammunition for each gun is in the SUV. Afu, you store the rifles under the seat where they will not be seen. Murad, I want you to double check that everything we need is in the Ford. Be sure to bring a couple of flashlights, and don't forget the plastic fasteners to wrap around the captain's wrists. Make sure we have something to stuff in his mouth to prevent him from yelling."

The men jumped at Zaim's commands, and within minutes, everything was placed in their vehicle.

Zaim looked around the two rooms, searching for any forgotten item, but he found none.

"Check your pistol, each of you. Make sure there is no bullet in the barrel but that you have it loaded with a full clip in the magazine. Make sure you each have an extra loaded clip with you."

One by one he said their names, waiting for each man to affirm that he was armed.

"Okay, let's go. It's a little early for us to be leaving, but I'll drive a little slower than the speed limit so as not to attract attention by speeding."

They rode in silence. Afu fidgeted with a button on his shirt sleeve. Murad watched the trees speed by outside the SUV's window, and Jibril and Imad rested their heads on the back of the seat, their eyes closed.

Zaim looked at his watch, 9:40. He did a little calculating in his mind and realized they were going to be arriving in town earlier than he had expected. At their current speed, they would be to the waterfront before 10:30, but he knew that driving too slowly might attract as much attention as driving too fast.

They arrived at the stoplights on Highway 61 at 10:25, and Zaim complained they were far too early to take their positions by the railroad engine that sat immobile on its stub of track. Engine 9 had been a museum piece for fifty years and wasn't going anywhere. But Zaim suspected that at this early hour of the night, people would be out walking their dogs, watching the dock lights, or maybe just enjoying the evening's fresh air off the lake.

Rather than taking the highway into town, he decided to stop at a small parking spot by Burlington Bay. He calculated it would be in the shadows of trees, and their black vehicle wouldn't be easily seen.

"We'll wait here for about twenty minutes," he informed the others. "By that time most people will have gone inside. There may be a drunk or two on the street, but we can avoid them."

The men sensed the tenseness that had begun to grip them, and no one was at ease in his seat. The evening breeze cooled the interior of the van, but they all had a thin film of sweat on their foreheads.

At 10:45 Zaim turned the key and the engine instantly came alive. He backed out of the parking spot under the spruce tree and headed for the waterfront, where to his dismay he found the street cluttered with people.

"Heathens," he muttered at the sight of revelers standing in groups, beer bottles in their hands.

It was a Saturday night, and one of the downtown clubs was hosting a wedding reception. The two hundred plus guests were enjoying the exceptionally warm August evening. Zaim turned up the alley behind the businesses and then cruised onto Main Street.

"We can't stay here right now. It would be foolish for us to try to get into the apartment undetected with all these people around. We'll have to wait somewhere else for a time."

He returned to the hidden spot by the lake to wait for the party to end and for Dunnigan's to close.

They sat in the shadows until almost one in the morning. A car's headlights appeared behind them, and for only a flash of time, they illuminated the SUV's interior, then swung away as the driver turned his vehicle away from them and headed up Burlington Road.

The car lights spooked Zaim, although through the trees he could not see the vehicle.

"We've sat here long enough. I'm afraid if we stay longer, we will attract attention to ourselves," he announced to the others.

Again, he started the engine and returned to the downtown area. This operation had not begun the way Zaim had planned. They were more than two hours off his schedule.

When they arrived, they found the party had slowed only a little. At least, Zaim supposed, they would be able to park among the many other cars and go unnoticed. He spotted a space near the back of the parking lot and pulled into it. From there they could see the captain's apartment, yet they were far enough from where most of the straggling revelers were gathered. Directly behind him was Engine 9. He noticed that the window he imagined must have been David Craine's was dimly lit from the inside, a sign he took to mean the occupant was home.

Sometime after 2:00 a.m., the crowd began to thin, and Zaim instructed the others to take their places.

"Jibril, it looks as though the street is empty. Walk across to your position near the corner of the building opposite Captain Craine's apartment. Wait there until you see Afu and me enter his building. Then come across, and be ready when we come down the stairs with him.

"Imad, when you see Jibril cross the street, pull the SUV up beside the door.

"Murad, from your hiding place, come up from behind and open both back doors, then position yourself on the opposite side. Our Mr. Craine will probably put up some resistance when we shove him into the backseat. You reach across the seat and pull him in, Jibril and Murad will shove, and I think he will not be able to prevent his abduction.

"When we are all in the car, Imad, drive out of town, west past the airport. We'll take care of the captain in the farthest pit up the Old Drummond Road and dump his body over one of the banks."

While the four watched, Jibril walked with some deliberation to where Zaim would have him wait in the shadows. Zaim looked at his watch. It was nearly 2:30, and yet the party down the street was still going on, although with far fewer participants. He could hear the music blaring, could see dancers moving and sweating inside, and occasionally, he spotted a drunk staggering into the shadows to relieve himself. The warning siren on the docks began its standard beep-beeping, signaling that the conveyor was being moved. Otherwise all seemed calm.

Just as Jibril was about to reach the cover the shadows, he was startled when a man in about his mid-forties lurched out at him and threw his arms around him. Jibril was in the arms of a falling-down drunk, and for an instant he thought he was being attacked. When he realized the situation, he thought of shoving the man's head up against the brick building. Then he realized the drunk was on the verge of caving in on his own accord.

Jibril steered the man around the corner and gave him a shove behind a dense stand of lilacs growing there. Almost in slow motion the man sprawled to the ground, and with a loud sigh as though he was crawling into a comfortable bed, he lay there, dead drunk as they say. Jibril sort of smiled, but his heart was still racing. He took his post, having no idea how long the others would have to wait for the street to become totally deserted.

About this time, the last patrons of Dunnigan's wandered out onto the sidewalk. A few walked slowly to their parked cars behind the apartment building. One couple walked hand in hand up the street, paying no attention to anything but each other. In minutes they were gone.

Jibril looked at his watch. It was 2:40, and the wedding party at the club had slowed considerably. Inside the building, only six or eight diehards were left, and they showed little inclination of folding for the night. Standing on the corner across the street from Dunnigan's, two men visited while they smoked cigarettes. Jibril watched as one dropped his to the sidewalk and ground it out with the heel of his shoe. They walked back to the bar.

Jabril slid down the wall to sit on the grass, thinking he might as well be comfortable while he waited.

CHAPTER
FORTY-SIX

IT HAD BEEN A SLOW NIGHT, AND BEN WAS HAVING a difficult time staying awake. He had already drunk three cups of black coffee, and the caffeine was having little effect on his brain. He rolled down the squad vehicle's window and decided to drive around for a while, thinking maybe the fresh air would revive him.

Ben stopped at the red light, the last traffic signal for anyone leaving the town heading east. It turned green and he decided to take a little used road angling off toward the lake. It was a rough road, not paved, and the washboard ripples on its surface mandated that drivers moved slowly.

As Ben maneuvered around the potholes, his attention was focused only on the road directly in front of him. In a few seconds he reached Burlington Road, a tarred surface paralleling the shore of Lake Superior. He came to a rolling stop at the intersection of the two roads and swung right. As the headlights of his vehicle swept across Burlington Road, he spotted a dark-colored SUV parked under the tree by the lake. In that instant, when his own headlights illuminated the interior of the SUV, Ben could see the backs of at least two heads inside the vehicle.

Acting as though he had seen nothing, Ben continued driving up the hill. The road led to South Avenue, and he turned right at the corner, and then drove toward the museum train engine.

His first impulse was to call in an alert, but the more he thought about what he might have seen, the less sure he was that he had spotted anything out of the ordinary.

He thought, "*That's a pretty common parking spot for people to sit and enjoy the cool breezes off the lake. Might be some people showing their friends the lake or perhaps a few kids stopping to have some alone time away from their parents. Or, and he smiles to himself, it might be the mayor and his girlfriend."*

Ben remembered the brouhaha when one of the newly hired city police officers had sneaked up on a similar car and shined his flashlight through its window. To say the least, the mayor had not found any humor in the situation.

Nevertheless, Ben was suspicious that what he saw just might be of importance. He decided to wait and see if anything more conclusive happened and decided to park his vehicle in the shadows behind old Number 9. He quietly climbed the steel stairs that led to the catwalk running the length of the engine's huge boiler. He sat near the front of the engine where he could see both the road leading to the docks and the back of David Craine's apartment building. He looked at his watch. It was almost 2:00 a.m.

He adjusted his posture to a more comfortable position, still well concealed in his nook high above the ground. Just as he settled back, a black SUV slowly pulled into the lot and parked between two cars under where he was sitting. Ben wished he could see inside the vehicle, but from his vantage point all that was visible was the top of the van. He thought it strange that no one stepped out, and at first he thought of going down to check. His directive had been to keep a low profile, and so Ben stayed hidden a while longer.

He was about to give up his post. Ben checked the time again, 2:25, and he thought he could be wasting his time. He assumed that the occupants of the SUV were drunk and were sleeping it off.

Quietly, a door to the van opened and a man stepped out. He looked both ways as if wary of being seen, and then walked with an exaggerated amble kitty-corner across the street toward the brick building on the other side.

Ben saw the outline of a person lurch out of the bushes and appear to attack him, but then it seemed that they were old friends greeting each other. The two disappeared behind the bushes, leaving Ben confused as to what he had just witnessed.

Before he could decide what to do, the car door on the other side opened even more cautiously, and another man stepped into the parking lot. Ben watched the figure slink from one shadow to the next and head for the back of David Craine's apartment.

He had seen enough, and Ben knew it is time to act. As quietly as possible he moved so that the front of the train engine blocked any view of him from the lot, and he quietly climbed down the opposite side of the steel hulk. From there, he had easy access to his squad, all the while being hidden from those on the other side. He slid into the driver's seat and began his call.

A sleep-muffled voice answered the other end of the line. "Lo," Deidre mumbled.

"Deidre, this is Ben. Something's about to happen down here at David's apartment."

As the meaning of Ben's words sank in, Deidre became instantly alert, and her heart began to pound against her rib cage.

"What's going on, Ben? Do you need backup?"

"I'm behind Engine 9 down at the waterfront. Here's what's happening. I think that black SUV from Brimson is parked here. One of the men has stationed himself in the shadow of the brick apartment house across Waterfront Drive from David's. Another is waiting behind David's place next to the alley. I assume the others are still in their vehicle. What do you want me to do, chief?"

Deidre doesn't hesitate. "I'm calling in some help for you, but, Ben, they won't be coming with sirens blaring. In fact, you may not know when they arrive. Can you get up on the engine again without being seen?

"Shouldn't be a problem, Deidre. Anything else?"

"Just stay quiet up there, but be ready to call for help. If I were you, I'd take your shotgun with you this time. You may need it before this is over. And, Ben, be careful."

DEIDRE JUMPED OUT OF BED AND BEGAN DRESSING. At the same time she had her cell phone in her hand, hitting the speed dial as she called. The phone rang five times before she got an answer.

"Hello, this is John Erickson," he mumbled through the fog of sleepiness.

"John, I don't have time to explain. Get over to my place as soon as you can, sooner if possible. I'm leaving in less than five minutes, and if you're not here when I pull out, you'll miss the excitement. Gotta go," and with those words she hung up.

Deidre raced to contact the other deputies on duty, but she was afraid to let the city police in on what was happening. She realized that John had never said anything to her about their involvement in the case, and she didn't have time for explanations. Then she put out an emergency call to the deputies not on duty.

As she was running out the door, she glimpsed a figure racing up her walkway. John was still trying to button his shirt, but he had made it. As they turned to go, the upstairs curtains of Mrs. Olson's house parted, and they could see her looking down on them.

"Doesn't she ever sleep?" John asked.

"Never."

The two piled into Deidre's white Lake County Sheriff's SUV and headed for the Law Enforcement Center. Along the way, she filled John in on what Ben had said.

"This is definitely a change in the situation," he understated. "We have to get over there for David's sake as soon as we can. Did Ben say if anything had happened to him?"

"No. It appears that the two men who left the SUV are look-outs. I would bet the others will be more involved. One will be the driver and the others the main actors. I think it will be best to take a few minutes to organize the other deputies before we go over. Ben will call if it appears something urgent is happening."

When they arrived at the Center, there were several deputies present. They gathered around Deidre.

"Jeff, you park around the corner to the right on First Street. Don't show yourself until you hear my call. Dale, position yourself at the end of the alley on Fifth Street. Don't allow anyone in the black SUV to drive out that way. John and I will block the opposite alley. Let's go."

Deidre noticed that the clock on the dash read 3:50, and she was aware that it wouldn't be too long before the eastern sky would begin to show signs of the sun tucked below the horizon of the lake. Surely something would happen before then, she whispered to John.

CHAPTER
FORTY-SEVEN

DAVID FLUFFED HIS PILLOW AND FOLDED IT in two so it had more depth. The pillow was old, and the feather stuffing was worn out from too much use. He flopped his head down on it but found no comfort. He flipped over, trying to find a position conducive to sleep, but all he gained was more restlessness.

Outside his window, the green shamrock sign continued to flash on and off, creating an emerald glow inside his room for three or four seconds and then casting the room into a relative darkness. The noise of the crowd below came through the wooden flooring, at times making his bed vibrate when the bass guitar amped up its voice.

David had tried to open a window and set up a fan to draw in the relatively cooler nighttime air, but the noise on the street made sleeping impossible. He had to shut the window, and the air in his apartment was stale and humid.

He sat up and folded down the thin blanket he had spread over himself at the beginning of the night. Now he straightened the wrinkled, soggy sheet and partially covered himself. One bare leg hung out from beneath the thin cloth. David couldn't decide if the sweat on his neck and face was from the over-heated room or if it was caused by the stress which was beginning to wrack his mind. Whatever, he couldn't turn off his thoughts and drift off to sleep.

He had all but given up on sleep, so he got up and relieved himself, filled a paper cup with water from the tap in the bathroom, took a drink, and wandered over to the window facing the side street. He pulled back the curtain just a bit and looked at the nearly deserted street, and he saw two men standing on the corner opposite Dunnigan's. Their cigarettes glowed red when they inhaled, drawing in oxygen to stoke the hot tobacco embers. One dropped his cigarette to the sidewalk and ground it out with his shoe. They wandered back to the bar.

He spotted a figure cross the street, walking straighter than most, but in the dim light he didn't recognize the man as a local. *Probably a tourist looking for a little excitement,* he thought.

A drunk staggered out of the bushes and threw his arms around the person who had just crossed the street. It appeared to David that the two knew each other, because they seemed to embrace, and then the more sober appearing of the two steered the beleaguered one back into the shadows, and the two disappeared from view.

On the way back to bed, David glanced at the digital clock on his bed stand. *Too soon to get up.* He smoothed the sheet, fluffed the pillow for the umpteenth time, and lay down. If he couldn't sleep, he figured he would at least rest as best he could. It would start to get light soon, not totally daylight, but it was that time of the morning when gray shapes would begin to form and the eastern sky would begin to brighten just a bit.

David lay still for a good half hour, and then could not be still any longer. Even though the noise downstairs and on the street had totally subsided by this time, he found his mind racing through a maze of thoughts. His stomach was knotted, and perspiration oozed from every pore. His sheets were damp with it.

He swung his legs over the edge of his bed and let his feet contact the floor. For at least five minutes he sat there, elbows on his knees, his head resting in his hands.

David got up and groped his way over to the medicine cabinet above his bathroom sink. He turned on the light, and in the mirror's reflection he hardly recognized the face looking back at him. The image was of a man older than what he thought he was. Discolored bags hung under his blood-shot eyes. His hair was mussed, and he had deeper creases in his face than he remembered.

He opened the cabinet door and took out a bottle of pain killer, flipped the lid off with his thumb, and allowed two tablets to spill out into his hand. He tossed them to the back of his throat, and gulped water from the same paper cup he had used before. His head throbbed from the tension he felt, and he rubbed the back of his neck, seeking some relief before the painkillers kicked in.

There was no use going back to bed. He knew sleep was beyond his reach, so he stripped off his sweaty underwear and washed up. He smeared on some antiperspirant, brushed his teeth, and took another drink of water.

He dressed in the near darkness, the only light coming from the dimly lit lamp he had left on all night.

David decided to leave for the Silver Bay Marina. By the time he got there it would be light enough to leave the harbor and begin his jaunt across Lake Superior to Cornucopia. He figured he would be able to find some peace in the quaint fishing village on the other side of the lake.

He slipped into his favorite boots. They had served him well in many different circumstances: hiking, boating, even climbing the trailhead to the Superior Hiking Trail at Castle Danger. He put on his battered baseball cap, and scanned the room for anything he might have overlooked. The digital clock on his bed stand read 3:55 a.m.

The pistol he had taken out of its hiding place the night before was still on the table. He looked at it and decided he was more apt to shoot himself than use it for protection. David slid the clip out of the gun's magazine and returned both of them to the closet. He was sure he would not have the will to aim it at another person, much less pull the trigger.

He looked around the apartment one last time, walked to the door, and opened it. Then he noticed that the lamp was still on. He walked across the room once more, turned it off, and left the apartment, being sure to lock the door behind him.

CHAPTER
FORTY-EIGHT

IN THE SUV, ZAIM GLANCED AT HIS WATCH. It was 3:55. He turned to Afu. "The street is quiet. It is time that we make our move."

Both car doors opened at the same time, and Imad quietly eased his shut behind him. He felt the latch catch and heard a faint click, then walked around to the driver's side and slid in where Zaim had been sitting. Imad watched Zaim and Afu slowly slink across the parking lot, keeping to the shadows as much as they could.

Ben, perched up on the museum engine, watched the entire scenario. As quietly as he could, he activated the radio fastened near his collar.

"Deidre, this is Ben," he said in as subdued a voice as he could and yet be heard. "The three men who were sitting in the SUV have moved. The one who had been driving and a smaller man are crossing the parking lot right now. The third is now the driver. Be ready for them to get to the apartment house in about thirty seconds."

Ben turned off his radio and crept around to the backside of the engine, then climbed to the ground. He slowly depressed his vehicle's latch, and using both hands on the door to muffle as much sound as possible, he pried it open just enough to slip in. He repeated the same muffling action to close the door, but did not fully engage the latch. He felt more than heard the latch catch halfway. Once inside he turned on his radio again.

"Deidre, can you see them coming across the lot?" Ben questioned. "Let me know when I should move out. I can't see a thing from back here."

He heard a click, faint because he had the volume turned down so low, then Deidre's voice. "Hang tight for just a few more seconds.

The two guys moving across the lot have stopped by the shrubs where the lot entrance divides. They are about halfway across. Now they're moving again. They're up to something, that's for sure. Give us to the count of ten and then come around the engine with your squad. You can block the path of the SUV. Ram him if you must to keep him from leaving."

Imad slipped the gearshift into drive and eased his foot off the brake pedal. The SUV crept slowly forward, its wheels hardly turning. It seemed to be moving as cautiously as was Zaim.

"No, wait. Abort that plan. He's beginning to move the SUV. Start your engine, but don't move until you hear from me," Deidre whispered into the radio.

After coming down the stairs, David reached the bottom landing. He pushed the entrance door open, hoping his departure at such an early hour would not disturb anyone who might be sleeping in the other upstairs apartment. He paused for a second and inhaled the fresh air blowing in off the lake. In the east, the sky had yet to turn pink, but there was a definite separation of the shades of gray above and below the horizon. By the time he made it to Silver Bay, the sun would be barely visible above the edge of the earth, and he would be able to see without a flashlight.

He didn't think he would need to bring anything with him. *Crusader, Too* was waiting in her berth at the marina. She was stocked with enough groceries for a few days, and she had plenty of gasoline in her tanks. Anyway, David knew it would only take him an hour or two to reach Cornucopia, maybe a little more. With any luck, he planned to be tied up at the wharf in the Wisconsin harbor and having breakfast at a familiar mom-and-pop cafe near the water's edge by 8:30 a.m. After that, he might just sack out for a few hours, taking advantage of the peace.

David smiled to himself when he remembered being irritated because his usual parking spot had been taken last night. All he would have to do this morning was take two steps across the sidewalk and jump in the rusty old Subaru. He turned the key and heard the engine rattle to life, put the car in drive and drove away without looking back, unaware that Zaim was only thirty yards from him, or that Murad and Jibril were already making their first move to intercept him. He was gone almost before they realized what had happened.

David made a rolling stop at the intersection, hardly slowing down and certain no one else would be driving down the street at that hour. He was a block up the street before the sheriff and her deputies could react.

He turned on his radio to a local golden oldies station and cranked up the volume. Jerry Lee Lewis was playing "Whole Lotta Shaken' Goin' On."

CHAPTER
FORTY-NINE

ZAIM AND AFU LEFT THE SHADOWS OF THE SHRUBBERY growing in the island where the entrance and exit to the parking lot split. They planned to cover the last bit of ground to Captain Craine's apartment building in a few steps, but just as they exited the shadows, David pushed the door open, crossed the few feet of sidewalk, and climbed into his own car. He drove away before Zaim and Afu could react.

Imad had driven up behind Zaim, who ran around to the passenger side and jumped in. Afu quickly got in the back.

"Quickly! Pull up to Murad and Jibril."

Zaim rolled down his window and shouted at the two, "Get in! We have to follow him," and the two men dove into the SUV.

They followed after David, being careful not to get too close.

"Stay a block behind him. It is evident he isn't trying to speed away. We'll follow him and find an opportune time to finish what we came to do tonight."

DEIDRE LOOKED UP FROM THE DASH OF HER SHERIFF'S VEHICLE in time to see David's car cross the intersection. The sight of his car so startled her that she was speechless for a second. The black SUV crossed seconds later, and it was evident the driver was following the Subaru.

"John, did you see what I saw?" she blurted out, recovering from her surprise. "That was David's vehicle with the men from Brimson following him."

John didn't have time to respond before Deidre was on the radio. "Ben, they're getting away. Go on South Avenue to Burlington, and see if they come by on Highway 61 heading east. No sirens or warning lights but make time getting there.

"Jeff, go to the stoplights on Seventh and Seventh. Radio if they head that direction. Don't use sirens or flashers."

She turned to John and with no hesitation took charge. "We'll follow behind a few blocks. I think we have time. They haven't broken any law yet, so we have no reason to stop them. As far as I know, it's not illegal to drive around at four o'clock in the morning, so we have no reason."

John looked at her, his jaw set and his face blank. He nodded.

Deidre's radio crackled as Ben signed on. "I was too late to intercept them. They were already a quarter mile past the intersection when I got there. I saw them disappear over the hill on Highway 61. Should I chase them?"

"No!" Deidre nearly shouted into the receiver. "Follow, but do not give chase. Stay far enough back so that they have a hard time spotting you, but maintain contact. I'll have Eric go to the Silver Bay marina. I'm guessing that is where David's heading."

She reached Jeff on the radio. "They are proceeding up 61 toward Silver Bay. John and I are on 61 now, Ben is ahead of us. Go up Highway 2, and cut across the Gun Club Road to Highway 3. Head down the West Castle Danger Road, and make sure they don't leave 61 without us knowing. That's quite a ways, so you'd better go with sirens and lights. If they stay on 61, you won't beat them to the intersection. If you don't see them coming up the West Castle Danger Road, follow 61 toward Silver Bay. Somewhere we are going to find them on that route."

A rather unusual parade formed heading up Highway 61. In the lead was David. He still had his car radio cranked up. By that time, Little Richard was belting out the words to "Good Golly Miss Molly," and David was wailing along with him. Away from Two Harbors and heading for the marina, he already felt a lightening of his spirit.

Following him by several hundred yards was the black SUV, but he was oblivious to its presence. The sun was about to rise above the lake, the road ahead was clear, and he was eagerly anticipating *Crusader, Too* leaving the harbor with him onboard.

The occupants of the SUV were fixated on the blue Subaru ahead of them, unaware that Ben was the same distance behind them or that Deidre and John would soon be joining them on the highway.

"There is a place ahead where the road narrows in a rock cut. Imad, be ready to speed up alongside him there, and we'll force him into the rock wall. Murad and Jibril, as soon as he is made to stop, rush out and pull him from his car. If we time it correctly, he will be too dazed to resist. There are a series of S curves just beyond Gooseberry Park. When he clears the park entrance we will move."

CHAPTER
FIFTY

DAVID ROLLED DOWN HIS WINDOW, allowing the crisp dawn air to fill his car. Just then he felt it jerk as though it hiccoughed. That was followed by another jerk and a couple of coughs from the engine.

"No," David groaned, and he turned off the radio so he could gauge the engine sounds better. The Subaru was making strange noises, and it was evident to him that it was about to die.

David turned where the sign read "Gooseberry Park," barely slowing down. His car sounded as though it was on its last gasp.

I might make it to the lot by the Visitor Center if I'm lucky, he thought, but the Subaru sputtered a time or two and the engine stopped completely. He steered to the side of the road.

David turned the ignition key off and then on again. He was rewarded only by the sound of the starter engine turning over, but not any sign of life from his car, not even a backfire. The sign by the side of the road read, "PARK OPEN FROM 8:30 A.M. TO 10:00 P.M." His watch said 4:30.

ZAIM WATCHED DAVID ABRUPTLY PULL into the park's entrance. "Hurry, Imad. He's seen us and is attempting to escape. I know a little of this park, and this is the only road in or out. We have him trapped unless he escapes on foot, but that is unlikely.

"The river gorge blocks his way to the north, and the lake is to the east. His only hope is to circle around to the highway, and we can block the walkway leading to it."

Imad floored the accelerator, and in seconds they were at the park. He wildly swung in behind David, stirring up a spray of gravel

212

on the shoulder of the road. The commotion startled David, and he turned in time to see the five men he recognized spill out of the SUV.

David knew the park well. He and Alicia had spent more days than he could count hiking its trails, wading in the river, and picnicking in its secluded spots. He hadn't been back much since her fatal accident, but not much had been changed over the years.

A shot of adrenaline surged through his veins when he saw Zaim and his crew careen down the narrow road in their SUV. David ran along an obscure trail leading to the river, hoping to cross the walkway under the bridge where he could make his way back up to the highway.

"Murad!" Zaim shouted. "Hurry down to the river. Take the right fork in the trail. There is a footbridge across the river. I want you to cross it and hide in the willow bushes. If Captain Craine tries to get away along that route, capture him. Shoot him if you have to."

"Afu!" Zaim barked, turning to the other three men. "Run up the trail to the left. Hurry past the visitor center and follow the paved path to where it meets the walkway under the highway bridge. Cross to the other side and hide behind the evergreens. If Captain Craine tries to cross there, stop him. Jibril and Imad, come with me. We will chase him down, because with the bridges secured, he will have no way to cross the river. We have him trapped."

As he raced down the footpath leading to the river, David could see Murad circling around to his right. Murad, years younger than David, traversed the terrain much faster than the older man. David figured by the direction he was heading that Murad was trying to get to the footbridge nearer the lake. That didn't much concern him, because Murad's direction was taking him away from where David wanted to go.

David raced down a lesser used trail, and he stubbed his foot on a loose rock, then tripped over an exposed tree root. He rolled a few yards down the trail and regained his footing, bruised but with no broken bones. Behind him he heard crashing and what seemed to him to be cursing, although he didn't understand the language.

He was thankful that he was nearing the bridge he intended to cross. David knew that once he reached the other side, it was only a few yards to the highway. He could hear the morning traffic beginning to move by, and he was quite sure he would be able to flag down help if he reached the road.

He heard the heavy thud of feet. Someone was running to his left and a little ahead of him. Through the brush David caught glimpses of Afu and calculated that it was too late to make it to the bridge ahead of him.

This left David one last option. Straight ahead and at the foot of a steep bank was the entrance to a shallow cave. Over the years, during periods of high water in the spring, the water level would rise enough to form a large whirlpool that gouged at the rocky bank. At that particular spot, the substrate was softer than the rest of the rock, and centuries of the bank being pummeled by boulders carried by raging water had carved a hidden niche. A large fractured boulder had fallen in front of the cave's entrance, leaving an opening barely large enough to crawl through. From the river, it looked to fill the entire opening. When the river receded in late summer, the cave was high and dry.

David slid down the solid rock bank, lost his footing and crashed to the abrasive surface below. He felt his shin being abraded as it scraped on the rough surface, and his ankle turned beneath his weight, sending a searing pain up his right leg.

For a moment, David was dazed by the fall, and then he breathed a sigh of relief to discover he had remembered the spot. The cave was only a half-dozen steps to his right. He squeezed into the opening before Zaim knew he had disappeared.

The cave was large enough that David could stretch out in a half reclining, half sitting position. It took a few seconds for his eyes to adapt to the dimness, but there was enough light coming through the entrance to allow him to ascertain how much damage he had done to himself.

His left elbow was scraped, and enough blood serum had oozed through the wound to begin crusting over. His right ankle was throbbing, but David was relieved to discover that he had full range of motion with less pain than he expected. Other than a few more minor scrapes and bumps he figured he came through the chase relatively unscathed.

David didn't know how long he could remain in this den without being discovered, but he planned to move as soon as he could. If he were to be located here, there would be no escape.

Zaim was beyond exasperation. One minute they were close to nabbing the Captain, the next he was gone, disappeared as if into thin air. He wondered if David Craine had fallen over the bank and was lying on the rocks below. Perhaps their problem had taken care of itself.

CHAPTER
FIFTY-ONE

"CAN YOU SEE WHAT'S HAPPENING UP AHEAD, BEN?" Deidre spoke clearly and calmly into the radio. She was driving as fast as the curvy North Shore road would allow. John glanced over at her, impressed at her concentration and collectiveness.

"I'm not sure what's going on. I'm on the straight stretch of road where the passing lane begins. I thought I saw David drive his Subaru through the park entrance, but I can't imagine why he'd do that. Certainly he knows that's the only way in or out and that he'll be trapped.

"That must have been him. The SUV followed, and I'm close enough to be sure they have gone into the park. Advise, please."

"Get there as fast as you can, Ben. No sirens yet, though. Surprise is still on our side, so stick with them and don't let anything happen to David."

Ben's answer was short. "I'm on it." Deidre heard the whine of his squad's engine rev to a higher frequency, and she could picture the vehicle jumping ahead as its accelerator was stomped to the floorboards.

By that time she was at the start of the straight passing lane on the two lane highway, and she floored the gas pedal. She and John felt the pressure of their headrests as the vehicle responded to her urging. In seconds the speedometer registered ninety miles per hour.

She saw Ben turn into the park's entry, and when she and John reached that spot, Deidre followed the route the others had taken. Only a few hundred yards into the park was a line up of cars. She pulled in behind Ben.

He was already out of his car, rushing to David's Subaru which sat nearly in the ditch off to the side of the road. The driver's side door was open.

Behind his car sat the black SUV, all four of its doors open as well. There was no mistaking that the occupants abandoned the two vehicles in a hurry.

Deidre and John jumped out of her SUV and sprinted up to where Ben was standing next to David's sedan. All three had their weapons drawn, not knowing what to expect. There was no one to be seen.

"We have got to find David before they do," Deidre said, stating the obvious. "My guess is that he would head to the walkway under the highway bridge. That's the only way he can get back to the highway from here.

"I don't think he'd head deeper into the woods or toward the lake. Either way would take him farther away from people and would only make it easier for those chasing him to kill him with no interference."

The three officers wheeled around when they heard another vehicle turn into the park. It was Jeff who had come down the West Castle Danger Road. Deidre relaxed a little.

"This makes four of us, five counting David, although I don't think he will be of much help against the others." She assessed the situation.

"Jeff, drive farther into the park, down to the station where they sell permits. There's a trail leading to the river from there. It intersects another trail running along the top of the river bank. Take up a position where you can look down at the footbridge crossing the Gooseberry. Make sure you have your rifle with. If David should go that way, you may have to use it to protect him. Be sure to take your field glasses with you. You'll have a good view of the river with them."

Jeff was already running for his squad by the time Deidre turned to Ben.

"I want you to go back to the highway. Station yourself on the stone wall overlooking the path leading to the base of the highway bridge. From there you'll have a clear view of the pedestrian walkway that goes under the bridge to the other side. I suspect that is the route David will try.

"Take your glasses and your rifle. Just be sure that whatever you do, you don't injure an innocent hiker, although I doubt if anyone else will be moving around in the park at this hour."

It took Ben nearly five minutes to get to his post, and by the time he did, Afu had run across the bridge's walkway and hidden in the dense stand of fir trees on the other side. Everything around him was quiet, although he strained to hear barely perceptible sounds far to his right and somewhat down the steep, brush-covered slope.

The deputy was most concerned about the bridge. Suspended beneath the road bed, about seventy-five feet above the raging Gooseberry River, a walkway provided a way for tourists to stand above the river and marvel at the magnificent falls. It connected the hiking trails on the east and west sides of the river and also provided access to the highway above.

Ben scanned the two sides of the river with his binoculars. Afu, trying to adjust his position so he could see if David was approaching, became visible for a moment, and Ben's back stiffened.

His heart still pounding. Ben sat patiently, being careful to not expose his position, and the forest was eerily silent. Nothing moved.

CHAPTER
FIFTY-TWO

BY THIS TIME DAVID'S LEGS HAD BECOME stiff and cramped. His bruises were beginning to deeply ache now that the adrenalin level in his system had dropped to a more normal level, and his ankle was beginning to swell against the cuff of his hiking boot. He dared not move for fear of giving away his precarious position.

The walls of the shallow cave were covered with condensation, and from above his head a steady drip of cold ground water spilled onto him and ran down his back. Involuntarily, he shivered.

A hot wave of fear surged within him when he heard footsteps approaching, and then he heard muffled whispers. It was that strange language again, and he understood nothing they said.

David deduced that there were at least two, maybe three people, and they were very near the narrow mouth of the cave. He buried his face in his arms and breathed in shallow breaths, fearful that they would hear any sound he might make.

Outside, Zaim turned to Jibril and Imad, and whispered, "He cannot have simply vanished. Jibril, you follow the river downstream on the chance that he is heading deeper into the park.

"There is a foot bridge a half mile downstream from here. It crosses the river, but don't take it. Murad is on the other side, waiting. If Captain Craine had gone that way, Murad would have captured him by now.

"Imad, climb back up the bank and head back to his car. He may have somehow slipped past us in the forest, but I think not. I will work my way upstream, which is the way I think he will be headed. Perhaps I can flush him into Afu's grasp. Hurry, now. Time is slipping away, and soon campers in the park will be waking and moving about. That will complicate matters considerably."

Each man moved out in his assigned direction, and in seconds, David heard only the sound of his own muffled breathing. He waited a full five minutes, and then decided he'd better make his move if he was ever going to.

He cautiously crept to the opening of the cave and tried to scan the surroundings, but from inside he had a very narrow field of view. He could see no one outside and hunkered closer to the light. As he neared the cave entrance his scope of the river bank became wider. None of his assailants were visible to him.

He took one step forward, then another, expecting to either be grabbed or brained at any instant. The most frightening point was when he emerged from what had seemed like his crypt. He pictured the men above him on the bank, ready to pounce. Taking two limping steps out into the light, he quickly turned and looked up. To his relief, all he saw were birch trees and ferns.

One silent step after another, David hobbled upstream, pressed against the rock wall of the riverbed as tightly as he could. A hundred yards ahead of him he could see the arches of the bridge spanning the gorge, and he inched his way in that direction. There was a walkway under the bridge deck for hikers, and he knew that if he could make it across, he could easily get to the highway and possibly into the safety of a passerby's car.

ZAIM REACHED THE BEGINNING OF THE WALKWAY and still had not sighted David. Below, the river raged over broken pieces of boulder, creating a maelstrom of fury. Across the span, he could make out Afu peering from around the thick cover of a balsam tree, and Zaim saw the rising sun glint off the barrel of the rifle Murad was carrying.

Zaim thought, *If the Captain came this way, he most certainly continued upstream. Afu would have taken care of him had he tried to cross. He must be trying to make his escape by using the trails above the falls.*

Zaim picked up his pace, hoping to reach the high falls before David could reach the more level terrain further upstream.

By this time, David was to the bridge, and its massive steel arches towered beside him. Although he was unaware, while he had been in his cave Zaim had passed him and was now ahead, moving to the upper falls. David placed one hand on the I-beam and curled his fingers around its flange. The steel was cold in his grasp and felt good next to his sweaty skin.

He peered over the edge of a vertical drop. Twenty feet below him was a massive block of basalt rock that had probably been cleaved loose and moved by the ancient glaciers that once covered this land. He wished he could somehow get down into the sheltering shadows of the crevice between the house-size block and the bank.

CHAPTER
FIFTY-THREE

STEALTHILY, DEIDRE AND JOHN MADE THEIR WAY through the underbrush, not exactly knowing which way to go. Every few seconds they stopped and listened, but any telltale sound was drowned out by the roar of water cascading over the two falls. Step by step they moved forward until they came to one of the many paved hiking trails that crisscrossed the park.

Without warning, they heard the sound of someone running heavily on the trail toward them, and two hikers, a young man and woman, charged into view. Their packs were still on their backs, but the straps to the covers had come loose and items were spilling out as they ran. The terror in their eyes was unmistakable.

They spotted Deidre and John and began to turn back.

"Sheriff," Deidre shouted out. "Stop! We can help."

For an instant it appeared as if the two were going to return to the direction from which they came, but then the man reached out and grabbed the woman, preventing her from breaking away. Deidre and John realized they, too, must have looked like a threat. Each had his pistol in hand.

"We're here to help. Calm yourselves as best you can," John said as he and Deidre approached.

Before they could ask what the problem was, the young lady stammered, "Man . . . there's a man . . . a gun!"

Deidre reached out and placed her hand on the girl's shoulder. "Take a deep breath. You're safe with us now. Calm down and try to tell us why you were running."

"We came over the slope on the other side of the bridge," the man began to offer, but then he had to stop and take another breath.

222

"Just as we approached the walkway under the bridge, a dark-haired man stepped from around one of the balsam trees. He had a rifle, and our first thought was that he would shoot us. Our only chance was to sprint across the walk and then up this trail. Can you tell us what's going on?"

Deidre's eyes widened as her system produced another shot of adrenalin. "Did you see anyone else? It's important that we know."

The two hikers looked at the officers with blank stares. Finally, the man responded. "We were too frightened to look around, but I don't think anyone else was there. At least I can't remember seeing anyone. But everything was a blur to me."

"If you continue up this trail and past the main building, you will come to the parking lot. There are three squad cars parked there. If you wait by them, help will be arriving in a few minutes. Whatever you do, don't come back down this way."

The hikers nodded and sprinted up the trail to a safer place, articles continuing to spill from their falling-open packs.

"John, David is down by the river and can't get across the gorge. The problem is we don't know if he is up or down stream. If you take that path," she said motioning to her right, "I'll head upstream. Take it slow. We don't know who we'll run into first."

"But we know at least one of them is by the walkway. The others could be there as well. Let's both head in that direction," John argued.

Without thinking, Deidre snapped back, "If they were all by the bridge, the hikers would have seen someone else. My guess is the person by the walkway is only covering one of David's possible escape routes. There's probably another stationed at the footbridge downstream.

"We'll cover more ground if we split up. Now go!"

John was not used to being bossed around, and for an instant his hackles went up, but before he could say anything he realized she was probably right.

"Deidre, be careful. There are real bullets in their guns."

A little chagrined, she looked at him and headed up the path toward the bridge.

Cautiously, John began to move in the opposite direction, and in a few seconds she was no longer in sight.

Deidre was alone in the most dangerous situation she had ever experienced.

Step by step she descended along the trail leading to the base of the bridge and the near side of where the pedestrian walkway started. Suddenly, she was startled by a scraping sound and a dull thud. She heard a loud moan coming from the direction of the river.

DAVID, GRASPING THE BRIDGE GIRDER AND LOOKING DOWN into the crevasse below him, was uncertain of what he should do. He had no idea what had happened to his pursuers, and he tried to calm his thoughts so he could reason out what should be his next move. He shifted his weight from his aching ankle to the other.

With no warning, what had seemed to be a solid rock ledge crumbled beneath his foot and he felt his hand torn away from the solid support his fingers had been wrapped around. For a sickening instant he clambered to find sure footing, but then he was falling through space for what seemed to him to be many seconds. Then blackness.

ZAIM HAD MOVED SEVERAL YARDS UPSTREAM along the bank, sure that at any second he would spot Captain Craine attempting to elude him and the others. He spun around at the sound of rocks falling followed by a muffled thud. Before he could react he heard a moan rise from the river gorge that made the hair on the nape of his neck stand upright.

DAVID OPENED HIS EYES AND TRIED TO CLEAR THE FOG from his brain. He had no recollection of where he was or what had happened. He looked up and at first thought he must be inside a chimney. Columns of rock towered above him, and through the channel they created he saw the blue sky high above. He tried to put the pieces together and wondered why he was lying on his back inside a fireplace.

Excruciating pain seeped into his consciousness, and he reacted with a loud cry, a mixture of a scream and a moan. He raised his head as best he could and looked at his leg. It was bent at a crazy angle as though his thigh had an extra joint, and his foot was pointing in a direction not in line with the rest of his leg. The sight sickened him and he turned his head to the side and vomited. David ached all over, and each breath he took required an effort to overcome the pains shooting through his ribcage.

DEIDRE WAS THE FIRST TO REACH THE BRIDGE ABUTMENT, and she could see the marks on the bank where someone had fallen over. She approached the edge and looked down. There was David lying in a crumpled heap at the bottom. She could see that he was barely moving, and she heard his moans above the sound of the running water going over the falls.

DAVID REGAINED HIS SENSES FOR A MOMENT and looked up. Peering over the edge of his chimney was the outline of a person. All he could see was a silhouette outlined against the bright sunlight behind it and the blue sky. He could make out a gun in the right hand of the person. The darkness of unconsciousness started to close in from the sides of his vision, but before everything went black, David heard a gunshot. Then he became unaware of the world around him.

DEIDRE, LOOKING DOWN ON THE MAN SHE WAS SUPPOSED to protect, did not see Zaim come around the point of rock upstream from her. He couldn't be sure what had happened, but he could assume.

225

The woman sheriff was intent on what was below her, and from the sounds bouncing from the rock walls, someone was down there and whoever it was must have been badly injured. It must be Captain Craine, he deduced.

Zaim was not going to wait to see what happened next. He couldn't wait, and reflexively, he raised his rifle and aimed at Deidre. He hurried his shot a bit as Deidre turned. The rifle cracked, and the pungent smell of gun smoke hung in the air. For Zaim it was as if time went into slow motion. He saw Deidre spin around from the impact of the bullet and saw her collapse to the ground.

SLOWLY, OR SO IT SEEMED TO HIM, DAVID regained his senses. His pain was still as intense as it had been, and he marveled that he was still alive. He tried to focus on the bank above him, and as his eyes adjusted, all he saw was blue sky. The figure with the gun in hand had disappeared, and he wondered if he had been hallucinating. He wretched and vomited. By now the pain had totally enveloped him. Again, David lost consciousness.

CHAPTER
FIFTY-FOUR

FROM HIGH UP ON THE POINT OF ROCKS ABOVE the trail, Ben had an open view of the walkway under the bridge. To his right he looked down on the footpath, and he could see the base of the bridge. His view upstream was obstructed by a dense clump of white cedar, but that didn't bother him. He reasoned that David or his pursuers would be coming from the downstream direction.

Ben scanned the visible area with his binoculars: the trail as far to the right as he could see, the base of the bridge, the walkway. As he focused on the patch of balsam trees on the far side, two hikers, a young woman and her male companion strode over the ridge and headed down the trail, walking confidently toward him.

As they passed the dense stand of conifers, Ben was startled to see Afu rise up from his position with a rifle in his hands. At the same time the hikers looked directly at the armed man in the bushes. Their utter surprise and fright registered with Ben, and he raised his rifle, placing the crosshairs of the scope on Afu's chest.

The couple ducked and burst into a mad sprint across the bridge, reaching the near side in only seconds. At the same time Afu cowered back into the trees. The hikers raced up the trail and out of sight. Ben's heart rate settled down somewhat, but he was now decidedly more alert.

Before he could completely gather himself, Ben heard more footsteps approaching from the downstream direction, and in seconds he recognized David cautiously moving up the trail. Something was wrong with his gate, and he limped as though his leg or ankle had been injured.

227

Ben steadied himself, looked through his rifle scope into the stand of balsams across the way. If Afu showed himself, Ben was determined to stop him from injuring David.

He saw his former teacher hobble up the trail, then stop by one of the bridge supports, and David looked over the side at the gorge below him. In horror, Ben watched the footing give way beneath David's feet, and he helplessly watched him catapult into space and disappear from sight. He heard a dull thud followed by a cry that was something between a scream and a gut wrenching moan.

Before Ben could move from his vantage point, he saw Deidre rush out of the trees and to the bank where David had been standing. He saw her look over the edge and pause. Then, from the one direction he was unable to cover, Ben heard the deafening roar of a rifle, and simultaneously saw Deidre spin and fall to the ground.

SECONDS AFTER DAVID HAD FALLEN DEIDRE REACHED THE EDGE of the bank and stared down at the crumpled heap lying on the rocks below. She was so shocked and intent on what she saw she had no awareness of Zaim coming around the point of dense cedars.

Without warning, she felt something slam into her chest on the right side. Then she felt more than heard the shock wave of a rifle blast. The impact twisted her around and slammed her to the ground. For an instant, nothing made sense, and she tried to find what it was that had struck her. Then she realized her right arm was numb and not working.

Deidre was only partially aware that her face had been pushed into the graveled path when she fell, and with her good hand she tried to brush the chunks of small rock away that were imbedded in her skin. She was confused that she couldn't seem to find her face. Through glazed eyes she looked up and saw a figure standing over her.

She saw Zaim raise his rifle and aim it at her head. She heard him curse her.

"You had to get in the way, didn't you?" he said, his voice sounding distant and echo like to Deidre. "It doesn't matter anymore," he continued, his voice almost calm.

"Someone must pay for what was taken from me. It might as well be you."

Zaim's finger began to tighten on the rifle's trigger, but before he could squeeze it, Deidre heard the roar of another gun, and Zaim pitched forward, lying so close to her on the ground that she could almost reach out and touch him. She heard him mumble something as he lay bleeding on the path.

Another shot came from the same place as the last one she had heard, but in her stunned condition, its retort hardly registered.

Before she lost consciousness, Deidre sensed someone sliding his arms under her and cradling her in his arms. She opened her eyes for a moment and saw John bent over her. Then all was black.

INSTINCTIVELY, FROM ATOP THE ROCKS WHERE DEIDRE had him stationed, Ben trained his scope on a thick stand of cedar trees to his left, and he caught a glimpse of someone moving toward the fallen Deidre. He followed the sound more than his sight until he saw Zaim burst into full view on the trail.

The dark-haired man rushed over to where Deidre had fallen and raised his rifle, ready to fire another shot. Ben could see his mouth moving as though he were saying something to her. Zaim's contorted face, the fear in Deidre's eyes, and the crosshairs of his scope centered on Zaim's chest all became clear to Ben in the same instant.

He squeezed the trigger and felt the recoil of his rifle jolt back against his shoulder.

CHAPTER
FIFTY-FIVE

JOHN WAS PUSHING HIS WAY OVER THE BRUSH-CHOKED bank downstream from the bridge. The red clay under foot and the steepness of the slope made for slow going, and he had to test each step he took or risk sliding in a crashing avalanche of arms and legs to the bottom. The sharp retort of a high powered rifle jolted him to a stop. The sound echoed off the steep river banks and seemed to come from everywhere at once.

He was experienced with firearms and could read much into the sound of a discharge. Sometimes there could be a sharp blast followed by a zinging that belied a miss and a ricochet. Or sometimes the sound could be more of a crack, and then a moment of stark silence indicating a shot that went far astray. But sometimes the sound could be more of a dull *BANG* that blended with a thud, meaning that the target was close by and something had been hit.

John heard BANG-whoomp.

Before he could move only a few feet, another shot was fired, this one from higher up the cliff above the bridge abutments. It was another BANG-whoomp. John knew from the sound that it wasn't good, and he leaped from the flat rock upon which he was standing and plowed through the brush, snapping off branches and dead stems as he ran. He heard one more BANG-whoomp.

AFTER WITNESSING THE SCENE ON THE OTHER SIDE of the bridge, Afu broke from his cover and started his rush across the bridge walkway. Ben swung around to his direction, and immediately focused his attention on the assault rifle Afu carried. Ben placed the

230

crosshairs of his rifle on the left quadrant of the sprinting man's torso, and for the second time squeezed the rifle's trigger. He saw Afu crumble to a heap on the concrete decking of the bridge.

Ben clambered down the face of the rock wall to the hiking path below and sprinted to where Deidre and Zaim had fallen. He arrived at the same instant that John came charging up the path from the opposite direction.

"Check on the fallen man," John ordered Ben. "I'll take care of Deidre." He got no argument from Ben.

He rushed to where Deidre lay on her side. Her left leg was folded back under her body, and her face was turned down into the gravel of the path. A puddle of blood had already formed under her, and John could see its origin, a rivulet of red running from her right side just above her breast.

He cradled her head in his hands and brushed the pieces of gravel and dry leaves from her face.

"No, no, not now. Not now," he mumbled over her still body. "Deidre, open your eyes. Don't give up. Come on, girl, move. Do something."

There was no response, and John held her limp form, and he wept.

Ben had spent the time hunched over Zaim, but now he stood up and in a controlled voice called dispatch over his radio.

"Jaredine, we've got a mess out here at Gooseberry Park. We have one officer down, perhaps dead. Also, two suspects are down, one confirmed dead, the other probable. There is a civilian who fell from a cliff, and I haven't assessed his situation, but it can't be good. It's not over yet, though. Three more suspects are still on the loose, and we may have more casualties before this thing is over. Send out all the help you can: the Rescue Squad, both ambulances, and mobilize all squads that are off duty right now."

He heard the dispatcher signal that the message had been received, and he cautiously moved to a protected spot where he could observe Afu lying on the bridge. There was no movement.

Ben slowly made his way up the trail and onto the bridge, keeping his handgun trained on the downed man. He knelt beside Afu and watched for any sign of life, a muscle twitch, the rising and falling of his chest. Then he did a pulse check. Afu was dead.

AS HE MOVED TOWARD THE LAKE, Jeff heard one shot rapidly followed by another, then another. An involuntary shudder moved up his spine, and he instantly became more observant. Just as he was about to move forward, out of the corner of his eye he saw movement to his left, and one of the men who had been under their surveillance came into view. As he walked along the bank, his eyes instinctively searched the downhill side of the path, making sure he didn't misstep and roll down to the river. Jibril walked directly under and in front of the bank upon which Jeff stood never looking up and being totally unaware that the deputy was so near.

"Stop!" Jeff ordered, and Jibril spun around to find himself staring into the barrel of the gun in Jeff's hand.

"Drop your rifle, raise your hands, and turn around."

Jibril obeyed, and Jeff kicked the abandoned automatic rifle into the brush. He placed a handcuff on Jibril's left wrist and ordered him to place his arms around a nearby tree. Then Jeff handcuffed Jibril's other wrist, rendering him a literal tree hugger.

He picked up his own rifle and headed to the bridge spanning the river below the falls.

IMAD WAS MAKING HIS WAY TO THE PARKING LOT when from the direction of the bridge he heard three shots fired in rapid succession. There seemed to be no space between the shots, almost as if they were fired from an automatic weapon.

Zaim had told him to return to the lot, and at this point, Imad was all too eager to obey his leader. He continued making his way uphill to where they had left the SUV, and with no hesitation, Imad walked out of the woods into a group of three deputies who had just arrived at the scene.

He gave up without a word.

AT THE BASE OF THE BRIDGE, JOHN CONTINUED to cradle Deidre in his arms, gently rocking back and forth as tears ran down his face. Ben came over and placed his hand on John's shoulder.

"John, let me take a look. We have to stop the bleeding. She's still with us, but we have to act, or we'll lose her. You hold her while I try to put pressure on the wound."

He tore back the part of Deidre's uniform that surrounded the small flaw in its fabric exposing a dime sized hole about two inches below her right collar bone. Red bubbles formed each time she exhaled, and her breathing was dangerously shallow. He reached into his back pocket and took out a clean handkerchief.

"Press this over the hole while I roll her so I can see the exit wound. Easy now."

Ben gently turned Deidre enough so he could see her back. The exit wound was larger and was also bubbling with each of her breaths. When Deidre inhaled he could hear a sucking sound.

"We have to compress this side, too. Hold her while I tear a piece from my shirt."

Ben pulled his shirttail out of his pants and ripped off a large hunk of fabric, folded it into a compress and placed it over the gaping hole. He lowered her back onto John's lap.

"The pressure of her body will seal the back. You hold the one on the front."

John looked at Ben with a blank stare but followed his directions.

"I can hear the sirens, and the paras should be here any minute now. They'll take care of her.

"I saw David Craine slip and fall over the bank. Hopefully, he still needs help."

Ben peered over the rim of the cliff and saw David lying on his back, his right leg twisted at a grotesque angle. He wasn't sure how many more dead he could face today, but he lowered himself over the edge and picked his way down to David.

CHAPTER
FIFTY-SIX

MURAD HAD CROSSED THE FOOTBRIDGE several hundred yards downstream. He was sitting on the cool, moss-covered ground behind a clump of willows, and from his vantage point he could scan the trail running on the other side of the river, as well as the narrow wooden footbridge. If Captain Craine attempted to escape using this route, he would be an easy target.

He shifted his frame to a more comfortable position until a succession of three gunshots caused him to start and his heart to race. The sound carried down the river gorge and echoed off the cliffs on either side. He could hear them continue to reverberate for what seemed like seconds, each rebound fainter the one before, and then there was silence. Even the birds and the squirrels fell silent, creating an eerie aura in the wilderness.

Murad hunched down lower in the vegetation, and scanned the opposite river bank. Surprised, he spotted Jeff slowly making his way along the precarious footpath. Murad made up his mind it was time to abandon his post.

He turned and, still crouching low, followed a trail that would lead him nearer to Lake Superior, but more importantly, it branched, the left fork providing an escape over the cliffs and into the dense forest above the river.

As Murad slowly worked his way up the steep trail, he looked back over his shoulder, and from that height he could see practically the entire river valley. From his vantage point he saw Jibril standing close to a huge birch tree, and then it dawned on him that his friend was not standing near it but was chained to it.

In the distance Murad heard sirens, many of them, getting louder by the second, and he really didn't have to think about it to deduce that they were approaching the park. Then he heard the characteristic sound of a helicopter. For a second he was frozen where he stood. He caught a flash of movement along the trail leading away from Jibril, and for an instant he saw Jeff making his way upstream.

Murad instantly recognized that now was the time for him to escape, and he continued up the trail and over the ridge high above the river. He abandoned his rifle under a scraggly spruce tree that at some time had been toppled by the wind, but he tucked his pistol in his pants.

He looked back one more time and thought, *"Better to live to fight another day than to die for a hopeless cause."*

Murad knew it would take a few days for him to make it to the Canadian border, but once there he could sneak across and disappear for a time. Who was to know, perhaps he'd come this way again.

WHAT WAS HAPPENING ELSEWHERE HAD NO IMPACT ON BEN. He could hear repeated moans that were hardly audible, and knew David must be badly injured.

Ben tested a sapling growing on the edge of the bank, and it appeared to be able to hold his weight. He swung his body around, and using the small tree as an anchor, lowered himself over the sharp rocky ledge. He thrashed with his legs until one foot caught a solid crack, and Ben eased his weight onto that foot.

Step by step, handhold by handhold he clawed his way down to the riverbed. As soon as his feet were on solid ground, he reached for his radio and once more called in to dispatch.

"Jaredine, this is Ben. You'd better call in Life Flight from Duluth. We have two coming in that look in bad shape, too difficult for the hospital in Two Harbors to handle. One has a sucking chest wound from a gunshot. The other took a twenty-five-foot fall off a cliff. He has a compound fracture of his femur, and I would guess multiple internal injuries. Both are unresponsive."

Jaredine acknowledged and placed the call to St. John's Hospital in Duluth. She had made this kind of call many times in the past, but these were not strangers she was talking about. They were her friends, and her voice carried a sense of urgency.

"This is dispatch out of Lake County," she said to the person at the hospital. "We need a Life Flight helicopter as soon as you can possibly get here. Send it to the parking lot at Gooseberry Falls State Park."

"What do you have? Did another tourist try to climb the rocks and fall off? Honestly, I sometimes wonder what they expect."

Jaredine's voice was curt. "We have an officer down from a gunshot wound and a civilian who fell twenty feet or more to the bottom of a cliff. Two suspects are dead, and there may be more casualties before the situation is resolved."

The hospital worker didn't answer but immediately buzzed the flight crew. "We have a situation at Gooseberry Park. Extreme trauma is expected involving multiple cases. Take off immediately. You'll be advised as you are in the air."

Then she turned her attention to Jaredine. "They are on their way. ETA, twenty-one minutes. I'll hang up now and contact the ER so they'll be ready. Call as soon as you know any further details about what we will be up against."

The dispatcher at the hospital knew some serious cases would be coming in, and before she could begin the alert process for the ER, she heard the characteristic *whoomp-whoomp-whoomp* of the chopper blades as the helicopter took off from its landing pad on the hospital roof. The hospital dispatcher said a silent prayer that they'd get there in time to do some good.

BEN CLAMORED OVER THE LOOSE ROCK and litter to David. He could see the man's chest rising and falling, but not in a rhythmic way that signaled normal breathing. Instead, David would take two or three quick, shallow breaths and then would lay motionless for

237

several seconds. Then he would heave a sigh, breathe a few more times, and again rest.

Ben knelt by his side, placed his fingers where he believed David's carotid artery would be and was rewarded by the feel of blood rushing through the vessel. It was a thin pulse, but, nevertheless, it was a pulse, weak, but a pulse.

"David! David, can you hear me?" he pleaded.

David responded with a low, guttural sound that seemed to come from his chest, but he managed to open one eye. It was only a slit, but it was a voluntary movement. Ben pried apart the lids, exposing David's pupils to the light. They were dilated, black discs that were far too large.

"David," Ben commanded. "Squeeze my fingers as hard as you can." He was surprised at the firm grip that enveloped his hand.

"That's good, David. Hang in there, and we'll get you out of here soon. Life Flight is on its way and should be here any minute. David, can you hear me?"

Again he saw the flutter of an eyelid.

"That's it. Don't go to sleep, David. Listen to me. Squeeze my hand again. That's it."

For what seemed like hours to Ben, he talked to David, each time getting a response, but each time he thought the response was weaker.

In the distance, Ben could finally hear the faint sound of the chopper blades, and they were getting louder by the second. He flinched when he felt someone place a hand on his shoulder, and he looked up. The paramedics had arrived, and when he turned he could see more rescuers lowering a stretcher over the bank and down to where he and David sat.

The paramedic knelt beside David and began to take vitals.

"There are some good signs here. We'll need your help getting him on the backboard, but first we have to straighten his leg. It'll look gruesome, but it has to be done. Hold his hips so we don't put stress on his back or neck."

Ben almost fainted when the medics pulled David's twisted leg somewhat straight, and David gave an involuntary scream of pain. But now it was time to slide the backboard under him, and Ben gathered himself for that task.

David was not a large man, but the stretcher and his body were dead weight to those carrying him. There was no viable way to get him to the top except up the face of the cliff. A trail came close to the river, but that was several hundred yards down stream. The stretcher bearers would have to wade through thigh-deep water to reach the trail from where they stood. One slip and David would be plunged into the river with the chance of being washed over the falls. They decided to go up the bank that Ben had come down.

Just as they had decided on their course of ascent, the para attending to David hollered above the noise of the racing river, "We've lost a pulse. He's gone into cardiac arrest."

The other medics ran to help. The attending paramedic already had the defibrillator out and was opening David's shirt.

"Clear!" he yelled as he placed the paddles on David's chest.

David gave an involuntary jerk as the electric shock surged through him. The medic relaxed a bit.

"We have a heartbeat again. Let's get him moved."

The stretcher was tied to ropes dropped from atop the rim and was more pulled than carried up the vertical drop.

By the time Life Flight had landed in the parking lot, the members of the rescue squad had David to the top of the bank and were carrying his stretcher up the path to the parking lot. Suddenly it dawned on Ben that Deidre was nowhere to be seen.

"Where's Deidre?" he asked in a panicked voice.

"It's okay, Ben. She's already in the copter, and as soon as we get David loaded they'll be off to Duluth."

"She's alive, then?" Ben asked, his eyes filled with tears.

No one answered him as they rushed by.

CHAPTER
FIFTY-SEVEN

DAVID OPENED HIS EYES, AND THE BRIGHT LIGHT was still shining above him, but the blue sky had disappeared. He was confused by the whiteness of everything, and his eyes tried to focus on something, anything. Eventually, he could make out his leg extended in front of him, also wrapped in white, and supported by a sling attached to a chain. He blinked his eyes again and tried to move.

From out of nowhere, a woman in a white uniform stood beside him and bent over him, and she placed her hands on his shoulders.

"Hello, Mr. Craine. Please don't struggle. You're safe and in the hospital in Duluth."

The nurse could see David sink back onto his pillow and bed.

"That's it. Relax. You've been through a lot, but you're in good hands now. I'm going to ask you to do some simple tasks. Close your eyes, and then open them."

David did as he was told.

The nurse reassured him, "Good. Now squeeze my fingers with both hands . . . excellent. Now just with your right hand . . . very good. Now with your left. That's wonderful."

David relaxed back on his pillow, a wave of relief sweeping over him. "How long have I been here?" he croaked, his voice dry and raspy.

"It's been eight days. I guess you've passed my next test, which was to try to speak. Now that I know you can, I need you to answer a few questions for me. Are you in any pain?"

David had to think for a moment, but forced out ,"No."

"Do you remember how you got here?

Again, "No."

240

"Do you remember anything of what happened to you?"

David hesitated. "The last I remember is pulling into Gooseberry Park. My car was missing—something wrong with the engine—and I didn't want to get stalled on Highway 61.

"Is that what happened? Did I have a car accident on the highway?"

"No, David. You fell from the bank down to the Gooseberry River's bed. Can you remember any of what happened after that?"

The fog shrouding his brain began to lift, and David tried to piece together the events of that day. "I seem to have an image of looking up at the sky and seeing a silhouette of someone. The sun behind was so bright I couldn't make out any details. Then I heard a crash. No, wait. It was a gunshot, wasn't it?"

"What else do you remember?" the nurse asked.

Again, David hesitated as more of the haze disappeared. "I remember hurting worse than I've ever hurt and seeing my leg bent at a terrible angle. Then I remember being placed on a board. After that, nothing. "Someone was shot, weren't they? Who was it? Can you tell me?"

Just then there was a knock on the hospital door, and David looked across the room. "Hi, David. I guess that would have been me."

Deidre smiled her warmest smile at him, but David reacted in shock, the expression on his face somewhat between surprise and angst.

"Deidre, what in the world . . . ?" he started to blurt out, but she shushed him.

"Take it easy. I look a lot worse than I feel right now."

David took in the sight. The right side of her face was a mass of scabs, dried and discolored. She sported two blackened eyes, the result of falling face down on the bare rocks after she had been shot. Deidre was sitting in a wheelchair, her right arm in a sling, and an IV tube trailing behind her to a stand supporting a bag of liquid. John Erickson had his fingers wrapped around the chair's handles, and he smiled. "Hello, David. Welcome back to the land of the living. I don't know which of the two of you looks worse. But I do know that it's absolutely wonderful to be here with you. The nurse buzzed us and asked that we come down. You and Deidre have some catching up to do. You've both got some stories to tell."

CHAPTER
FIFTY-EIGHT

THE DAY AFTER THE INCIDENT IN THE PARK, Ben received a visit at the Lake County Law Enforcement Center from Enos Pratt, the FBI director of the Duluth area. "Well, hello, Ben," Enos said as he extended his hand.

Ben was impressed with the man's bearing. "Hello, Director Pratt."

"Enos is just fine with me. I've come to speak to you personally for two reasons. First, we need to know as much as possible about what happened at the park. If I understand it correctly, you were set up on a rock outcrop above the walkway. What were you able to observe from up there?"

"Well, sir," Ben began. "I had a wide open view of the walkway under the bridge and a partially obstructed view of the trail running along the river gorge. I could cover whoever came and went pretty well from up there."

"And I understand you had a sniper rifle with you."

"Not really. Well, I suppose you could call it that. It was a Remington .270 with a scope, something that can be bought at any sporting goods store."

Enos sat silent for a moment, thinking. "You handled it well."

"Thanks," Ben responded, shifting himself a little self-consciously in his chair.

"As best as you can remember, what exactly did you observe before your actions."

Ben took a deep breath before beginning his story.

"I had just hunkered down on the flat rock above the trail when a pair of hikers, a young man and woman, came over the knob on the other side of the bridge. As they stepped around a clump of small balsam trees, one of the suspects stepped out from behind the evergreens. He had an assault rifle, and when they saw him, they sprinted across the bridge. He seemed to be as surprised as they were and ducked back under the cover of the branches."

"I see," Enos interjected. "Can you describe this couple?"

"They were both slender in build, looked to be in good physical shape. It was difficult to judge height from where I sat, but he was taller than she by about six inches. He had black curly hair. She had straight blond hair. Both were quite fair skinned."

"You observed all that in the roughly five seconds you had as they ran across the bridge?" Enos' right eye brow raised, quizzically.

"Yes, sir." Ben shifted uncomfortably in his chair.

"What happened next?" Enos entered something on the notepad in front of him.

"David Craine came limping up the path, and he stopped, supporting himself on a bridge beam as he looked over the edge of the drop down to the river. As he leaned out, the edge of the bank gave way, and I saw him fall over the edge. Then I heard him hit the rocks below.

"Sheriff Johnson rushed up the trail and looked over the bank where David had fallen. It was then I heard a gunshot from my left. Deidre, Sheriff Johnson, was spun around and fell to the ground."

"How long did it take her to get to the scene after David Craine fell?" Enos wanted to know.

"Only a few seconds. I can't give you exact timing, because in this kind of situation, time seems to become compressed."

"Then what?" Enos asked.

"Then the tallest of the suspects came running from my left. He stood over Deidre with his rifle raised. I could see his mouth move as he said something to her. That's when I shot, and he went down.

"The other man, the one on the other side of the bridge, broke cover and was sprinting to the scene, and I took him out."

"What did you do then?" the director wanted to know.

"I slid down the embankment as quickly as I could and rushed over to where Sheriff Johnson lay."

"Why didn't you pay more attention to the suspect you had shot on the bridge?"

"He was the farthest away, and anyway, I was quite certain he was dead."

"How were you certain of that?

"The crosshairs were centered on his left thoracic quadrant when I pulled the trigger. It was a lethal shot."

"Okay, so you reached Sheriff Johnson and the other suspect. What did you find?"

"Agent Erickson had arrived just before me. We checked Sheriff Johnson first. She was unconscious but breathing, although the wound on her chest was sucking with each breath. We applied compresses as best we could to seal the wound, and he assumed the care for her. Then I checked on the condition of the suspect. He was alive, barely.

"I left Agent Erickson with Deidre and scaled the bank to look at David Craine. Shortly after, the paramedics arrived and took over. I guess that's all I can report to you, sir."

Enos Pratt rocked back in his chair and tapped his pencil on the table. Otherwise the room was silent as the sweep second hand of the clock made two revolutions. Then he spoke.

"Ben, I have to tell you, I'm impressed with the way you conducted yourself up there. Your observations are right on, and everything you've told me matches the facts perfectly. Good work. That brings me to the second thing I wanted to talk to you about. The organization is always on the lookout for new talent. We're currently accepting applications for prospective agents. I'd like you to submit your paperwork. I can't make you any promises, Ben, but I think you stand a good chance of being accepted." Enos smiled at Ben in a knowing way.

Ben was dumbfounded. He sat in stunned silence until finally he stammered, "Yes, sir, I'd like that."

Enos stood and extended his hand. Ben followed suit, and they shook on it as if closing a business deal.

"Oh, and Ben. In your report, you said the suspected terrorist mumbled something in a foreign language. What was it again?"

"He kept repeating, 'Dania, Dania.' Do you have any idea what that means?"

"No, I don't. Our interpreters don't know either. It appears to be some inconsequential rambling of a dying man.

EPILOGUE

THE WARMTH FELT GOOD ON DEIDRE'S SHOULDERS as she sat on the sandy bank of the Sucker River, her back to the mid-May sun. Her physical wounds had healed, and only when she faced the mirror in her bathroom and she saw the still purple-red scars did it seem real. Everything else seemed like a recurring bad dream. She thought over all that had happened these past few months.

Finally, John had been able to reveal to her all he knew. As soon as David had opened the flash drive left behind on his boat, he had contacted the FBI. They, in turn, had jumped at the opportunity to set up a sting operation, using David as their contact person. She still marveled at the courage he had shown by allowing himself to be placed in the crosshairs of a terrorist organization. His involvement had been kept a secret, not only to protect his cover, but also to ensure that everyone involved, including the Sheriff's Department would not make any suspicious moves.

In the distance, far out on the lake, she saw the speck of a boat cruising on its way to the Wisconsin shore, and she wondered if it was her Mr. Craine, now more a hero in her eyes than ever before. It had taken time, but his wounds were healed sufficiently so that he was ready to take *Crusader, Too* out the first day that open water permitted. He had told her his plan was to cruise the Wisconsin shoreline the entire summer, spending as much time around the Apostle Islands as possible. He thought he would stay out of Canadian waters for a long time.

And then there was Ben. He had recommended to the county board that Jeff be appointed acting sheriff until Deidre could resume her duties, saying he thought Jeff deserved the chance. Along with

247

the FBI, the department had requested a search warrant to go into the hunting shack up in Brimson. It was immediately granted by the sitting judge. Ben was in charge of the investigation from the Sheriff's Department's end, and he, along with several members of both agencies collected enough explosives and other items to form an airtight case against Jibril and Imad.

Three months later, Ben was informed that his application to join the FBI had been accepted. He resigned from Lake County and began the rigorous training required of his new post.

Deidre, her back still to the sun and her mind far away in thought picked up some pebbles and one by one tossed them into the smooth-running stream.

"So where are you now?" John asked her. He was lying on his side behind her, acting as her back rest.

Deidre rocked back, putting more of her weight on his chest. She reached back and ran her fingers through his hair.

"Thinking, just thinking," she said.